Pocono Flying Lessons

a novel

C.A. Pensiero

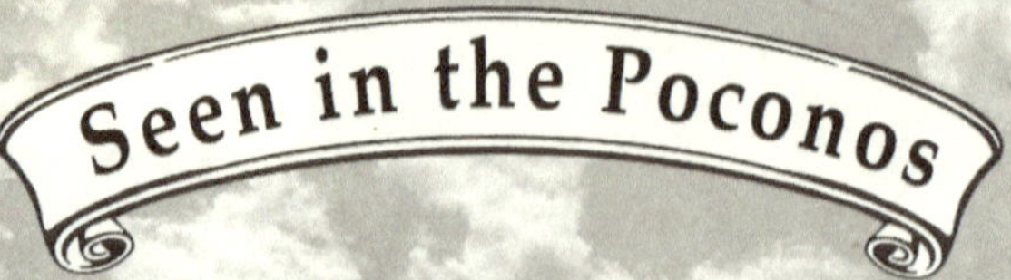
Seen in the Poconos

Pittsburgh this way
Mount Pocono Airport
The Pocono Classifieds

Small Mountain Coffee

Lovers' Cove

LOU'S
Dirty Water Dogs
Pickle Me Poconos
Festival
SOUTH FORK
Fishing and Hunting Club 226 MILES

Seen in the Poconos

Big Pocono Mountain

Shawnee chairlift

Honeymoon Hideaway

Published in the United States of America by
Park Strip Press

ISBN 979-8-9938647-0-9 (paperback)
ISBN 979-8-9938647-1-6 (eBook)
ISBN 979-8-9938647-2-3 (audiobook)
ISBN 979-8-9938647-3-0 (hardcover)

10 9 8 7 6 5 4 3 2 1

To Melissa . . . happy birthday!

Maybe there was a way out by flying. Maybe our restless blood could find frontiers in the illimitable air.

—F. Scott Fitzgerald

Love is such a beautiful thing.

—DJ Romeo, booth magician

Prologue

July 4th

Samantha Casselberry was on her way to see fireworks. After all, it was her birthday, and her parents always took her to see fireworks on her birthday.

She perched on bare-skinned knees in the backseat of her parents' Subaru station wagon. The cracked brown vinyl pinched her skin. She leaned her face out the window, letting the wind tumble her hair. She loved the way the Pocono air smelled on her birthday. Sticky pine sap and campfire smoke.

She slipped her hand into the wind and tilted it.

The wind caught her palm and lifted it.

She tipped her wrist and it dipped. Tilted again and it climbed.

Up.

Down.

Up again.

Today she was six, which already felt much older than five. She needed one whole hand and then one finger to count her age now. Pretty soon, she'd have to start using her toes.

From the front seat, her mom turned and smiled. "Perfect night for fireworks." The sky was clear; a light breeze stirred the pines as the sun dipped behind Big Pocono Mountain. Her dad rested his hand on her mom's knee, and she laced her fingers through his.

Her dad drove quickly up the winding mountain road, as the radio played *The Boy From New York City* by The Manhattan Transfer.

"Ooh-wah, ooh-wah," her mom sang along over her shoulder.

"Tell us about that boy from New York City," Samantha sang back, still flying her hand out the window.

They kept singing as Samantha's hand rode the air current, twisting left and right. Tight fingers made it climb. Tilted fingers sent it diving at her command. She flew her hand above a rumbling stream beside the road, then arched her fingers and let it soar high above the treetops.

She knew there wouldn't be any fights today—no fights about the lights getting shut off, or how long they had before the money ran out. Not on her birthday.

There wasn't as much work in the Poconos as there used to be. Her dad worked construction, but there wasn't any construction to work. Her mom said he could clean insulation out of one of the old resorts; her dad said he needed a special license, and they didn't have money for it.

His pant legs were usually dusted with flakes of dried concrete. Samantha liked picking the tiny bits out of his whiskers.

But today was different. That morning her dad had painted her toenails with her mom's candy-apple-red nail polish. His hands were hard and calloused, but he held her foot like it might break. When he finished, he said, "I want you to know how much I love you."

When her favorite part of the song came on again, she leaned back inside the car and sang the bouncy "ooh-wah, ooh-wah" part into her dad's ear. His whiskers scratched her lips.

Then her mom sang the line about the boy from New York City.

"You two are silly," he said. Then he dropped his voice right on cue, rumbling out a long, goofy "Yeeeahh."

Samantha shrieked with laughter and leaned back out the window.

They passed an old log cabin that had been turned into a candle shop, lit by hundreds of tiny white twinkling lights. Samantha flew her hand over its roof, focused hard on holding it steady without using her arm. Next, they passed a famous Pocono honeymoon resort: LOVERS' COVE. Her mom said couples came from all over the world to take baths in their heart-shaped bathtubs. Samantha wished she had a heart-shaped bathtub.

Her dad eased off the gas. Just past the resort's entrance, a white-tailed deer bounced through the trees—quick and light, its tail flashing. Samantha turned her head to watch it leap once, then vanish like magic. She had seen them on this road before, sometimes coming out from nowhere. Her dad was watching for other deer and the slower speed made her hand descend toward the ground.

They were almost there.

Big Pocono Ski Area sat at the top. They'd lay a blanket by one of the chairlifts and watch fireworks from 2,131 feet up.

You could see forever from up there. Practically into New Jersey.

As the road leveled beside a lake used for snowmaking, a car approached from behind and began to pass. Her dad sped up. Samantha flew her hand over the roof as it went by.

The other driver looked over. Their eyes met. She smiled at him.

He smiled back—a dreamy, floaty kind of smile.

She closed her eyes and imagined herself flying. Hair in the wind. Hand to the sky. Not pretend flying.

Real flying.

The air changed. Cooler. Tilting.

The wind lifted her. She was rising. For real.

Her mom's singing cut off mid-note.

Samantha opened her eyes.

The lane lines slid sideways in the windshield. Her dad's hands jerked the wheel. Her mom made a small sound—half gasp, half prayer.

Then a sharp pop, distant and ugly, like someone stepping on an empty soda can.

Glass burst.

—ooh-wah, ooh-wah—rising and dipping in its bright little loop.

There was a hard slam and then another, heavier, and then weight left her stomach.

Samantha's head snapped forward. A white flash. A roar like the wind had teeth.

And then cold hit her like a slap.

Water.

She was in water.

Waist-deep in the shallows of the snowmaking lake, dress soaked and heavy, legs sinking into mud. She clawed at the slippery bottom and stumbled, coughing, the shock stealing her breath. The world rang like a bell inside her skull.

She turned—spinning in place—looking for the car.

The Subaru was on the bank, folded around a tree at the lake's edge, the front end crushed inward like someone had balled it up in their fist. Steam hissed from under the hood. The radio still played, tinny and cheerful.

"Ooh-wah, ooh-wah…"

She waded through mud and water and climbed onto the bank, palms slipping in wet grass. Her knees scraped on gravel. She didn't notice. She ran to the Subaru, sobbing.

Her dad was slumped over the steering wheel. His face was wrong. Still. Blood smeared the windshield in red streaks.

So much red.

"Daddy?"

She looked for her mom.

The passenger seat was empty.

Up ahead, a car sat just off the road. A man stood beside it. A deep dent buckled the right rear fender.

Their eyes met.

She waited for the dreamy smile—hopeful for something. Anything.

But there was nothing.

Only the cold turn of his shoulders as he looked away.

Then he drove off, leaving her alone on the mountain road that was supposed to take her to see fireworks.

PART I

Thrust

CHAPTER 1

Don't Be Icarus

July 4th—Twenty Years Later

The stall was coming when the wings started to talk—light buffet, then harder.

Nose high. Airspeed bleeding off.

Eric glanced at Nasser. White knuckles. Braced like impact was inevitable.

Below, the Pocono hills rolled out in green ridges. Not many good fields if the engine quit.

An old instructor's joke: *Your students are always trying to kill you. Every single one of them.*

The stall horn screamed.

Nasser panicked—slamming the ailerons and mashing the rudder.

The Cessna snapped off into a spin, a wing dropping as the nose sliced down toward the trees in a tight, twisting spiral. The horizon rolled. Sky. Trees. Sky again. Dropping fast.

Eric kept his voice level. "Fly the airplane."

Nasser frantically pumped the yoke, yanking the ailerons side to side.

"Just fly the airplane, Nasser." Eric nodded through the windshield. "See those houses down there? They're getting bigger."

Nasser's eyes were wide. "Eric, the houses are too big!"

"Fly the airplane."

"I am trying, Eric! It will not come out of the spin!"

"PARE—power, ailerons, rudder, elevator. You've got this."

Without looking, Nasser reached for the throttle but grabbed the bright red mixture knob instead. Pulling it would kill the engine. Eric bumped his hand off the knob.

Nasser didn't notice. He went right back to slamming the yoke.

"I am trying! It is not working, Eric!"

Eric glanced down at Nasser's foot jammed on the pedal. "You're pushing the wrong rudder."

"My airplane."

Nasser let go immediately.

Eric took over. Power to idle. Ailerons neutral. Rudder full opposite rotation. Elevator forward. Wait.

The Cessna stopped spinning. Still plunging, Eric nudged the yoke forward a little harder, broke the stall, then eased the nose back up.

They leveled at just under 3,000 feet.

"I am sorry, Eric."

Through the windshield vent, Eric caught a trace of campfire smoke.

"Let's just hope someone can pry this seat cushion out of my ass later."

Nasser didn't respond.

"It's okay," Eric said. "We'll practice them again. You did one thing really well."

Nasser looked over. "I did?"

"You let go of the controls when I said to."

Nasser turned back to the window.

Eric watched the airspeed settle. "Ever hear of Icarus?"

"The boy who flew too close to the sun?"

"That's right. His father built the wings," Eric said. "Warned him not to climb too high."

"And he did not listen."

"Nope. Didn't listen."

Nasser was quiet.

"So what's the lesson?" Eric asked.

Nasser thought about it. "Do not be Icarus?"

Eric considered that. "That's one way to put it."

"I will not be Icarus, Eric."

"You already weren't." Eric nudged him. "You listened. Keep it up."

Eric let his hands fall back to his lap. "You have the airplane."

Nasser slowly placed his hands and feet back on the controls.

Eric had been grinding out flight time at Mount Pocono Aviation—long hours, low pay, but that's how young pilots got their hours and unlocked an airline interview. He was close—eight months, maybe. Especially now that he had a side gig flying a twin-engine cargo plane for Bruce Payne a few nights a week.

"Let's head back," Eric said. "We'll do a few landings, then we're done."

"Okay," Nasser said. "Uh… how do you want me to get us back, Eric?"

"That's your call."

Nasser frowned and reached for the chart on his knee-board. "Well… I could tune two VORs. Triangulate. Plot the radial and—"

"Or—" Eric pointed through the windscreen. "See that peak? Mount Pocono Airport's just past it. Fly toward the peak."

"Oh. Yes, that would be much easier."

"It's called situational awareness," Eric said. "Always know where you are."

"I will try to have more awareness, Eric."

"It'll come."

Nasser banked the Cessna toward the peak.

The cockpit was hot. No air conditioning in the 150, and the July sun pressed straight through the windshield. Sweat ran down Eric's temples, and his Ray-Bans kept slipping on his nose. He dug a crushed box of tissues out of the side pocket, slid off his glasses, and wiped his face.

He glanced over at Nasser.

Nasser still wore his bomber jacket—thick leather, zipped up, like it was 1943 and he was in a B-24 over Western Europe. All he needed were a white scarf and Snoopy goggles.

Eric almost laughed, but he didn't have room to talk. He sported Ray-Ban Aviators—never his style, but every pilot he knew had a pair. They'd looked good on Tom Cruise in *Top Gun*. He wore them because Sam liked them. That was reason enough.

"Still wearing the bomber jacket in this heat?"

"Yes," Nasser said. "It is my flight jacket."

"You know you can take it off, right? The FAA doesn't require leather."

"If I take it off, I am just a regular man," Nasser said. "With the jacket, I am a pilot."

Eric wiped his lenses clear. "Fair enough."

Nasser nudged the trim wheel until the pressure came off the yoke and he could fly with his fingertips, like Eric had taught him. The altimeter held 3,000 feet.

Below, the forest rolled away—green in every direction.

"This country is beautiful," Nasser said. "So much green."

Eric glanced from the trees to the panel. "You're holding altitude. Nice."

"Thank you, Eric." Nasser nudged the trim wheel a little too far.

Eric felt the nose begin to creep up.

"I wish my parents could see this," Nasser said. "They would love it."

"Where do they live?"

"Jounieh. Lebanon," Nasser said. "Near Beirut."

The Cessna climbed another fifty feet.

"It may have looked like this once," Nasser said, eyes on the horizon.

"It doesn't anymore?"

Nasser shifted. "No. There are not many trees left where I was born."

The VSI ticked up.

"How come?"

"War."

Eric paused. "I'm sorry."

"It's okay, Eric."

Eric tapped the altimeter with his pen. "Watch your altitude."

Nasser jolted. "Oh—" He corrected, bringing the nose back down to 3,000.

"My father sent me when I was fifteen," Nasser said. "To live with my uncles."

"You ever going back?"

"America is my home. I have a better life here."

"Because you're flying?"

"Yes. I have wanted to fly since I was a young boy," Nasser said. "Flying is not possible there. But here in America you can be anything."

Eric nodded. "That's true." He squinted out at the ridgeline. "I guess they don't exactly love Americans over there, huh?"

Nasser shifted, then let out a small laugh—more at Eric than at the question.

"Eric," he said, "you make many jokes." He glanced over, a quick grin. "I like that."

Eric smirked. "Dangerous habit."

"But . . ." Nasser lifted one shoulder, almost apologetic. "Just so you know—some words, I try not to use. It's not my style. My religion."

Eric blinked, then nodded. "Got it. No problem."

Nasser's smile held. "Thank you. And for the record—I could explain politics all day, but…" He looked back outside. "It is best to keep politics out of the cockpit."

Eric nodded. "Politics and religion," he said, then pointed ahead. "You see the airport yet?"

"I think so, Eric. Right side of the peak."

"That's it," Eric said. "Let's go do some landings. I need to get home soon. Got a trip to Newark tonight."

The Cessna bumped through the rising summer thermals. Eric felt Nasser stiffen beside him.

"So, you are flying the Bruce Goose tonight?" Nasser asked.

"Yep. Probably get a little over an hour of multi time."

"Why is it called that?"

"Tail number's N600SE," Eric said. "From the ramp it looks like it spells GOOSE."

Nasser considered it. "Like Howard Hughes' Spruce Goose."

"Yeah. H-4 Hercules," Eric said. "Biggest wooden airplane ever built. Flew once and never again."

Nasser opened his mouth, then thought better of it.

Eric laughed. "Don't worry — the Bruce Goose actually flies. I'm building my hours, and it's multi-engine time."

Nasser pulled the carb heat, enriched the mixture, and eased the power back as the Cessna descended toward pattern altitude.

"Just hope your wife never sees that cargo plane," Nasser said.

"She wouldn't like it. Especially not tonight. I'll miss her birthday."

"Your wife has a Fourth of July birthday?"

"Yep. Sam's lucky," Eric said. "She always gets fireworks on her birthday."

CHAPTER 2

Birthday Girl

Eric spotted his wife, Sam, through the upstairs window as he wheeled his old FJ Cruiser into the cluttered parking lot of their apartment complex. She leaned over her desk, framed in late-afternoon light, most likely chasing another small-town story for *The Pocono Classifieds*—a free weekly newspaper with a staff of five and barely enough ads to meet payroll.

It wasn't the job she'd dreamed of after graduating from NYU with a degree in journalism and big plans. But when her uncle landed Eric an interview—after patching a hangar roof for the guy who owned a struggling flight school—she packed up and moved back to the Poconos with him.

Eric would teach flying lessons at the local airport during a time when airlines were furloughing and flight hours were drying up everywhere.

"We'll figure it out," she'd said. "I can write anywhere."

She wrote about flea markets, the new antique shop in Swiftwater, the chrome-edged diner in Tannersville that still refused to upgrade its pie case after fifty years, Christmas trees in the library at Skytop—and the psychic shop wedged between Herring Bridal and Trip's House of Vapes—finding stories in the place she once called home.

Sam glanced down from the window as he lifted the birthday cake from the back seat. She pushed back from the desk and hurried to the door of their second-floor apartment. He hesitated outside, cake in hand. He didn't want to tell her Bruce Payne had texted.

Trip tonight newark and back.

There were plenty of hungry instructors who would take it. Multi-engine time was hard to come by and he needed the hours. He stared at the apartment door. At least they would have a few hours tonight for dinner and cake. He shifted the cake to his other hand.

The apartment door swung open before his hand reached the knob. Sam stood barefoot in the doorway, beaming. She wore a white tank top and pale blue shorts, her skin warm from the sun. A silver toe ring caught the light as she shifted her weight onto one hip. Her dark hair was pulled into a loose ponytail, a #2 pencil jammed through it like an antenna—eraser worn flat, the wood chewed and scarred.

"You got me a cake."

"Happy birthday," Eric said, juggling the cake and his flight bag.

She kissed him and held on to his neck.

"Baked it yourself?"

"Yep," he said, carrying her into the narrow kitchen-slash-dining-room-slash-bicycle-storage. "Right before my last flight."

Sam let go, as Eric placed the cake on the counter. He crossed to the small desk against the living-room wall. He pulled his logbook from the drawer, flipped to the next blank line, and filled in the date, the aircraft type, and the hours. Every flight brought him closer to 1,500 hours—the bare minimum just to get noticed—and to his dream of flying for the airlines.

He always logged his flight time the moment he got home—his progress slower than he'd hoped. Sometimes flights canceled for weather—especially in winter. Sometimes for maintenance—especially in the summer, when the airplanes flew nonstop. Some students burned out. Some simply quit. Flying lessons were expensive.

"I swear, these Hobbs meters shortchange me," Eric said. "Feels like my flights are always longer than they say."

"Maybe you lose track of time in the sky."

"Maybe," Eric said. "But if I'm still sitting in the plane thirty minutes after shutdown and not getting credit for it?" He tapped the logbook with his pen. "Over a year, that adds up. That's fifty hours." He capped the pen and closed the logbook.

The apartment was cramped, everything arranged to make the most of their limited square footage. A secondhand couch faced a small TV balanced on milk crates. The kitchen barely had room for a table for two, its linoleum worn thin in front of the sink, two ten-speeds hung from hooks bolted into the ceiling.

She had made it home: mason jar wildflowers on the windowsill, string lights around the doorframe, vanilla candles trying to cover the building's mustiness. A faded Fourth of July red, white, and blue top hat with stars perched on the corner of the bookcase from the night they met.

"How were your flights today?"

"Fine. Except when Nasser tried to spin us into the ground."

Sam froze. "Wait—what?"

Eric lifted a hand. "No—sorry. Bad choice of words. It wasn't a big deal. It was more like a baby spin. We never really got into a full spin." He gave her a quick squeeze as he passed. "I had it under control before he even realized. He pushed the wrong rudder. That's all."

"Maybe save the spiraling-toward-the-earth stories for after cake," she said, without turning.

"Hey. I'm fine. I promise."

Sam turned back to the counter, slowly.

"So," he said, pinching a bit of frosting from the cake, "this frosting is really sweet."

Sam froze, studying him. "You have to fly tonight, don't you?"

He nodded.

"Bruce?"

"Yep."

Sam sighed. "Let me guess. If you don't take it, another instructor will."

"I only need 800 more hours," he said. "Then we're out of here."

She put her plate down harder than necessary. "There's something off about that guy," she said. "I really don't like him."

"It's multi time."

Eric grabbed two mugs from the cupboard—her chipped NYU mug and a Pittsburgh Steelers mug—and placed hers on the table with the chip turned away from her mouth.

"He acts like flying his junky old airplane is supposed to be some kind of gift."

"The airlines love multi time."

"Yeah, as long as it's safe."

Eric wiped his hand on his pants. "Of course it's safe. His planes get inspected by the FAA."

She nodded—almost believing him.

"Once I get the hours, we can start sending out apps," he said. "It'll be worth it."

She stepped toward him. "I don't mind being back here, you know."

He spun her around and wrapped his arms around her waist. His hands slid over her ribs, slow and familiar, holding her tight against him.

She leaned back into him and let him hold her there, the tension easing but not gone. "I know. I'm being selfish," she said. "I don't want to watch fireworks by myself."

"I know." He stayed where he was, arms still around her. "But I do have a surprise for you."

"You already got me cake."

"I know. I got you something else too."

"What is it?"

"A surprise."

She frowned.

"Better not be expensive," she said. "You know we're broke, right?"

"I'm taking you somewhere. Birthday trip. Just a day late."

"Where?"

"You'll see."

She poked his ribs. "What do you have up your sleeve, mister?"

"You'll see."

CHAPTER 3

Don't Drop Her

Eric drove his shoulder into the hangar door.

Metal dragged along metal. The rollers fought the track with a high, scraping whine that carried across the ramp. He leaned into it again until the door gave a few more inches and a narrow gap opened.

A small gray blur shot through first.

"Hey—"

Wilbur hit the concrete at a trot, tail straight up, ears clipped tight against his head. His wiry coat stuck out in uneven tufts. He didn't look back.

"Where's Bruce?" Eric said.

Wilbur ignored him and made a beeline for the left main tire inside, nose down, circling once before planting himself against the rubber and sniffing hard.

Eric shoved the door wider and stepped in.

The air inside was stale and sour—bird droppings, avgas, old rubber. Twilight leaked through a cracked Plexiglas pane high on the wall, just enough to outline the airplane in the middle of the floor. The concrete was mottled with old spills layered over older ones. Near the back wall, a propeller blade leaned in the corner. Shelves sagged under stacks of yellowed Trade-A-Plane magazines and oil-stained manuals. A workbench sat buried beneath alternators, hoses, and coffee cans filled with bolts.

Wilbur thumped the tire once with his paw and looked up at Eric as if to say, Well?

In the far corner, a dog bed lay half-hidden beneath a moving blanket draped over bald tires. A stainless bowl sat beside it, water line halfway down, rim crusted white. The hangar stayed cool in July and held heat in January. Wilbur had made it his.

Eric coughed and stepped fully inside.

Dust hung in the air. He lifted his foot over a coil of safety wire, ducked beneath a jagged strip of sheet metal hanging at eye level, and made his way to the back wall. The fuse box was older than he was—its metal cover bent at one corner. He reached in and twisted the single ceramic fuse.

The high-bay lights blinked once.

Twice.

Then burned steady.

Wilbur barked at the sudden glare and retreated toward the open door, settling where he could watch both Eric and the ramp outside.

The airplane came into view all at once.

N600SE.

The Piper PA-31-350 Chieftain sat low on her gear, aluminum skin dulled to a flat gray. "Casket gray," one of the mechanics had said, tapping the skin with a screwdriver.

The left flap hung a few degrees lower than the right. An access panel near the tail was held down with duct tape gone brittle at the edges. One cowling bore CLOSE ME in fading red Sharpie.

As Eric walked closer, a pigeon burst from the left propeller hub and shot out through the door. Wilbur jumped, then stood stiff, pretending he'd meant to.

Eric stopped at the intake and peered inside.

No nests.

He ran his hand along the fuselage as he began the walk-around, palm skimming rivet lines and shallow dents. Outside, the old Ford fuel truck downshifted on the access road.

Wilbur followed him halfway around the wing, then lost interest and circled back to the wall, curling into his blanket.

Eric crouched beneath the wing and pulled the sump drain. Blue fuel ran clean into the tester. He wiped a streak of oil off the dipstick, checked the level, and slid it back in. When he flicked the landing light on, one side stayed dark.

He leaned closer. The lens was spider-cracked.

"Figures," he muttered.

He stepped back and looked at her.

Dull aluminum. Uneven flap. Tape holding what shouldn't need tape. But the control surfaces moved. The props turned. The gauges usually stayed in the green.

That was enough.

He grabbed the first tote and hauled it into the cabin. Five plastic bins. A dented cooler wrapped tight in gray duct tape. Two plain cardboard boxes with shipping labels he didn't read. The cooler thunked against the floor; he shoved it forward with his boot and cinched the cargo net tight.

Bruce's voice echoed in his head.

"You fly smart, you land it, everybody goes home."

Eric lifted the next tote.

"You get scared every time a screw falls off, you'll never build the hours."

The last box was heavier than it looked. He adjusted his grip and slid it in beside the others.

"You want the hours. I want the freight delivered."

That was the deal. Night departures in weather. Hand-flying approaches into airports with a single non-precision approach. Newark at midnight. Albany in freezing rain. Boxes labeled *farm equipment* that felt like bricks.

Multi-engine time.

He climbed back down and looked at the tail number again.

N600SE.

Around the airport, people talked. Three thousand hours. ATP. Clean logbook. Then Route 611 on New Year's Eve.

Flashing lights in the rearview mirror. After that, no airline calls. Just freight.

Eric closed the cabin door, walked around once more, then climbed into the left seat and pulled the door shut behind him.

He'd taken the Goose through icing that rattled the boots, crosswinds that shoved her sideways on short final, and one night over Allentown when half the panel went dark and the radio hissed like it was dying.

She always made it home.

He slid into the seat and pulled the little red logbook from the side pocket. Hobbs time. He wrote it down without rounding.

"Here we go."

He ran his start flow from memory. Boost pump on. Mixture rich. Props full forward. Throttle cracked.

He leaned out. "Clear prop!"

The left engine coughed on the first crank and caught on the second, shaking the nose. The hangar filled with vibration. The oil-pressure needle hesitated at the peg. He tapped the glass.

It crept into the green.

Outside, runway lights blinked on in sequence.

He tried the right engine.

Whine.

Nothing.

He released the starter, counted under his breath, adjusted the throttle, nudged the mixture.

"Come on."

He hit it again.

The starter groaned, then the prop barked and the engine caught—rough at first, then holding.

Both engines settled into an uneven idle. He eased the throttles back to a shaky thousand RPM and scanned left to right. Oil pressure—green. Fuel flow—steady. One ammeter lagged low; he rapped it once with his knuckle until the needle jumped.

Avionics master on.

The radios snapped to life in a burst of static. Panel lights glowed. Nav. Strobes. One by one.

He didn't say the checklist out loud. His hands moved through it anyway.

He fed in power and the Goose rolled forward out of the hangar. The mains hit the same crack in the concrete and thumped hard before smoothing out. A light crosswind nudged the tail; he held it straight with his feet.

Blue taxi lights slid past on either side. The field was awake now—runway bright, hangars outlined in sodium glow.

He keyed the mic, the transmit switch dangling from the yoke on a dried rubber band.

"Mount Pocono Traffic, November Six Zero Zero Sierra Echo, departing Runway Five, Mount Pocono."

At the hold short, he ran the engines up—magnetos, props, mixtures, gauges.

A corner of white stuck out of his jacket pocket. He pulled it free.

A napkin from the cake, chocolate icing smeared across it—HBD traced into the frosting with her finger, a crooked heart, a frowny face.

The engines shuddered at run-up power.

He folded the napkin once, slid it back into his pocket, and rolled onto centerline.

For her.

Throttles forward.

The engines answered with a full-throated shake. The left stumbled once; he caught it with rudder before the yaw built. The Goose surged.

70.

80.

He held her down a second longer, then eased back.

They were climbing at 200 feet per minute.

He kept the nose where it would hold—just shy of mushy—watching the vertical speed needle struggle upward.

Newark was thirty-two minutes ahead. No autopilot. No GPS. Just the compass, the VOR, and the dark stretching forward. It was enough.

High above, contrails crossed the sky in straight white lines. A pair of strobes blinked far overhead, steady and indifferent.

He held the climb through 3,500 feet. I-80 came into view below—headlights eastbound, taillights west—threading through the valley. He trimmed, leaned the mixture a notch, and kept going.

5,500 feet over the Delaware Water Gap. The river cut clean through the ridge, a black ribbon between darker hills. Mount Minsi to the south. Tammany to the north.

He'd hiked there once.

Sam had walked ahead of him, reading lines from an old railroad ad she'd found in an archive.

"No route brings quite as much delight—as cleanly road of anthracite."

He hadn't understood the line.

He'd understood her.

A jet passed overhead, low enough this time that he could make out the faint blink of its tail light against the stars.

He checked his altimeter again, held the heading, and kept climbing.

Advection fog pooled in the river valleys below, thick and low against the dark. The Goose rode through light bumps, the wings flexing once, then settling. Panel lights cast a weak green glow across the gauges. Oil pressure steady. CHTs stable. Fuel flow where it belonged.

Ten minutes out.

The left engine coughed.

The nose yawed left.

Right rudder.

He pushed hard, eyes snapping to the panel.

Fuel pressure good. Oil pressure holding. Temps steady.

He reached for the checklist without looking.

Fuel pump — ON.

Mixture — full rich.

"Come on."

Throttle — idle.

Don't drop her.

The engine stumbled again, then caught. The prop bit clean air and the yaw eased. He fed power back in slowly.

The airspeed steadied.

Oil pressure still in the green.

Fuel flow steady.

He kept his foot in the rudder another second before easing it off.

"All right," he said quietly.

The checklist went onto the right seat.

The airplane smoothed out.

Then—

A bright flash off the left wing.

CHAPTER 4

Circle the Lady

A red flare burst off the left wingtip, then another, then another.

Below him, New Jersey flickered alive—red over Hackettstown, white strobes near Morristown, blue popping somewhere west of Parsippany. Closer in, over Paterson and Clifton, whole neighborhoods pulsed at once—backyard mortars rising from cul-de-sacs, park shows firing in sync, little towns competing with bigger ones. Every town had its own sky.

At 5,500 feet, the Goose slid through drifting smoke from shells that had climbed too high. One exploded close enough to wash the cockpit in white. He held the climb.

Guard frequency crackled—121.5—then strings, then cannon fire. Someone had keyed up Tchaikovsky. The 1812 Overture boomed through his headset, tinny and distorted and completely inappropriate.

He almost laughed. He reached over and turned the volume down.

The right seat was empty. He glanced at it once, then back outside. Fuel flow steady. Oil pressure good. Cylinder temps where they should be. Trim set. Keep going.

Manhattan rose ahead, lights tight and vertical. He eased the power back, let the nose drop and started down.

"New York Approach, November Six Zero Zero Sierra Echo, VFR request Bravo transition, landing Newark. Information Echo."

A voice came back thick and fast.

"Zero Sierra Echo, squawk two five five two. Descend and maintain two thousand five hundred."

He dialed it in.

"Zero Sierra Echo, radar contact. Descend to one thousand two hundred. We'll take you down the river. Fireworks tonight. Altimeter two niner niner four."

"Down to twelve hundred. Two niner niner four."

"You see the big building all lit up nice and pretty for the fourth of July?"

"Affirmative."

"Follow the Hudson southbound. Stay at twelve hundred. Abeam the Empire, contact Newark Tower one one eight point three. Happy Fourth."

He banked south and settled at 1,200 feet, the Hudson sliding beneath the nose. Fireworks burst level with him now—some below, some rising to meet him. The grand finale went off over the harbor, white light filling the windshield and flashing across the cowling. The Statue of Liberty stood under it all, torch steady, copper washed red and blue.

He held altitude.

Abeam the Empire State Building, he switched frequencies.

"Newark Tower, November Six Zero Zero Sierra Echo, twelve hundred over the Hudson, inbound for Runway Two Niner."

"Zero Sierra Echo, number three. Circle the Lady. We'll call your base."

"Number three. Circle the Lady."

He rolled into a left bank and let the Goose trace a wide arc around the statue, keeping the torch just off his wingtip. Below, heavies lined up for 22 Left—wide bodies dropping out of the dark, landing lights steady and bright. One touched down. Another followed.

He tightened the turn slightly, adjusted power, watched spacing.

Second circle.

Third.

"Zero Sierra Echo, make left base Runway Two Niner."

"Left base."

He broke off the orbit, dropped flaps, reached for the gear. As he turned final, one last shell climbed slow from the river, hung for a second, then split into white.

On guard, a voice came through the static.

"Happy Birthday, America."

He kept his eyes on the runway.

"Sam would've liked this."

CHAPTER 5

Sticky Brain Glue

Eric showed up right on time for his 8 a.m. lesson with Isabella, clutching a large plastic coffee cup. His sunglasses did little to hide the dark circles.

Instead of flying straight back to the Poconos, he'd spent four hours stranded in a maintenance hangar off Taxiway Zulu on the cargo side of Newark Liberty, watching two mechanics wrench on the Goose's left engine until nearly one in the morning. A routine round-trip had turned into an all-night ordeal after the engine refused to start once the cargo was offloaded.

"Why'd you shut it down, kid?" Bruce Payne had asked over the phone.

Maybe it was the lack of sleep—but for once, Eric explained himself. He told Bruce Payne why he hadn't left an airplane with a spinning prop unattended on the Newark ramp. Nothing was more dangerous: an idling engine, blind spots, people walking around. Any ramp controller would've shut him down in a heartbeat.

There was a pause on the line.

"Alright," Bruce said finally. "Yeah. You're right."

A breath through his nose. "That place is a zoo after midnight with all the freight dogs."

Eric stayed quiet.

"I'm not pissed you shut it down," Bruce went on. "You don't leave a prop turnin' at night if you don't know what you're doin'. That's basic."

Eric told him about the hiccup over Jersey.

"Okay," Bruce said. "Then we're not flying it home like that."

"You sure?"

"I don't know." His voice hardened. "Tell them to call me before they touch anything expensive."

By the time Eric touched down back in the Poconos, it was past 2:30 a.m.

One hour in the logbook. *1.0.* Four-plus hours on the ground—waiting, barely awake—under harsh, bluish-white hangar lights.

The call with Bruce hadn't been half as bad as the call with Sam. She'd stayed up, waiting. When Eric finally called to say he was stuck in Newark, he didn't mention the engine trouble—just said the Goose was "giving him trouble." It was easier to worry her a little than to terrify her.

He'd crawled into bed beside her and pressed close. She was warm. She was asleep. He closed his eyes.

Eric leaned against the Piper Warrior, coffee in hand, running on less than four hours of sleep. He and Isabella climbed into the cockpit, buckled in, and taxied toward Runway 5. Quiet frequency. No traffic. A perfect morning for her final lesson before the checkride in the afternoon.

By tonight, she'd be a Certified Flight Instructor, teaching her own students.

Isabella was one of his favorites—and one of his best. Fourth-generation pilot. Her great-grandfather flew with the Tuskegee Airmen in a P-47 with the 332nd Fighter Group—the Red Tails. Her grandfather dodged SAMs over North Vietnam in an F-4 Phantom. Her father flew a Boeing 777 long-haul—Hong Kong, Paris, Dubai. Isabella had been in airplanes before her feet could reach the rudder pedals. She'd been to Oshkosh a dozen times before her first formal lesson, soloed on her sixteenth birthday, and knocked out her private at seventeen—instrument and commercial not long after. Flying was in her blood.

She adjusted her headset and scanned the engine instruments. "Oil pressure's in the green. Suction's good. Fuel pressure stable. Ready for run-up?"

Eric folded his hands loosely in his lap like a bored passenger. "All yours."

She advanced the throttle smoothly to 2,000 RPM and called out the checklist items, one by one. Carb heat—check. Magnetos—left, both, right, both. RPM drop within limits.

"Impressive. You almost sound like a real instructor."

She shot him a look. "Try to contain your excitement."

"I'm just waiting for you to hang your purse on the mixture knob again."

She groaned. "One time. One time—and I was joking."

"You said, 'Is this where this goes?' like you were dead serious. I almost jumped out of the airplane."

"Anybody ever tell you that's a bad idea without a parachute?" she said, adjusting her Ray-Bans.

"Good to know," he said. "You're really getting this CFI stuff. You must have a good instructor."

"He's all right," she said. "After he's had his coffee."

Eric took a sip.

"Ahhh." He glanced at her. "Sorry—you were saying?"

She brought the throttle back to idle. "Mixture full rich. Trim set for takeoff. Doors and windows secure."

"And no handbags attached to critical engine controls?" Eric added.

"Wait." She held up both hands and glanced around. "Have you seen my lip gloss?"

Eric shook his head. "Jeez. And here I thought I might actually survive this lesson today."

She rolled her eyes and taxied toward the runway. "Hopefully you remembered your parachute this time."

The takeoff from Runway 5 was textbook. In the right seat, Isabella had the controls—light touch, eyes always scanning. The Piper Warrior skimmed along the ridge, its low wing slicing through a July-blue sky. Below, the runs at Camelback Mountain were all green, grassy hills waiting for winter.

Eric slouched in the left seat, legs sprawled, arms crossed, playing the bored private student.

"So," he said, voice flat, "are we almost in Jersey yet, or what?"

Isabella smirked. "Depends. Did you file a flight plan with Wawa as our alternate? I think you need more coffee."

"See?" Eric said. "That's the kind of sass the FAA loves in a new CFI."

She gave the yoke a slight nudge left, banking smoothly toward the ridgeline. "You told me to treat this like a real lesson."

"Right." He sat up, adjusted his seatbelt, and pointed at the panel. "So, here's the real lesson. Teaching is building blocks. Start simple. Nail the basics. Don't jump straight to P-factor. Demonstrate a takeoff without enough right rudder. Then one with no right rudder at all. Then it clicks: what happens when the downward-moving blade takes a bigger bite of air than the upward-moving one."

"Got it," Isabella said.

"And most important—don't ever tell them the wrong thing," Eric said. "In fact, don't give them an answer if you aren't 100% sure."

She glanced over. "Even if I think I'm 90% sure?"

"Nope. Not even 99%. If you don't know, say so," he said. "Offer to look it up later. But don't guess. Law of primacy."

Isabella nodded, eyes back outside.

"The first thing a student hears sticks," he said. "Right or wrong. Teach it wrong, and that bad info gets cemented."

"My dad installed the water lines to a faucet backward when I was a kid. To this day, I still have to think about which side's hot."

"Primacy," she said. "Sticky brain glue."

"Exactly. Sticky brain glue. That's how you build safe pilots—and keep them from breaking airplanes."

The engine droned. Wind slipped past the fuselage.

"So," Eric said, stretching. "You ready for the next lesson?"

"Probably not."

The Warrior droned along.

"If I do anything stupid today, stop me. I got about three hours of sleep."

"That's terrifying."

"Welcome to the life of a CFI," he said.

Isabella adjusted her grip on the yoke.

Eric reached down and pulled the throttle to idle. "Engine failure."

The nose dropped.

It got quiet. The vibration stopped.

"What now, brand-new instructor with a brand-new student?" he said. "And don't just push the throttle back in like last time. We're pretending."

Isabella gave a tight nod. "Roger that, Captain."

She scanned her instruments and trimmed the Warrior for best glide.

She glanced over. "You pulled the power," she said, "but you forgot something."

"Carb heat," she added. "Unless you want our engine turning into a Slush Puppie."

She didn't wait for approval. Isabella reached forward and pulled the carb heat knob. The engine coughed once, RPM dropping as it settled into a rough, uneven idle.

Eric stared out the window. "Good catch." He frowned. "Slush Puppie?"

Isabella tightened her grip. "Best glide—set. Trim for 73 knots. Pick a spot." She adjusted the trim again. "Looking for a place to land."

"Lots of trees out there," Eric said. "Trees are bad."

"There," she said, pointing. "Highway. Two lanes. Minimal traffic. No telephone wires."

Eric monitored.

Isabella held best glide and calmly banked into a descending turn toward the highway.

"Radio call?" he prompted. "Pretend."

"Engine failure, Mount Pocono traffic," she said. "Warrior Four Two Charlie, over Camelback mountain, engine failure, descending south of the field."

"What frequency are we on?"

"UNICOM. Or 121.5 if I had to—and I'd declare an emergency."

"Nice."

"Mixture full rich. Switch tanks." She glanced at him. "Can you switch tanks? Left to right."

"Got it." Eric reached down. "Oh—hey. There's my pen. I knew I dropped that somewhere."

"Mixture rich. Switch tanks," she repeated, eyes flicking to the selector. "Which you left on the left tank. I'd go to right."

He gave her a look. "Just checking."

"Sneaky," she said. "I'm not falling for that again."

"Now you're getting it," Eric said. "Never trust your students. Remember—they're all trying to kill you."

Isabella kept her eyes forward. "I was wondering when you were going to say that."

Eric grinned and looked back outside.

The road widened in the windscreen.

Isabella continued aloud. "Carb heat—on. Mags—both. Master—on. Engine instruments—check for signs of life. If it were real, I'd go for restart now."

"Sharp," Eric said. "And when you land, land with the traffic."

"Roger that. Landing with traffic. Avoiding a head-on with an imaginary cement truck."

She held the descent. Calm. The road swelled in the windscreen. Lane markings thickened. Guardrails rose. The tops of trees separated into individual crowns. The road stopped looking flat.

At 300 feet, Eric eased the throttle back in, and the engine roared to life.

"All right, that's low enough," he said. "Let's try to stay out of the emergency room today."

Isabella exhaled.

"I was kind of hoping you'd wait another five seconds. I was lining up for a really nice touchdown."

She pulled back, and the Warrior climbed away from the ground.

"Yeah, but the drivers start to get nervous below fifty feet."

"Fifty feet? Yeah, right."

"Airspeed, altitude, or brains," Eric said. "You only need two."

Isabella held up two fingers, counted silently, then looked over at him. "Lucky you."

Eric glanced over, then sighed at the sky. "This is the thanks I get for passing on priceless aviation wisdom."

Isabella laughed. "You walked right into that," she said. "You're the one who said never trust the student. I'm just being a good one."

"All right, hotshot. Let's climb back to pattern altitude, and I'll show you how not to enter the downwind." He smirked. "Besides, I'd rather be lucky than good."

Isabella rolled her eyes. "Are you going to keep this up all day?"

"Nah," Eric said, stretching. "That's about two hours. Let's head back."

Isabella glanced at the clock on the panel. "Two hours? We've only been up a little over one."

"Right—one hour," he said quickly. "My brain's still back in Newark."

"You need coffee."

"I need sleep." He glanced at his watch. "Wake me up on short final."

"Roger that."

PART II

Drag

CHAPTER 1

Land of Love

"You are now entering the land of love." Sam read the words painted in gold across the red, heart-shaped sign along the road to the famous honeymoon resort, Lovers' Cove. The paint had dulled just enough to suggest it had once gleamed. "Eric Andrew," she said, "are you taking me to a little love nest?" She leaned forward, chin resting on her knees, bare feet propped on the dashboard as she took it all in.

Eric kept his eyes on the road.

Sam smiled. "It's okay. I've always wondered about these places."

Keeping his eyes ahead, Eric said, "I just wanted it to be something . . . different. For your birthday."

Her smile widened. "This is not what I was expecting."

They rounded a bend and the entrance hit them like a dare: a giant wooden archway flanked by two concrete cupids—one winking, one blowing a kiss—their edges worn by years of weather, their expressions permanently committed. The resort's name was announced again in looping red letters:

LOVER'S COVE

Eric slowed the FJ Cruiser and lifted his sunglasses, hooking them at the collar of his flight jacket.

"Wow," he said. "They are not subtle."

Sam squinted at the sign, her toes tapping lightly against the windshield in a slow, absent rhythm. "I hope that apostrophe's wrong."

"Huh?"

"It says *Lover's Cove*—the apostrophe's after the *r*, before the *s*," she said, still studying the sign. "That makes it singular. If it were *Lovers'*, the apostrophe would go after the *s*." She tilted her head. "Unless this place belongs to one very ambitious lover."

Eric looked at the sign, then back at her.

"You can take the girl out of NYU," he said, "but you can't take NYU out of the girl."

"Well, ya know . . ."

The road narrowed into a winding driveway, cracked asphalt bordered by low stone walls tangled with ivy. Every fifty feet, a heart-shaped sign appeared, each offering a faded gold affirmation in looping cursive:

Hold Hands, Hold Hearts.

Your Forever Starts Today.

No Refunds—Just Love.

Sam glanced over at Eric. "Was not expecting that last one."

"What does that even mean?"

"Not really sure," she said. "At least it's spelled correctly."

"They really went all in," she straightened up for a better view.

As they crested the hill, the full grounds of Lovers' Cove spilled into view—like a postcard from another time. Walking paths looped through flower beds and overgrown shrubs, some still trimmed into hearts or swans.

Couples were everywhere.

A young couple pedaled past on a tandem bicycle. Another pair giggled beneath a faded white gazebo. A man in a T-shirt that read JUST MARRIED carried a woman piggyback while she wore a pure-white veil of tulle and glitter. A rowboat glided across the manufactured pond.

On the far shore, a paddleboat shaped like a giant swan hugged the edge. Eric squinted. "Tell me that's not a giant swan-boat."

"Oh, it's a giant swan-boat."

To their right, they passed tennis courts. Rosebushes had grown wild along the edges, their blooms drooping with neglect. One man swung and missed, the ball thudding into the net; his partner giggled, jumped into his arms, and kissed him anyway.

The next building was Lovers' Spa Pavilion—a retro 1970s spaceship of tinted domes and dulled chrome. A faded sign out front read:

Couples Mud Baths — Chocolate Fondue Bar — Candlelit Saunas.

"Chocolate and saunas?" She tilted her head, reading the sign again. "That sounds kind of . . . messy."

Eric looked at her, then back at the pavilion.

Farther in, private villas sat among the pines—stone chimneys, red doors, roofs curling at the edges. White string lights zigzagged from eave to eave; even in daylight, a few flickered weakly, refusing to die.

Then, the main lodge rose at the top of the slope—tall and grand, but slightly outdated—painted beams stretching upward, windows dulled by dust. A frayed red carpet led to double glass doors. Above them, a neon sign buzzed in lipstick red, fighting to stay alive:

The Heart of the Cove.

Eric pulled the FJ into a spot marked by a red sign:

Reserved For Sweethearts Only.

They sat for a moment, taking it in.

"It's like a giant Valentine's Day card."

Sam turned to him, wide-eyed. "That's it. A Valentine's Day card from the seventies."

He rubbed the back of his neck. "I wasn't sure if you'd like this, to be honest. I heard a commercial on the radio yesterday morning and booked it on my phone."

Sam's eyes sparkled. "It's kitschy and kind of great at the same time. Honestly? I'm liking it. And I love that you wanted to bring me here. I just—" She shook her head. "I didn't even know places like this still existed."

Relief crossed Eric's face. He looked over, sheepish. "Yeah. The pictures looked different on the internet."

She squeezed his hand. "It's wonderful. This is going to be fun."

They got out and walked toward the lodge. Behind them, a swan-boat drifted into the reeds and got stuck. Another couple watching from a nearby bench started clapping, and the man in the swan-boat, his sweetheart beside him, waved like he'd planned the whole thing.

"Welcome to the land of love," a bellhop called, hurrying past as the glass doors—plastered with hearts and cupids—whooshed open.

CHAPTER 2

Champagne Wishes and Heart-Shaped Dreams

Inside, Lovers' Cove looked like it hadn't updated since 1978: plush red carpet worn thin in traffic lines, neon hearts sputtering along the walls, marble columns chipped and yellowing, mirrored ceilings throwing the tired light back at itself. *You Take My Breath Away*—not the fighter-jet one, the other one by Rex Smith—played a little too loudly from somewhere unseen, the speakers crackling like they hadn't been touched since the song first hit the charts. A crystal chandelier rotated in the center of the lobby, its prisms cloudy and nicotine-dulled, scattering uneven light across the room. Near the entrance, an ice sculpture of two swans locked in a frozen kiss melted into a shallow tray.

Sam looked around. "Wow," she said—half awe, half disbelief.

Eric glanced at her, unsure whether to be proud or embarrassed.

“This is like the commercials,” Sam said. “When I was little. I forgot about them.”

Eric took in the wallpaper—chubby pink cherubs with arrows. “It’s like Cupid opened a timeshare—”

“Welcome to Lovers’ Cove,” the receptionist said brightly. Her name tag read Brigitte™. “Checking in for a romantic escape?”

Eric started to answer, caught on the tiny ™, and stalled—just long enough to be weird.

Sam slid in. “Yes. We’re here for the champagne wishes and heart-shaped dreams package.”

Eric turned to her. “We are?” He blinked once, then shut his mouth.

“I don’t know,” she said. “That’s what the commercials used to say.” Then she half-sang, half-spoke the lyrics, playful and nostalgic:

“Champagne wishes and heart-shaped dreams,
In the Poconos, love is more than it seems . . .”

Brigitte kept smiling, patient as a professional.

Sam’s voice trailed off when she caught Eric’s look.

“But,” Sam said, rccovering, “we’ll take . . .”

Eric tried again. “We want one of the champagne-glass rooms.”

Brigitte beamed. “Of course you do. All suites come with a Champagne Tower and a heart-shaped tub. May I also recommend a round oversized bed that rotates beneath a mirrored ceiling?”

“We’ll take it,” Sam said.

As Brigitte typed, Sam drifted to a life-size Cupid statue holding a stack of brochures for couples’ archery lessons.

“Hey, look.” She held one up. “We can shoot love arrows tomorrow after breakfast.”

Eric took the brochure. “Why would we be doing archery?”

“It’s Cupid, Eric,” Sam pointed at the statue. “Love arrows. Romance.”

“Oh.” He nodded once, like he’d known all along. “Sure. Cupid. Obviously.”

She raised her eyebrows—twice.

Brigitte handed Eric a keycard on a heart-shaped keychain. “You’re in Champagne Suite Seven,” she said. “One of our premium suites. Décor inspired by Venus and Adonis.”

“Right,” Eric said automatically, taking it.

Sam grabbed his hand and tugged him away from the desk.

As they turned to go, Eric glanced back at Brigitte’s name tag. Brigitte winked.

They headed down a hallway. Eric squeezed Sam’s hand.

“What was up with the ™ on Brigitte’s name tag?” he asked.

Sam didn’t even slow down. “Yeah, I didn’t get that one either.”

A suite door swung open and warm chlorine air, plus the slow pulse of *Let's Get It On*, spilled into the hall. A guy stood there in a towel, suds clinging to his shoulders, gripping a silver ice bucket. Behind him, his wife, was dripping and toweling off in the pink light, bubbles hiding nothing. She saw them and shrieked, "Alex!"

Alex lunged and slammed the door so fast the latch clacked.

Eric paused, watching Sam for a reaction.

Sam kept walking and called back, a little too bright, "You're good—we didn't see a thing!"

A few steps later, Sam slipped out of her sandals and hooked them together by the straps, walking on without breaking stride.

They stopped at the door to Suite Seven. A glittery decal above it read:

. . . *where dreams bubble over.*

Eric opened the door. Strawberry-scented air hit them full in the face. Sam squealed in delight, her bare feet sinking into the plush carpet.

Eric took one look around. "Okay. I may have underestimated this place."

CHAPTER 3

The Heart-Shaped Tub

Suite Seven looked like it had been designed by a magazine ad—bold, glossy, and slightly out of date.

A round bed sat beneath a mirrored ceiling, upholstered in crushed red velvet. At the foot, two swan-shaped towel sculptures faced each other, necks curved into a heart. Fake rose petals were scattered across the comforter, trying hard. In the headboard, a metal slot and a handwritten note suggested that the bed could be made to vibrate.

A fake fireplace flickered in the corner, throwing jittery orange light across metallic wallpaper embossed with vines and cherubs. A red velvet loveseat faced it, cushions permanently impressed. Above it, a television played an instrumental version of *Lady*, by Kenny Rogers.

The minibar held tiny bottles of amaretto and schnapps. Two cans of whipped cream sat beside the chocolate-covered strawberries, because of course they did.

In the bathroom, sunk deep into the tile, sat the heart-shaped tub—glossy and exact. It didn't hug a wall. The room had been built around it. Under the red heat lamp, the porcelain looked permanently pink under the heat lamp.

The centerpiece was the Champagne Tower: a seven-foot champagne-glass hot tub on a mirrored platform, bubbles churning beneath pink recessed lights. A short spiral staircase wrapped around the base, its brass handrail worn smooth by thousands of honeymoon hands.

They stood there a moment, taking it in. Lovers' Cove tried hard. Like a guy in a wrinkled suit at the edge of the party.

They fell onto the loveseat and Eric rubbed Sam's legs, slow and absent at first. With each pass, his hand drifted a little higher, brushing the hem of her dress, then slipping just beneath.

She shifted against him, then slid her toes along the leather of his left boot, hooking the heel. With a tug, she pulled it halfway off. The second foot joined in, pressing until the boot thudded onto the carpet.

"Next."

She did the same with the right boot, her toes curling just enough to catch the edge until it slipped free.

She put her phone on the floor.

"Stop wasting time." She stretched. "I planned on being very naked tonight."

"Where do we do it first?"

"Definitely the heart-shaped tub."

CHAPTER 4

Cocktails and Cuddles

The Love Lounge was buried beneath the main lodge, tucked into the basement, pretending to be a naughty secret the resort didn't know how to keep. A velvet rope cordoned off the stairwell. A heart-shaped sign read:

TONIGHT: Live DJ — Couples Dancing — Cocktails & Cuddles.

"Did that sign say 'cuddles'?" Eric asked, glancing back at the sign.

Sam hooked her arm through his. "It's legally required here, my love."

Eric turned. "My love? I kind of like that."

At the bottom of the stairs, the lounge opened into a cave of dim light and mirrored columns. The ceiling glittered with fiber-optic stars. A disco ball spun slowly, scattering pinpricks of light across tables and faces.

The bar curved in a half-moon. Champagne flutes stood in neat rows from one end to the next. The bartender—a man with a bushy mustache and a permanent smile—caught their eye and gave them a quick, knowing wink, as if welcoming them to the club.

Eric shook his head, amused. "I think everyone here is in on it." He reached for her hand, and together they slid into the crowd.

The dance floor was outlined in red rope lights blinking to the beat of a glitter-soaked disco track—music that sounded like tight pants, cologne and platform shoes.

The DJ, in a red bowtie and a glittery jacket that caught every light in the room, stood behind a glowing, heart-shaped booth labeled DJ ROMEO, his head bobbing as if he'd been doing this since 1978.

Rod Stewart's *Do Ya Think I'm Sexy?* pulsed through the room.

"DJ Romeo, huh?" Eric said. "I'll bet he plays a lot of love songs."

"I wouldn't call this a love song," Sam replied, watching a few couples lean into the groove. "This song practically unbuttons its own shirt."

Eric stared at her, deadpan. "You've been saving that one, haven't you?"

She didn't answer. She pretended to unbutton the top button of her shirt—slowly, deliberately—and then turned back to the dance floor.

Eric rolled his eyes. "Wow."

She giggled.

They found seats near the dance floor—white linen draped over the tables, silk roses rising from tall blue-and-white Ming vases.

"These are beautiful," she said.

"Even the menus are heart-shaped," Eric said. Then, almost to himself, "Shocking."

Sam lifted one, turning it in her hands. "Oh my gosh, they are."

Before they could open them, the lights dimmed. DJ Romeo leaned into the mic with the silky confidence of a man who'd built his entire life around late-night FM radio.

"All right, lovebirds… this one's for the classics. No filters. No auto-tune. Just two hearts—and the Long Island maestro himself. Let's take it back . . . to *Just the Way You Are*."

The smooth electric piano filled the room.

Sam dropped her menu.

"Oh my God."

"Seriously?"

"I love this song," she said.

"How did I never know this about you?"

She was already reaching for his hand. "Dance with me."

"How could I possibly say no in a place like this?"

They stepped onto the glowing dance floor. The electric piano moved first, buttery and patient, each chord settling into the room like it had nowhere else to be.

Then the saxophone eased in beside it—warm, breathy, unhurried—sliding between the notes, softening their edges, lingering just a heartbeat longer than expected. Together they wrapped the song in something slow and human, the piano laying the ground and the sax leaning close, as if the music itself were dancing cheek to cheek.

"I feel like we just wandered onto an episode of *The Love Boat.*"

"Shhh," Sam said, smiling into his shirt. "Just dance with me."

CHAPTER 5

The Legend of Frank Sinatra

Their waiter, wearing a sash that read, LOVE AMBASSADOR, poured their champagne. "Your prix fixe entrées will be right out," he said. "Tonight's main course is chicken cordon bleu with heart-shaped twice-baked potatoes."

Eric lifted his glass, laying it on thick. "To love. And blue cheese—and I do mean cheeeese." He motioned around the room.

Sam clinked her glass against his. "It's Swiss, actually. Chicken cordon bleu."

"Right. Swiss. I meant Lovers' Cove cheese."

"To *Lovers'*—plural possessive—Cove. May it never, ever modernize."

At the next table, a couple in matching Just Married T-shirts giggled like teenagers, leaning over the centerpiece candle and slurping opposite ends of a single spaghetti strand. It snapped too soon, globs of sauce splashing the bride's shirt.

Eric's phone buzzed. He read the text. "Isabella passed her checkride."

Sam's face lit up. "She can start instructing now?"

"Yep. She's probably already on the schedule. I knew she'd pass." He turned his phone off and slipped it into his pocket. "She's sharp. Headed to the Air Force Academy in the fall."

"I love her," Sam said. "She's funny."

"Yeah. She really is."

Midway through dinner, a man in a tailored red blazer moved from table to table, shaking hands and trading easy conversation. His pocket square was folded with precision. His cologne—faintly citrus, unmistakably expensive—lingered after he passed. He walked with the posture of someone who had hosted hundreds of nights like this and expected every one of them to matter.

When he reached their table, he paused, smiled with practiced ease, and rested one hand lightly on the back of Sam's chair—just enough to suggest familiarity, not intrusion.

"Good evening, folks," he said. "And how are we treating you tonight?"

Eric opened his mouth to answer, but Sam got there first. "We're being treated like royalty. I love the Ming vases on all the tables," she said, playing along.

The man chuckled—low and smooth. "That's what we like to hear." He gestured toward the vase. "My partner's obsessed with blue-and-white ceramics. I've never really understood why. But in a good relationship, you don't have to understand everything. You just have to stay true." He looked at them. "Sometimes love is admiring the obsession, even when it doesn't make much sense to you." He let the thought settle, then added, "Being in love isn't about agreement—it's about attention."

Sam nodded, letting him finish.

"I suppose, after all these years of watching couples come and go, I've learned two things."

Their host held up a finger. "The first—you can always tell when two people are truly in love." His gaze shifted to them, not invasive—just observant.

"It's there," he said. "In the way people look at each other. In the pauses. The quiet between words."

He nodded once, satisfied.

"And you two?" their host continued. "You look each other in the eyes."

Sam looked at Eric and smiled. "And the second?"

He lifted a second finger.

"Every breakup happens for the same reason," he said. "One person simply decides they can do better."

Sam's smile faded.

She felt Eric's hand tighten around hers, then loosen again.

Their host extended a hand. The cuff of his shirt was monogrammed in pale blue silk.

"David Roseman," he said. "My family's owned Lovers' Cove since 1962. Welcome."

He shook both of their hands with practiced ease—firm but unhurried, as if the gesture itself had been borrowed from *Casablanca* and rehearsed until the wrist knew exactly when to let go—his thumb lingering a moment longer than necessary, his expression already anticipating their reaction.

"That's a long time," Eric said.

"My grandfather started it all," David Roseman said, not quite boasting, but enjoying the memory. "Back when heart-shaped bathtubs were considered scandalous."

"Wow," Eric said.

David Roseman leaned in, lowering his voice like a man trading in secrets. "You know that saxophone solo in the Billy Joel song you were dancing to earlier?"

"*Just the Way You Are?*" Sam asked.

David Roseman smiled, pleased. "That solo was performed by Phil Woods." He let the name sit. "One take. Billy Joel wanted something that sounded . . . inevitable. It ended up on *The Stranger*."

Eric looked up. "Who's Phil Woods?"

Sam squeezed his hand.

"Lived right here in the Poconos." David Roseman said. "One night in '89, Phil played here for three hours. People came by the busload. It was mythic." He paused. "I snuck into the club that night and watched from behind the ficus while my father mixed a rye Manhattan at the bar that Lady Randolph Churchill herself would've expected."

"Wow," Eric said. "Behind the ficus."

Sam's toe found his under the table. Firmly.

David Roseman looked at them a moment longer, as if measuring something unspoken. He didn't fidget. He didn't scan the room. He gave the impression of a man who had nowhere else to be—and no need to prove it. He straightened the edge of their tablecloth. Instead of gliding to the next table, he pulled out the empty chair beside them, brushed an invisible speck from his blazer sleeve, and sat down like someone who had spent a lifetime making others feel at ease—and knew exactly how much space to take.

"I have to say," he began, folding his hands, "it's always nice when a couple like you finds us. You truly look like you're in love. I can see it."

"We are," Sam said.

"Some couples come here chasing something they saw in an ad." He opened his palms. "But you two?" A measured pause. "You brought it with you."

He studied them another moment, satisfied.

"Lovers' Cove is amazing," Sam said. "It feels like a memory I didn't know I had. They used to run commercials when I was little. Maybe that's it."

"We like to think we're preserving something that mattered."

His gaze drifted across the room.

"Places like this were built for devotion." He gestured gently around them. "For belief."

"Belief in what?" Sam asked.

He met her eyes. "That two people could come to the Poconos and forget about the rest of the world. Just to be with each other. If only for a little while."

"Like a theme park for sweethearts," Sam said. "But there's real love here. You can feel it."

"Then you understand."

Sam's eyes glistened. "I've been writing stories about the Poconos," she said. "There's so much here. People just… drive past." She glanced around the room. "Places like this—they're slipping away."

Eric recognized the look. She wasn't pitching anything yet, but she was already somewhere ahead of him. When Sam believed in a story, she didn't let go.

David Roseman folded his hands neatly. "Ah. So, you're a writer."

"Journalist," Sam said. "For *The Pocono Classifieds*. Free paper. Weekly—but we're still standing."

David Roseman nodded, adjusting the corner of a cloth napkin before setting it back down in a perfect square. "I've seen it. Yes, of course. We look forward to it every week."

"That's wonderful to hear." She doubted he waited by the mailbox for it each week—but she liked imagining that he might.

"Who doesn't drive around the Poconos and wonder what stories are hiding inside those abandoned honeymoon resorts? I try to capture things like that."

"My family built five honeymoon resorts here in the Poconos," he said. "Only Lovers' Cove is still open."

He paused.

"The others have . . . crumbled away."

His eyes drifted around the room before returning to them.

"The first one still stands." He paused. "Technically."

"Wait," Sam said. "Your family built one of the very first Pocono honeymoon resorts?"

"We did. Honeymoon Hideaway." He held the name a moment. "It's still there," he said. "Still standing."

He tipped his chin toward Eric; Eric returned the gesture.

"In its day, it was the crown jewel." He adjusted his cuff. "People planned their weddings around it."

His voice warmed as memory took hold. "My father used to say that if you threw a dart at a Long Island phone book in '63, you'd hit someone who'd honeymooned there."

"He even built a runway," David Roseman added.

"Couples used to fly into your resort?" Sam asked.

"They did," David Roseman said. "Some of our—shall we say—better-heeled clientele."

Sam turned to Eric. "Have you ever seen that runway from the air?"

"Not that I know of."

"It's on the ridge, behind the main lodge," David Roseman said. "Just a landing strip and a few parking spots. There's a small hangar with steps that lead down to the resort."

"I'll look for it next time."

"Our couples at Honeymoon Hideaway enjoyed candlelit dinners and strolling violinists," David Roseman went on. "They returned to suites named *Colosseum of Desire, Temple of Ecstasy, Venus in Velvet.*"

"Venus in Velvet," Eric repeated.

Sam's toe found his foot beneath the table—then pressed down hard. She didn't look at him.

"But," David Roseman said, and something in his face cooled, "eventually our couples had better things to do than drive three hours from Queens."

He adjusted a cufflink—square-cut sapphire set in platinum.

"Though I'll admit," he added, "my father refused to modernize. No televisions. No telephones in the suites. He believed mirrored ceilings and heart-shaped tubs would be enough."

Sam sighed. "A private runway and heart-shaped tubs—and no cable TV." She shook her head, amused. "That actually sounds perfect."

"He believed romance didn't need modern technology," David Roseman said. "He was right, for a long time. Until he wasn't."

"What about the other resorts?"

"Gone," David Roseman said. "Bulldozed or abandoned." He smoothed the pleats of his slacks. "One of our old lots is the U-Haul depot now."

"I would love to see one of the original Poconos honeymoon resorts," Sam sighed, "Could I go there to research a story?"

David Roseman shook his head.

"Unfortunately, you couldn't get in. It was gated off at the main road years ago," he said. "It's quite far back—down a long drive."

"How about a tour?" Sam asked.

Eric grinned. He knew his writer wife well.

David Roseman considered her, then shook his head. "That wouldn't be possible. It isn't a museum." A polite nod. "It's seen better days." He met her eyes. "And I'd hate for it to become an elegy. Some things are better remembered as they were."

"No," Sam said quickly. "That's not what I have in mind at all. I'd like to research the old majesty—to capture what time left behind, in a sense. That's what interests me."

David Roseman listened, nodding once. When he spoke, his voice was calm and settled.

"I'm afraid that won't be possible," he said. "An exposé on my family's crumbling resort is not something I'd ever want to see. I've never considered opening it, and I don't intend to."

He let the words rest—firm—then nodded, just enough to keep the moment intact.

He turned to Eric. "So, you're a pilot?"

"How'd you know?"

"She asked if you'd ever seen our runway," David Roseman said, smiling. "I put it together."

“I’m a flight instructor at Mount Pocono Airport.”

“I’ve always wanted to learn to fly. My partner once gave me a coupon for a lesson.” He adjusted the crease at his cuff, eyes drifting briefly toward the far window. “I never used it. I’ve often regretted that.”

Sam jumped in. “If you ever change your mind, I know a good instructor.” She put her arm around Eric. “Free lesson for a tour?”

Eric looked at her.

David Roseman stood. “I’ll have to keep that in mind.” He smoothed the front of his jacket with a single, practiced swipe. “Enjoy your eve—”

He stopped himself, nodded politely to the couple at the next table, then smiled warmly at the bride splattered with marinara sauce, as though this were exactly the type of romance he specialized in. Then he turned to go.

“Wait,” Sam said.

He stopped.

“The apostrophe,” she said, rushing now. “On your sign. At the entrance. It’s wrong.”

David Roseman paused. Then he turned back.

Eric glanced at Sam, then back to David Roseman, offering a small, apologetic shrug.

“The apostrophe,” David Roseman asked. “Is wrong?”

“It says *Lover’s* Cove,” she said. “Singular possessive. But it should be *Lovers’*. Plural possessive.” She hesitated, “Unless the resort belongs to one very . . . busy person.”

Eric, without thinking, lifted a hand and traced a small, useless apostrophe in the air, nodding solemnly.

David Roseman nodded slowly, as if searching his memory for a long-forgotten grammar rule. He studied her, and something shifted behind his eyes.

"We'll have to fix that."

He glanced up at the disco ball, then back at her, turning his wrist in that easy, deliberate gesture that was unmistakably David Roseman.

"Have you ever heard about the time Frank Sinatra came to Honeymoon Hideaway?" His eyes twinkled, like he'd just uncorked a bottle of myth.

Sam blinked. "Sinatra? The Frank Sinatra?"

"The very one," he said, pleased with himself. "Summer of '68. He was in the area—Philly, maybe New York—and stopped in for a nightcap. Next thing you know, he's at the piano in our lounge."

He gestured toward the far end of the room.

"Mind you, it wasn't just any piano. A Steinway Model D. Most lounges settled for a Model B—fits better in a tight space. But my grandfather believed in resonance."

He rested his hand flat, as if feeling it through the floor.

"Said the D hums in the floorboards. Full concert grand. Gleaming ebony. Massive."

Sam's eyes brightened. "Is the piano still there?"

"It is," David Roseman said. "They had to remove the door frame to get it inside. My grandfather was furious. Once it was in—it was never coming out."

Eric watched him closely, not interrupting, not quite buying it.

"Wow," Sam said. "I would love to see that piano."

David Roseman nodded, considering.

Eric glanced at her, then at David Roseman, then back at Sam.

"What did he sing?" Eric asked.

"Bartender said Sinatra and the piano player walked in, did a full set that ended with '*Come Fly With Me*,' and walked out like ghosts."

Sam leaned in. "Really?"

"No set list. Just the Steinway, and a scotch," David Roseman said.

Eric frowned. "Why would he do that?"

Sam nudged him with her knee.

David Roseman laughed. "Because he was Frank Sinatra."

He glanced between them, candlelight catching his face.

"There are no photos. No recordings. No proof." He gave a small shrug. "Some legends are better when you don't insist on verifying them."

He let that thought settle.

"Yeah, right," Eric said.

David Roseman looked back to Sam.

"My grandfather would never have missed that apostrophe," he said. "Details mattered to him. I shouldn't have missed it either. It will be corrected. Thank you for seeing it."

He reached into his blazer and handed Sam a crisp, heavy business card—matte ivory, his name embossed in raised silver.

"Call me with your story idea," he said. "Maybe one day I'll show you the Steinway."

"That's my personal number," he added. "At the bottom."

Then he turned with a practiced flourish and moved on—already smiling at the next table.

Sam stared at the empty chair for a moment. "That man knows exactly how to make an exit."

Eric let out a low whistle.

"He just gave you his personal number. And promised to fix an apostrophe. I think you might be the only person he's ever promised to do anything for."

Sam looked down at the card in her hand, then back at the empty chair. "It wasn't about the apostrophe. He probably just cares about the same things I do."

Eric nodded, still watching the room reset itself around David Roseman's absence. "He floats in and floats out right on cue," he said. "After dropping a couple of legends."

"You know," Sam said, "I kind of believe him."

Eric squeezed her hand. "I do too, honey."

"I said kind of."

CHAPTER 6

Love Is Such a Beautiful Thing

"Ladies and gentlemen," DJ Romeo purred into the microphone, his voice dripping with velvet, "this one goes out to anyone who's ever been struck by Cupid's arrow . . . hit by his crossbow . . . or simply sideswiped by passion." He smiled to himself. "In the hot tub of love." A few appreciative laughs rippled through the room. "It's the Bee Gees with," he lowered his voice, "*Too Much Heaven*."

"Did he just say hot tub of love?"

"Shh," Sam said, already pulling his hand. "DJ Romeo is speaking my language."

They stepped onto the floor, joining the swaying orbit of couples beneath the disco ball. The lights softened, and then—there it was—that first dreamy falsetto of Barry Gibb curling into the room.

Sam pulled herself close to Eric. She rested her head against his chest and closed her eyes. He folded his arms around her, grounding her in something quiet and unbreakable. Their bodies finding an off-beat rhythm—charmingly imperfect. But somehow, still perfect.

The music carried them, her breath rising and falling with his, his hand at the small of her back, her palm resting against his chest.

The kitsch kept glittering, but the joke was gone. For a moment, it felt like Lovers' Cove was a place built just for them. A silly fairytale that had somehow turned real. Around them, the cheesy décor faded into background magic.

"This place is really over the top, isn't it?" Eric said.

"Yes."

DJ Romeo's voice returned.

"Ooooh, love is such a beautiful thing,"

"And I see you two lovebirds there in the middle—

"That's right, you two.

"Spin her, kid.

"Spin your precious love around—

"and take her to your highway to the sky.

"Take her there, kid."

Eric looked at Sam.

"Did DJ Romeo just call me out . . . with song lyrics?"

Her eyes sparkled as she tilted her head.

"I don't know. Did he?"

"I think he did."

"He did, huh?"

Her mouth curved into a slow smile.

"Well?" she said, voice low, daring.

"What are you going to do about that?"

Eric looked around.

"I have to spin you now."

He leaned in. "It's a matter of honor."

Sam stepped back just a little.

Without breaking eye contact, she slid out of her heels. One. Then the other.

They landed with soft clicks.

Barefoot in the glow of the mirror ball, toes curling into the floor, dress skimming her thighs like starlight on water, she offered her hand.

"I'm ready to go to your highway in the sky."

He gazed at her—barefoot, fearless, offering him her hand—half disbelief, half victory.

"Jesus Christ."

He stepped back, took her hand, and sent her into a twirl.

She spun, laughing, her dress flaring out in a glittering halo of light and color, like a silk pennant caught in a sweet, invisible breeze. The mirrored lights fractured into diamonds. The music swelled. The stars in the ceiling circled overhead.

DJ Romeo leaned hard into the microphone, eyes closed, one hand to his chest, singing along off-key with absolute conviction—drawing out the refrain like an oath he'd taken years ago.

"Love is such a beautiful thiiiing . . ."

At the edge of their orbit, the LOVE AMBASSADOR drifted to a stop. He'd been carrying a tray—champagne flutes balanced on napkins—but the tray hung there in his hands like it had suddenly lost its meaning. His sash caught the mirror-ball light. His mouth fell slightly open. He wasn't scanning tables.

He was just . . . watching Sam twirl.

Watching the way the whole room arranged itself around her. Watching the way Eric's hand anchored her and sent her outward, like he'd turned love into a simple, physical law.

The LOVE AMBASSADOR took one slow step forward without realizing he'd moved—a man pulled by music. His shoe nudged the edge of the dancefloor. He caught himself before he fell, but not before the tray tipped—one champagne flute wobbling, liquid trembling at the rim.

A tiny gasp rippled from a nearby table.

The LOVE AMBASSADOR froze.

And in that frozen beat—half-kneel, half-stumble, tray angled like an offering—DJ Romeo saw the whole thing and decided what it meant.

DJ Romeo—without missing a beat—boomed into the mic:

"THAT'S RIGHT! GET DOWN ON ONE KNEE FOR LOVE!"

The crowd erupted.

At the end of her twirl, Sam teetered—just a little—and Eric was already there, steady as a promise, catching her lightly and pulling her close as the room roared around them. Their laughter burst out, tangled and right, turning the music into something simply—beautifully—true. Her breath, warm at his neck. His arms, tight around her. The impossible lightness of everything that mattered. Everything that was real.

"I swear," Eric said, brushing her hair back behind her ear, "I can't take much more of this. I'm about ready to pick you up and carry you off this dance floor . . . forever."

"Promise?"

"*My precious love.*"

He kissed her forehead. Right in the middle of the dance floor.

Like a promise.

Cheers. Laughter. Applause like a wave breaking. Even the LOVE AMBASSADOR—still caught in the spell—let out a breathy laugh, as if he'd been chosen for something holy and ridiculous and didn't dare refuse it.

Up in his booth, DJ Romeo bobbed to the beat, head low, jacket catching the light, like a magician who had conjured the evening from thin air and was seeing it through to the very last note.

The music fading out, the final notes drifting through the room like perfume, as couples held each other closer—some swaying, some kissing, some just letting the moment wrap around them like silk as a tender silence settled in—the hush of a night no one wanted to end.

Outside, the wind stirred the pines, as the lights dimmed inside, and somewhere high above Lovers' Cove—

the stars spun on, unaware.

Or maybe not.

CHAPTER 7

A Perfect Little Heart

Later that night, with the Bee Gees still playing in their heads and the unmistakable heat of desire between them, Eric and Sam made their way back to Suite Seven. Sam slipped into a Lovers' Cove robe labeled *Hers* and disappeared into the bathroom. Eric flipped the switch beside the seven-foot champagne-glass hot tub. Bubbles churned to life, the cloudy glass still towering like a monument to indulgent love. He poured champagne into two flutes from the mini-bar.

From the doorway came a sing-song call:

"Oh, my love?"

Eric turned. Sam stood in the doorway, still wrapped in the resort's white robe. She loosened the belt and let it fall away.

"I'm going in."

She turned and began to climb the spiral stairs, hips swaying with theatrical purpose. She lingered halfway up, glanced over her shoulder, then slowly turned to face him—arms raised like a game show hostess revealing a prize.

"A little birthday love."

His eyes moved over her—red-painted toes, bare legs, soft curves, skin glowing gold in the low light. And just below her belly button, where her body narrowed—a perfect little heart.

Eric froze.

"Wait . . . is that—"

He was already peeling off his shirt. "I don't even care."

She giggled and bolted, bare feet flashing on the velvet steps as she took the spiral two at a time.

Eric lunged after her, shirt half over his head, his slacks bunching at his knees. He kicked them off as he chased her up the stairs. He caught her at the landing and together they slid into the champagne-glass hot tub. The mirrored ceiling reflected their naked bodies, framed in candlelight and bubbles.

CHAPTER 8

4-Ever

The following morning was bright and clear as they walked around the lake hand in hand. Sam glanced at Eric then tipped her chin toward the line of swan-boats sat tethered to the dock.

Ten minutes later, they were afloat.

Eric did the pedaling while Sam leaned into him, letting her toes slip into the water, drawing slow, carefree circles as the sun warmed her skin. A pair of ducks flapped across their path and Eric had to swerve, if that's what you call it in a giant swan-boat.

Next, they tried archery. Eric fired one arrow directly into the ground about five feet ahead. The instructor—a retired gym teacher in his sixties wearing a Lovers' Cove visor—told him he was "sweet but hopeless."

An old walking path curved through a grove of pine trees. The outlines of old fire pits and benches marked where decades of couples had once sat under the stars. The stones were weathered. The wood faded.

Then Sam slowed and pointed. "Aw, look."

On the trunk of a thick pine, the bark had been scarred long ago by a heart, carved deep, the letters still clear after all this time:

JON + BROOKE

1979

Eric ran his fingers over the carving.

"Think they're still together?" Sam asked.

"Sure. Jon's an airline pilot. Brooke's a drug rep. They live in Denver. He coaches wrestling. She collects novelty shot glasses."

"Or maybe they're boring and happy," Sam said. "Carwashes. Yoga. Matching SUVs."

"Or" Eric added, "Brooke's a stripper. But a classy one. With a retirement plan."

Sam gave him a shove. "Brooke deserves better than that."

They leaned back against the tree, looking up through the thinning canopy. The forest heavy with all the old hopes and dreams.

"Well, hopefully they're happy," Sam said.

"They are," he said as he put his arm around her.

They stood there for a while longer, breathing in the morning—two more names, two more lives, now part of the same long, unfinished story of Lovers' Cove.

After packing up the FJ, they pulled onto the winding driveway out of the resort. Sam leaned her head against the seat, watching a couple fumble with a set of bows at the archery range. The woman tried to aim while her partner stood behind her. The arrow fell straight to the ground.

Eric slowed near the entrance to the main lodge and pulled over.

"Hang on," he said. "I forgot something."

"What do you mean?"

"I need to run into the gift shop."

"Wait. Eric, I don't need any more gifts."

But he was already jogging up the steps and disappeared inside.

Sam watched a couple trying to load a cooler onto a giant swan-boat. The man slipped, flailed, and tumbled into the lake. His partner jumped in after him, trying to rescue both him and the half-submerged cooler.

Sam shook her head.

"This place is insane."

A few minutes later, Eric came back with something in his hand. He slid into the driver's seat and held it up proudly: a tiny souvenir pocketknife. Cheap steel, plastic handle, *Lovers' Cove – Pocono Mountains* stamped in fading gold letters along the side.

"You bought a souvenir knife?"

Eric winked.

On the way out, he turned onto a gravel side path that led into the woods. They got out, shoes crunching on the stones, and walked until Eric found a good tree.

He knelt. Pressed the blade to the bark. Carved carefully, hand steady, tongue caught between his teeth. Sam watched, her hands tucked into the back pockets of her jeans, her heart full. When he finished, they stepped back to admire it.

A heart. Inside:

ERIC + SAM

4-EVER

Back in the FJ, they didn't say much. The gravel crunched beneath the tires as they pulled back onto the long driveway. A couple on a tandem bike wobbled past.

Sam leaned forward, plugged in her phone, and scrolled. Then, with a private smile, she pressed play.

Van Morrison's *Have I Told You Lately* filled the speakers—earnest and grounded, its warmth carrying a love that didn't ask for anything back.

Eric glanced over, locking eyes with his wife. Then, without breaking her gaze, he slid on his Ray-Ban Aviators and turned back toward the road.

Sam reached across the console and laced her fingers through his.

"I love you."

Eric looked over.

"I know. I love you too."

They drove like that, fingers laced, back to the real world.

CHAPTER 9

Muffin Wrap

The office of *The Pocono Classifieds* sat like a shoebox above a coffee shop in downtown East Stroudsburg. The newspaper was the only free weekly in the area that still ran its name in italics, because Constance believed it made the paper feel avant-garde yet urgent. And no one ever disagreed with Constance.

The paper paid the coffee shop downstairs five hundred dollars a month plus a full-page ad—inside cover, once a week—for the office space. By midmorning, a trace of espresso and burnt cinnamon drifted through the floorboards. *"Campfire S'mores Lattes are back!"* was drawn with marshmallows and flames on the chalkboard by the entrance downstairs, and Lukas had announced to the newsroom that he was already on his third cup.

Sam was at her desk near the window—the pane cracked in the corner, taped over with duct tape and a Post-it note that warned, DON'T LEAN. Her workspace was a patchwork of mostly dead pens, mismatched notepads, and a thrifted floral-shade desk lamp Eric had found for her. The glow from their weekend at Lovers' Cove hadn't worn off her yet.

"The best part was floating around on a giant swan-boat," he'd joked that morning at breakfast.

She knew what part he'd liked best: the champagne-glass hot tub, or the vibrating bed under the mirrored ceiling. It definitely wasn't the giant swan-boat.

"I figured it out," Lukas said, leaning back in his chair like he'd just brokered world peace. "My thing. My next big thing. And you're going to want in."

"Am I?"

"You ready?" He was practically vibrating. "My new podcast."

She turned toward her desk. "What is it?"

"It's called *Expired*. Every week I check expiration dates in my fridge—yogurt, hot sauce, condiments. I taste-test whatever's borderline and people try to guess if I'll survive."

"You're not serious."

"I already have theme music. It's just a ticking clock with, like, ominous cello underneath."

Sam stared at him. "You're eating expired food?"

"For the content," he said. "Also, the suspense."

"That's just food poisoning."

"Or we pivot," he said. "We taste-test similar soft drink brands. Like Coke and Pepsi. Generic cola versus name brand. See if we can actually tell the difference."

She took a sip from her water bottle.

"That's not terrible."

From the other side of the room, Constance didn't look up from her screen.

"They already did that," she called. "It's called the Pepsi Challenge. It's been over since 1985."

Lukas deflated slightly. "Okay, but this is recent."

"It's not recent," Constance said. "It's retro. And it lost."

Sam was working on a feature article about a local business, Jewels by Liz—a hand-beaded jewelry store run out of an old bank building on Crystal Street. She'd just returned from an interview, where the owner, Liz, had shown her a collection of their bracelets made from beads and copper wire, each named after local Pocono landmarks: Delaware River Driftwood, Camelback Mountain Sunrise, Bushkill Valley Fog.

"They're meditative to make," Liz had said, stringing tiny turquoise stones through the wire. "I honestly think people are tired of the mass-produced stuff. They truly want to feel connected to where they live."

It was a good quote. Maybe a little long winded but it was honest. Rooted. Sam had underlined it twice in her notes. Now the cursor on her laptop blinked, daring her to get poetic about wire-wrapped stones.

"Make it big and epic," Constance had said that morning, balancing a chai latte on a stack of Pocono tourism booklets.

"But make it unpretentious too. You know. Folksy. We really need her to buy ad space."

Sam took a sip from her water bottle, fingers hovering over the keyboard. Outside her window, a fresh stack of *The Pocono Classifieds* sat on the café bench down on the sidewalk. A man walked up, grabbed one, and wrapped his muffin in it.

Sam looked back at her screen like she hadn't seen it.

Larry from Larry's Auto had pulled his ad from the paper last month. "Why cut down a bunch of trees to print stories I already scrolled past a week ago?" he'd said. "Same stories already got meme'd to death online before the paperboy chucks a newspaper into my bushes."

Constance had nodded like she understood. Then she'd gone upstairs and slammed a stapler against the broken copier until it stopped jamming.

Sam couldn't really argue with Larry. People didn't read the news the way they used to. Nobody clipped newspaper articles anymore.

Still, she felt the loss—not just of the news, but of the connection. She thought of Liz naming bracelets after local landmarks, trying to hold onto a place with beads and wire.

She glanced again at the stack of papers outside her window. She tried typing:

In a town like this, the smallest stories are the ones that last the longest.

She deleted it.

She leaned back and let the chair squeak.

If the paper folded, there would be no community protests or home-grown rallies to save it. Just a stack of leftover papers for the recycling bin.

Or muffin wrapping.

What scared her more was how quietly it might happen. How few people would even notice it was gone. But she wondered—if the paper vanished, would anyone even care? Or would they just refresh their feeds?

Outside, a gust scattered the paper stack. A copy fluttered off the bench and onto the sidewalk.

Last winter, an elderly woman had left a note on Sam's desk after her husband passed away: "Thank you for the wonderful article about his garden club this summer. It made our grandkids happy."

That mattered more than anything she'd written all year. Maybe that's why the idea of Honeymoon Hideaway stuck in her mind. She had a feeling that some stories weren't lost at all; they were just waiting for the right person to find them. She wanted to tell stories people would keep. Stories they'd hang on refrigerators. Fold into photo albums. Read out loud at holidays. That was the type of story Honeymoon Hideaway could be. She turned back to her keyboard.

The office walls of *The Pocono Classifieds* were mostly bare except for a curling fire code notice and a bulletin board cluttered with thumbtacked classifieds: Missing Cat, Barn Sale, Part-Time Dishwasher Needed.

The free weekly was held together by five people, a second-hand printer that jammed, and the stubborn belief that local stories still mattered.

Constance, a former features editor from New York, had come to the Poconos, bought a canoe, started a newspaper with her savings, and began working on the Great American Novel. Amelia, the ad rep, who talked a big game about full-page spreads but mostly sold business-card size ads to realtors, and increasingly, an alarming number of massage parlors. Bartek, the layout guy—an InDesign virtuoso with a preference for Helvetica. And Lukas—the intern-slash-reporter-slash-social media manager—who wore sunglasses indoors, Hawaiian shirts, and a bucket hat. He channeled Hunter S. Thompson, wrote headlines as if he were up for a Pulitzer, and treated every pancake breakfast like it was Watergate.

"Hey, Sam," Lukas called from across the room, holding his phone like it was a direct line to the Pentagon. "You hear about the haunted chairlift up at Shawnee?"

She didn't look up. "No. But I'm guessing you're going to tell me."

Lukas shoved off and rolled his chair over with journalistic urgency and promptly crashed into her desk. "Security guy posted in a Facebook group. Swears one of the old lifts came on by itself. Lights flickered on, motor started but get this . . . nobody was even up there."

Sam looked up. "And you believe this?"

"Some people say it's just a wiring issue. Others are saying it could be the ghost of a ski instructor who fell off the very same chairlift back in 1997."

Sam took a sip from her water bottle, capped it, and stared at him. "You ever consider writing horror instead of reporting?"

"Constance said I could do a sidebar if I get a quote from the ghost."

"Try not to fall off the chairlift," she turned back to her article.

The cursor still blinked at her. She wondered how many people would even read her article about the beaded bracelets that Liz made and named after local Pocono landmarks. Her eyes drifted lower—to the bench outside the café as copies of *The Pocono Classifieds* still fluttered in the breeze, untouched.

CHAPTER 10

Waldo Pepper

9:18 AM—Sam:
You gave me a bruise

9:19 AM—Eric:
no I didn't

9:19 AM—Sam:
Oh really?
(photo attachment)
(Her shoulder in *The Pocono Classifieds* bathroom mirror. A faint purple mark near her collarbone.)

9:20 AM—Eric:
that not a bruise

9:20 AM—Sam:
What is it then, Dr. Young??

9:21 AM—Eric:
take shirt off
Can't tell

9:21 AM—Sam:
No Way !

9:21 AM—Eric:
Im not as smooth as Dr Romeo???

9:22 AM—Sam:
It's DJ Romeo, my love.
An NO! Somebody will see!

9:22 AM—Eric:
Nobody will see.
I promise

9:22 AM—Sam:
No!!
Evidence of what?

9:22 AM—Eric:
evidence that I won

9:22 AM—Sam:
Won what?

9:23 AM— Eric:
champagne hot tub
Olympics

9:28 AM—Sam:
You know I did.
I still smell like chlorine.

9:29 AM—Eric:
YUM
you mean romance

9:31 AM—Sam:
Lukas just asked if you fell off a swan-boat.

9:32 AM—Eric:
Tell him...
nm.

10:14 AM—Eric:
Nassers will be here to do more carrier
Landings

10:15 AM—Sam:
Don't scream.

10:16 AM—Eric:
yea.

10:17 AM—Sam:
You should log that.

10:18 AM—Eric:
0.4 screaming

11:42 AM—Sam:
You eating lunch?

11:45 AM—Eric:
Airport vending machine
Gourmet coffee

11:45 AM—Sam:
I'll make spaghetti.

11:47 AM—Eric:
Flight cancelled damn

11:47 AM—Sam:
Why???

11:48 AM—Eric:
Maintenance
altimeter reading 300 high
they've been staring at it for 2 hours

11:49 AM—Sam:
That's annoying.

11:50 AM—Eric:
Sat around all morning
didnt log a thing

11:52 AM—Eric:
Maybe I should just log it anyway.

11:53 AM—Sam:
LOL

(He stares at that.)

11:54 AM—Eric:
I'm kidding

11:55 AM—Sam:
I know.

11:57 AM—Sam:
Don't.

(He reads that twice.)

11:58 AM—Eric:
Don't what.

12:03 PM—Sam:
Just . . . don't.

12:05 PM—Eric:
You're hot

12:07 PM—Sam:
Am I?

12:08 PM—Sam:
I still smell like chlorine.

12:09 PM—Eric:
YUM

Nasser was at the airport when Eric arrived, hunched over a stack of flight manuals on the picnic table outside the terminal. Cool breeze through the trees. Pine and avgas. Eric approached, coffee steaming in his hand, and couldn't help but laugh. Nasser looked up—bomber jacket as always. But now there was a white silk scarf at his throat.

"You ready to hop in the Curtiss Jenny and fly some loop-de-loops over the county fair?" Eric called.

"Good morning, Eric," Nasser said. "You look like you did not sleep at all."

"Lindbergh stayed awake thirty-three hours to cross the Atlantic," Eric said. "Four hours crisscrossing Jersey in the middle of the night is nothing."

"Sorry, Eric."

Eric nodded at Nasser's neck. "Speaking of Lindbergh—where'd you get that thing?"

"What thing?"

"The scarf."

Nasser looked down, full of pride. "My wife bought it for me."

Eric shook his head. "You look like an old barnstormer. Only about a hundred years too late."

"Yes. We streamed *The Great Waldo Pepper* the other night. It is all about the barnstormers," he said. "I'm going to buy it."

Eric blinked—then it clicked. "Of course," he said. "Waldo Pepper and the outside loop."

12:37 PM—Sam:
(photo attachment)
(Shirt and bra off in *The Pocono Classifieds* bathroom mirror.)

Eric glanced down at his phone mid-sip and choked. He coughed once and pocketed it fast. He looked up. Nasser's eyes were on his manuals—then not. Then back.

"Nasser," Eric said, "you are by far the most motivated student I've ever had."

"Thank you, Eric."

Nasser cleared his throat. "Your wife is . . . very supportive."

Eric went still. "My wife?"

"Yes." Nasser nodded quickly, then realized what he'd just said. "I mean—my wife. My wife is supportive. She buys me scarf."

Eric stared.

Nasser blinked. "But also your wife. Supportive."

Eric looked away. "Right."

"So, anyway. If you liked *The Great Waldo Pepper,* read *Biplane,* by Richard Bach."

Nasser nodded, eyes on manuals. "I loved it. I want to learn everything about flying."

"Let's start with some landings," Eric said, standing. "Need to get you ready for your first solo so I can cut your shirt off."

"Shirt. Tail." Eric corrected himself.

"Yes, I believe I will do much better today," Nasser said, gathering his manuals.

Eric nodded at the scarf. "That wasn't fashion, by the way. It was for wiping oil off your goggles—those engines leaked like hell."

"Yes. Good. I will be prepared."

Eric started to laugh. "Our Cessna 150 doesn't have an open cockpit, so I doubt you'll—" He stopped.

Nasser hesitated, then added quietly, "Please tell your wife I am very sorry, Eric."

CHAPTER 11

Hangar Talk

"Airplanes don't care about your feelings, kid," Bruce said. "An engine failure at thirty-nine thousand feet over the Atlantic doesn't care if you're offended."

He laughed once, short.

The hangar light buzzed overhead as Bruce stood on the step ladder, one arm buried in the open cowling of the Goose, a beer balanced against the nacelle. Wilbur stirred from beneath the workbench and padded over to Eric, nails ticking on the hangar floor. Eric reached down and scratched behind his ears. The dog leaned into his leg and gave a huff.

"Freight's gotta be in Teterboro before six," Bruce said, tightening a fitting. "After that, the Hudson crossings jam up and nobody can get into the city. Miss the slot, you miss the check."

Eric leaned back against the tool chest, one hand still resting on Wilbur's head. "Can't help bad weather or airplanes breaking."

Bruce stepped down and wiped his hands on a rag already black with grease.

"You know airplanes have two of everything, right?"

"Yeah."

"Two pumps. Two alternators. Things fail. That's by design. They build 'em with backup for a reason."

Wilbur gave a short, sharp bark, then settled again. Bruce didn't look at him.

Eric crossed his arms. "Backup's not the same as ignoring it."

"I'm not saying ignore it," Bruce said. "I'm saying you don't ground a plane every time it's missing a bolt. You fix what'll kill you. The rest? You monitor."

"And if you guess wrong?"

Bruce looked at him steadily. "You don't guess," he said. "You decide." He tapped the side of the fuselage with the wrench. Wilbur yapped once. "Freight doesn't wait for perfect, kid."

Eric shifted his weight. Wilbur circled once and lay down beside his boots. "Neither do airlines."

Bruce smiled. "Now you're thinking." He took a pull from the beer. "And timing? That's everything. Airlines hire till they fire. You hit the window, you're in. You miss it, you're flyin' checks for another ten years."

Eric nodded.

"I don't want to miss it," he said finally. "I want to build something decent for Sam. A real life."

Wilbur thumped his tail once against the concrete.

Bruce studied him. "That's the right instinct," he said. "You just can't let feelings run the airplane, or your home life." He put the beer down and ran his palm along the wing root like it was an old dog. "One little mistake," he said quietly. "New Year's Eve. That's all it takes. One night. One wrong decision. Doesn't matter how good you were before it."

Eric watched him.

"I wasn't even drunk," Bruce muttered. "Just tired."

He paused.

"Doesn't matter." Bruce stared past Eric, somewhere beyond the nose of the Goose. "Read something once," he said. "Some pilot wrote it. Said somewhere between lift and gravity, a man figures out what to hold onto, when there's nothin' else." He shrugged. "Problem is, most guys don't figure it out till it's too late."

Outside, a truck backfired. Wilbur lifted his head and barked toward the hangar door.

"You think the airlines cared that I had three thousand hours?" Bruce said. "You think they cared I'd never bent metal? That I'd never scared a passenger?" He shook his head. "They don't care." He wiped his hands again. "They don't care how you got your hours. They don't care if you flew freight in the middle of the night or taught some kid to stop stalling in the pattern. They don't care what you sacrificed. They care about one number."

He turned and looked at Eric.

"You hit the number, you're in. You don't hit it, you're not."

Eric held his gaze.

Bruce picked the beer back up.

"You fly smart, you land it, everybody goes home. You get scared every time a screw falls off, you'll never build the hours."

He took another pull. The can made a small hollow sound against his teeth.

"And you keep your paperwork clean," he said, like he was adding a final item to a checklist. "They don't play games with paperwork."

Eric didn't answer.

Bruce squinted at him. "You ever been ramp-checked, kid?"

"No."

"You're lucky." Bruce wiped his mouth with the back of his hand. "Ain't fun. They ask questions like they already know the answers." He nodded toward the Goose. "But I got records for everything. Gotta be that way, or they'll shut you down."

He paused, listening to the buzz of the hangar light.

"Nobody sues if you land it," Bruce said, and the words ran together at the end. A hiccup snuck out of him like it had been waiting. He frowned at it, annoyed.

Wilbur's ears twitched.

"And nobody checks a Hobbs meter unless something goes wrong," Bruce added, quieter.

He finished the beer and tossed it toward the trash. It missed and clattered near Wilbur.

Wilbur barked once.

"Sorry, Wilbur," Bruce said, rolling his eyes.

Bruce squinted at him.

"You know what makes an airplane fly, kid?"

"Sure. Bernoulli's principle."

Bruce shook his head.

"Newton's third law of motion."

"Nope."

Eric waited. "What then?"

Bruce lifted the beer and grinned.

"Money," he said. "That's what makes an airplane fly."

Eric didn't smile. Wilbur gave a small bark.

"I learned that January first," Bruce added. "Fuel costs money. Parts cost money. Hangars cost money. You don't move airplanes without it."

He picked up the wrench again and climbed back up the step ladder.

"You know how long you can fly an airplane upside down?" he called down.

"No."

"Till the engine quits."

Bruce barked a laugh and went back to work.

CHAPTER 12

Snoopy Goggles

Eric leaned over before the engine run-up. "All right. Same plan as last time—touch-and-goes until we get smooth landings. Smooth meaning no bounces and fewer screams of terror from me."

"I do not think you screamed," Nasser said.

"I wasn't sure if you landed or were shot down."

Nasser laughed. But Eric could already see the tension building—the tight grip on the yoke, the shallow breaths. Nasser wasn't afraid of flying. He was afraid of failing.

That was harder to fix.

Takeoff: clean. Climb-out: a little slow but Nasser corrected. They turned crosswind, then downwind—1,000 feet over the treetops.

"Carb heat on," Eric said. "First notch of flaps."

"Okay," Nasser replied, voice clipped.

"Picture the runway like a hallway," Eric said. "You're walking the airplane down it. You're not throwing it through the door."

They turned base, then final. Nasser's hands tightened again. Approach: too high. Airspeed: too fast.

Eric watched.

Then calmly.

"Eyes down the hallway. Don't stare at the numbers. Ease it down. Don't dive for it."

Nasser pitched up and flared too high. Eric caught the yoke before Nasser could push forward. The Cessna 150 bounced—hard. Floated. Then bounced again, harder. A puff of tire smoke bloomed beneath them.

"Okay," Eric said evenly. "Go around. Full power. Let's do it again."

Nasser shoved the throttle forward, cheeks burning under his sunglasses. His white scarf drooped like a surrender flag.

"That was my carrier landing," Nasser joked weakly. "You know—*Top Gun*."

"Well, I wouldn't call that *Top Gun*," he said. "That was more like *Hot Shots! Part Deux*."

Nasser frowned, climbing back to pattern altitude. They turned crosswind, then downwind again.

"Okeydokey," Eric said. "This time, imagine you actually like the runway. Imagine you want to kiss it—not slap it across the face."

Nasser adjusted his scarf.

The second landing floated longer. Settled. Still a little firm—but better. Much better.

"All right, that one floated a little bit," Eric said as the wheels chirped on. "Next time, don't round out so early."

Nasser shook his head. "I thought I had it."

"You did," Eric said. "Just held it too long."

Nasser pushed in the throttle and retracted the flaps on speed as they climbed out.

"Timing's everything," Eric said. "First woman to fly across the English Channel was Harriet Quimby in 1912. Wore a silk flight suit."

Nasser glanced over. "I never heard of her."

"Nobody has," Eric said. "The Titanic sank two days later."

Nasser pulled the carb heat and eased the throttle back.

"Let's do a few more, Waldo Pepper."

Third landing. No jokes. No tension. Nasser flew a smooth, even pattern. Final approach: on speed. The runway threshold rose up to meet them. The Cessna 150 floated—perfectly—and kissed the runway with a smooth, straight touchdown.

"Nice," Eric said. "That's the one."

Nasser looked over. "Whoa. I did it."

"You didn't force it," Eric said. "You let it land. That's the way the pros do it."

Three more landings. Each one better than the last. When they taxied back, Nasser's grin was wide. Eric nudged him on the shoulder as they shut down. "Not bad, Nasser. Waldo Pepper must've rubbed off."

They climbed out onto the tarmac. Nasser tugged at his scarf and looked back at the Cessna 150, a flicker of confidence in his eyes that Eric hadn't seen before. "I think I get it now."

"Good," Eric said, then shook his head. "But if you show up in a leather helmet and Snoopy goggles for your next lesson, I'm quizzing you on the FARs until lunch."

"What are Snoopy goggles?"

"I'm sure you'll figure it out. Come on, barnstormer. I'm going to try to get a nap. I've got a flight in the Goose tonight."

Nasser followed him across the ramp, his white scarf flapping in the morning breeze.

CHAPTER 13

Don't Lose an Engine

The Goose sat tail-heavy on the ramp at Payne Aviation, nose too high.

Eric walked around her once, then again. His hand went to the usual places out of habit—tire, strut, fuel cap—then stopped. He kept looking past the wing, through the open door, at the freight.

Dozens of boxes marked: TIME SENSITIVE – FRAGILE were stacked in the Goose like cardboard Tetris.

He paused at the cabin door and leaned in, scanning for paperwork. No clipboard. No folder. No weight and balance. No load manifest.

Inside the hangar, Bruce was wiping oil off his hands with a black rag that was already soaked through. He was working on one of his other airplanes. The cowlings were open.

"Hey Bruce, did you weigh that all yourself?"

"She's ready to go," Bruce Payne said. "You're welcome."

Eric glanced at the Goose again. "Look how she's sitting."

Bruce looked him over.

"You're young. Your wife's young."

"She'll remarry."

He laughed.

"Hell, she might even upgrade."

Eric didn't smile.

Wilbur padded out from behind a stack of oil cases near the back wall of the hangar, nails ticking softly against the concrete. The little terrier-schnauzer mutt blinked up at Eric, tail wagging in cautious half-circles.

Eric crouched without thinking and scratched behind his ears. "Hey, buddy."

Wilbur leaned into the touch, then trotted back toward the open hangar door as if satisfied the night's business was in order.

Bruce gave a short laugh, like Eric had missed a great punchline. "Relax. It's a joke. You worry too much. I weighed everything." He jerked his thumb toward the Goose. "You've got seven hundred horses on the wings and blue sky. Point her down the runway and give her hell, kid." He turned back to the open cowling. "That old bird can take it."

"If I lose an engine on takeoff, Bruce, she won't climb. Not with all that weight. You understand what I'm saying? I'll be in the trees before the gear's up."

"Then don't lose an engine." Bruce laughed.

"Bruce, it's not that I don't want to fly her. I'm just trying to make sure she's not overloaded."

Bruce tossed the rag onto the toolbox. "This business isn't easy, kid. You know what overnight delivery pays? Everybody wants Amazon speed on a dollar-store budget." He nodded toward the Goose. "I need that plane in Teterboro before the George Washington jams up, so I can pay you Friday."

"I'm not flying an overloaded airplane, Bruce."

Bruce started to walk away, then stopped. "Airlines don't care how you get the hours. Just that you get them, fast."

"You know what airlines ask about first?" He didn't wait. "DUIs. Jumping from job to job. That kind of thing."

Eric shook his head. "It's over weight."

"Okay, kid. I gotta get someone else, then." Bruce walked over to his toolkit and picked up his cellphone.

Eric followed. "No, I've got it, Bruce."

Bruce clapped him once on the shoulder and laughed.

"Great news, kid." He laughed. "I'll get you a Starbucks card."

Eric laughed. "Don't worry about it."

He walked back out to the Goose.

Too heavy.

He buckled his harness and adjusted the seat.

Battery master switch—ON.

The panel buzzed with the dim glow of instruments and switches.

The fuel quantity tanks were only showing a quarter full.

Yep, she's over.

He didn't need the numbers.

She was over max gross.

By a lot.

His hand hovered over the mixture.

Shut it down.

Beacon—ON.

The red light began its rhythmic flash.

Navigation lights—ON.

Fuel pumps—ON, the electric whine pressurizing the lines.

Abort.

Mixture controls—FULL RICH.

Props—HIGH RPM.

Cowl flaps—OPEN.

"Clear prop!"

Engine start sequence: left engine first. Starter engaged. Oil pressure. A cough and rumble as the old Lycoming turned over and held.

Then the right engine—equally stubborn but finally catching and settling into a rough idle.

Engine run-up: both engines to 1700 RPM. Magnetos. Engine instruments in the green.

The engines sounded tired.

Should've refused the flight, but the idea of a termination echoed in his head.

Airlines don't hire fired pilots.

He announced his taxi plan on UNICOM and began the slow roll toward the runway, the overloaded Chieftain sluggish even on the ground.

At the hold-short line, he completed the *Before Takeoff* checklist: controls free and correct, flaps set, trim set, fuel pumps on, mixture rich, props high RPM.

One final scan of the engine instruments.

He should refuse the flight.

Instead, he pushed the throttles up for takeoff.

The airspeed barely moved.

The engines roared. Throttles fire-walled.

She's too heavy.

The airspeed slowly crept up.

At 85 knots, Eric eased back on the yoke. The nose lifted, but she wouldn't budge.

Then—

Bang.

The left engine coughed like it always did.

It coughed again.

This time, it quit.

Completely.

CHAPTER 14

Uncle Sam Top Hat

Five years earlier

It was the Fourth of July, and the streets around Bleecker were alive—paper flags in storefront windows; two men in matching red, white, and blue seersucker standing beneath a fire escape, both wearing a tall Uncle Sam top hat; the smell of roasted peanuts; street-cart guys slinging dirty-water dogs loaded with mustard, the best kind. A fire hydrant ran at the curb, puddling water in front of a bodega that blasted classic rock too loudly, the bass rattling a stack of milk crates. Coffee and beer drifted out of open doors. Sirens wailed somewhere uptown, fading into laughter and the clink of ice in plastic cups.

Test fireworks popped in the distance, echoing off brick and steel in The Village. New York was dressed for its big night. Everyone kept looking up, waiting for the sky to light off.

Everyone except the boy.

The boy stood at the edge of the sidewalk; hands stuffed in a flight jacket watching a group of street musicians gathered beneath a rusted fire escape. They made music from anything—upside-down five-gallon pickle buckets, scratched cymbals mounted on broomsticks. A bass player thumbed a single string tied to a mop handle, wedged into a plastic tub.

They fell into a rhythm, and then—somehow—a harmony. A cappella. Raw. Beautiful. They started with wordless doo-wop harmonies, then eased into *The Boy From New York City*. The sound melted into the night as a crowd gathered, drawn like moths.

As the musicians eased into harmony, the two men in matching red, white, and blue seersucker began arguing: hands cutting the air, words swallowed by the music. One of them turned abruptly and pushed through the crowd. The other followed, reaching for him. In the scramble, one of their hats slipped free and tumbled to the sidewalk.

The boy bent and picked it up, holding it out as the second man passed.

"Hey—your hat."

The man didn't stop. He waved a hand without looking back. "Keep it."

The boy stood there a second longer than necessary, the ridiculous hat in his hands.

Then he glanced up.

That's when he saw her.

She was near the edge of the crowd, half in shadow beneath a string of flickering lights zigzagging between the buildings. A pink sash crossed her red, white, and blue sundress:

BIRTHDAY GIRL.

Her hair was pinned up like she'd tried and then given up. In her hand, a tiny American flag. She wasn't waving it. Just holding it—twisting the plastic pole without even realizing.

The musicians leaned into that doo-wop refrain—soft "ooh" harmonies—and the air changed, like the song had been waiting for the birthday girl. Her face tightened. She looked like a ghost had whispered through the harmony.

The birthday girl was crying.

The girlfriends around her didn't notice.

But the boy did.

He couldn't stop looking.

And then the birthday girl looked back, and for a second, everything in the world went still. Her fingers stopped twisting the flag.

When the musicians finished and the crowd clapped, the boy took one step, then another—like the distance between them suddenly mattered.

"Happy birthday," he said, unsure how close to stand.

The birthday girl looked up, startled. "How did you know it's my—" She touched the sash like she'd forgotten she was wearing it. She let out a short, faint laugh and wiped a tear from her cheek with the back of her hand. "Thanks," she said, her voice cracking. "Sorry. That song . . ."

The boy nodded. "Yeah. It was beautiful."

"No, I mean . . ." The birthday girl said, looking up at the brick facade like it could shield her from the memory. "It was playing on the radio when my parents died. Car accident. July Fourth. I was six." She shook her head. "I don't know why I'm telling you this."

The boy stepped closer. "Because you wanted me to know—" He stopped. "I mean . . . wanted me to know why you were crying."

The birthday girl looked at him again. "Are you the boy from New York City?"

"No," the boy said. "Pittsburgh. Just in for the fireworks."

"Good," the birthday girl said. "Because I don't like that song."

"Then I still have a chance."

"And you came to The Village to stand in a crowd and listen to street drummers?"

"We were on our way to the pier," the boy said. "A guy dropped his hat. I picked it up. Then I saw you."

He was still holding the ridiculous top hat—slightly crushed, completely his now.

A red flare streaked up in the distance.

The show had started.

But neither of them looked at the sky.

They stood under the rusted fire escape, face to face, in a crowd full of noise and strangers—an island of stillness.

Above them, the city lit in fire. windows flashed blue, then red, then white; the colors blooming and fading unseen, while the street musicians started a new song.

And so did they.

CHAPTER 15

Ground Effect

It had to be this takeoff.

Not good.

The propeller windmilled, the roar replaced by silence on the left wing.

He was out of runway.

He could jam on the brakes and pray as he skidded off the end—or continue the takeoff and try to clear the trees.

There was no stopping now.

"Goddamn it."

Instinct took over.

Eric jerked the Goose into the air, then immediately lowered the nose, keeping her barely a foot above the runway.

Ground effect.

Eric could feel every rivet straining. Every bolt holding the overloaded airframe together.

Gear up.

The right engine screamed at full power.

The airspeed indicator froze.

83.

Then.

84.

85.

He needed 90.

Each painted runway stripe erased a second he didn't have.

Eric's left hand gripped the yoke, knuckles white. His right hand firewalled the remaining throttle.

The dead propeller windmilled, dragging the left wing, yawing the aircraft.

Dead foot. Dead engine.

Behind him, unsecured cargo slammed against the cabin walls as the Goose skimmed the runway.

Identify. Verify. Feather.

The left propeller slowed—then stopped spinning. He felt the increase in airspeed and the pressure off his left leg.

87.

The ground effect cushion was fragile.

It wouldn't last.

The threshold markers flashed beneath the nose—white rectangles marking the end of the runway.

88.

The trees loomed ahead, a black wall of pine and oak.

Gravestones

Eric fought the instinct to pull back too early.

Not yet.

Let the speed build.

Trust the training

88.

The runway ended. The ground dropped into a shallow ditch, then rose again toward the tree line.

The Goose hung suspended—too heavy to climb, no runway left to land.

Wait.

Not yet.

Wait.

Then—

90.

Now.

Eric pulled back, slow and smooth.

The Goose lurched into the air, heavy and wounded. One engine dead. One screaming. She clawed skyward, wallowing, trying to yaw, trying to spin.

Trying to die.

Jesus.

Eric refused to let her.

Don't drop her.

He crushed the right rudder pedal, locking it in place. The yoke shuddered.

"Come on, Goose."

He eased back and kept the climb shallow—just enough to slip over the treetops.

The Goose groaned.

But she obeyed.

One engine howled.

One was dead weight.

He banked left in a wide arc. If she stalled now, she'd fall like an anvil.

Goddammit Bruce.

300 feet.

400.

He turned to base and dropped a notch of flaps.

Training didn't prepare you for this.

He lined her up for final, pulled power back on the single screaming engine, and felt her shudder as the airspeed bled off. The Goose descended through the darkness.

A wounded bird.

He mashed the throttle back to firewall.

Oil temperature climbed into the red. Eric heard metal grinding—engine eating itself one revolution at a time.

The prop was still turning.

But for how long?

He had one shot.

The runway lights stretched ahead—two parallel rows of white cutting through blackness. Eric's hands worked the yoke, leg mashed the rudder.

One landing.

No mistakes.

No go-around.

85 knots—fast, but he needed it.

The Goose wanted to sink. The engine wasn't quite enough. Eric nursed the throttle, adding power just enough to arrest the descent.

200 feet.

The runway looked different with the crab angle he held.

Pull some power.

Less rudder.

100 feet.

The engine coughed.

Choked.

Then screamed back.

The oil pressure needle dropped toward zero.

50 feet.

The threshold flashed below.

The sink rate increased.

They were coming down whether he wanted to or not.

Eric flared at the last possible moment and greased the mains onto the runway.

The tires chirped once.

Rudder straight, yoke forward, throttle idle.

On the ground.

The Goose rolled down the centerline, slowing—

Then finally—

Eric reached for the mixture controls. The engine decided first. With a final mechanical death rattle, the right prop jerked to a stop.

The Goose rolled to a stop in the middle of the runway.

Then came the ticking of cooling metal.

Both engines were cooked.

Eric sat frozen, hands still gripping the yoke. Adrenaline sharpened every sound. Sweat ran into his eyes. His chest heaved. He was alive.

He stared straight ahead at the runway lights, blinking into the dark. He couldn't let go yet.

A tractor rattled in the distance.

Bruce.

The clatter grew louder, bouncing across the grass and onto the runway shoulder, engine barking louder than it should. A tow bar dragged behind it, hopping on the pavement.

Bruce climbed down before it had fully stopped, baseball cap backward, rag in his hand like this was just another inconvenience.

"Hurry up, kid," he called. "Let's get her off the damn runway before somebody calls the state police."

Eric opened the door and climbed out slowly. His legs felt rubbery. Gravity felt heavier now.

Bruce walked a tight circle around the nose, eyes moving from the left prop to the right.

"What happened?"

"Engine quit on takeoff."

Bruce nodded once, taking it in.

"Nice job," he said. "Most guys would've balled it up in the trees."

Eric didn't answer. His throat felt thick.

Bruce hooked the tow bar to the nose gear. "Come on. Help me steer her."

They moved fast guiding the Goose as she rolled off the runway and toward the hangar. The tires thumped over seams in the pavement.

Inside the hangar, Bruce pulled her into place, straightened the tow line, and killed the tractor. The sudden silence rang.

For a second neither of them spoke.

Then Bruce said, too casually, "Looks like you fried both engines?"

"Looks like it."

Bruce made a low sound in his throat—half impressed, half sick. He stared at the dead props like he was trying to will them to turn.

"Jesus," he muttered. Then, louder, like he could muscle the moment back into something manageable: "You got her back on one. That's… that's good flying, kid."

Eric didn't answer. His hands still felt like they were gripping the yoke.

Bruce scraped a thumbnail across his teeth and looked at Eric again, eyes narrowing—not angry, exactly. Counting.

"That's gonna be… what—two overhauls?" Bruce said, mostly to himself. "If we're lucky. If we're not lucky, it's mounts, too." He let out a humorless laugh. "There goes my Christmas."

"You loaded her heavy."

Bruce's eyes flicked once—fast—then back to the props. "She's a Chieftain. She's built for freight."

"She was over."

Bruce exhaled through his nose. "You didn't have a scale, kid. Neither did I."

"You told me you weighed it."

"I told you she'd go."

"That's not the same thing, Bruce."

Bruce stepped closer, lowering his voice like they were in church. "Listen. If that airplane doesn't move, I don't get paid. If I don't get paid, I don't pay you. I don't pay the mechanic. I don't pay the hangar. I don't pay the insurance. You think any of that gives a damn about your feelings?"

Eric's laugh came out wrong—thin. "Yeah. I noticed. The airplane didn't give a damn either."

"You could've said no."

"And then what?" Eric said. "You fire me?"

"I call someone else."

Eric's throat tightened. "So you pushed."

Bruce's face hardened—then softened again.

"I didn't push you," he said. "I gave you the job. You want to make this business personal, you're never gonna get any hours."

"I almost didn't make it over the trees."

"I know," Bruce said, quick—too quick. "And you didn't die. Because you're good. Because you fly smart."

"Because I got lucky."

"Luck ain't part of it, kid." He tapped the cowling with a knuckle. "Luck don't turn wrenches. Or buy fuel. Choices do. You chose to fly it. You chose to bring it back. That's your job, if you want it."

The hangar went quiet.

Bruce stepped to the cabin door and swung it open.

"Alright," he said, clapping his hands once, brisk. "Let's—" He stopped himself. Swallowed. Tried again. "Let's see what we've got in here."

He reached in and grabbed one of the plastic tubs. Set it down. Then another.

Eric stood by the wing root, still replaying the takeoff—runway stripes, the airspeed stuck, the trees coming.

Bruce lifted a third tub. This one he didn't set by the others. He shifted it toward the back corner of the hangar—where the shadows were deeper.

A sharp bark snapped through the space.

Wilbur.

The little terrier-schnauzer mutt appeared from behind a stack of tires, trotting into the light like he'd been asleep five minutes earlier. He planted himself in front of Bruce and yapped again.

Bruce froze with the tub in his hands.

"Jesus Christ," he muttered. "Dog thinks he's Geraldo Rivera."

Wilbur yapped again and followed Bruce's feet, nose glued to the tubs.

Eric finally looked over. "What are you doing?"

Bruce didn't look at him. He dropped the tub—then straightened, wiping his hands on the rag.

"Cleaning up," he said. "What's it look like?"

Wilbur sniffed the tub once, satisfied, then trotted back to his corner and curled up like the whole case was closed.

Eric stared at the tubs. Then at Bruce. Then at the Goose.

He turned and walked out.

Bruce watched him go.

He stood there a moment longer, listening to the metal tick as it cooled.

"Luck is part of it," he said, to nobody.

CHAPTER 16

Subway Shoes

The Pocono Classifieds office smelled like cinnamon scones and printer ink. It was Tuesday: acoustic guitar drifting up from the coffee shop downstairs, an inbox full of unread submissions, and Amelia yelling into the phone over coupon placement—this week about why a divorce lawyer's ad could not, under any circumstances, run next to the ad for Herring's Bridal.

Sam sat beneath a crooked corkboard filled with clipped headlines and photos of long-gone interns, tapping at her keyboard. On her screen: a working headline—*The 4:30 a.m. Club: Inside the Wild World of Poconos-to-NYC Commuters.* Beneath it, a subhead she hated but couldn't improve: Meet Wayne "Subway Shoes" Callahan, the man who's turned commuting into a lifestyle.

Her phone lay beside her laptop, next to a water bottle and an unopened granola bar. She hit play.

"You gotta layer your socks. That's the key. Bus is freezing, train's boiling. And you time your bathroom break at Delaware Water Gap—never before, never after."

In the video, Wayne lifted his cuffs to reveal three pairs of socks.

Sam leaned back and stared at the water-stained ceiling tile. Wayne had built a website—The Pocono Commuter—with bus schedules, espresso reviews, and a wildly confrontational message board called Let's Talk Tolls. The guy was sweet. The story was thin. But it could work.

Across the room, Lukas was swearing at the printer again. Bartek had one earbud in, humming just loud enough to annoy no one as he laid out an ad for Hagan's Appliance and TV:

FINAL DAYS—EVERYTHING MUST GO

Sam turned back to her keyboard. She reread the paragraph about Wayne "Subway Shoes" Callahan and his sock-layering gospel, typed a sentence, then deleted it.

By afternoon she'd pivoted to a follow-up on the fiercely contested canoe race championship at Lake Harmony—a beloved annual showdown where rival resort staff, volunteer firemen, and at least one guy in a Viking helmet battled for bragging rights, a paddle-shaped trophy, and a year's worth of free chicken wings at Piggy's BBQ.

Bartek squinted at his screen and muttered, "Comic Sans? Are these people serious?" Lukas had one AirPod in and typed loudly enough for everyone to know he meant business. Across his monitor scrolled a draft headline: "Is Lake Wallenpaupack the New Loch Ness?" Beneath it sat a blurry photo of what looked suspiciously like a log.

Constance snapped her fingers at him. "Lukas, that story is not going on the front page."

"It's local," Lukas said. "It's weird. It's clickable."

Amelia covered the receiver with her hand. "We don't even have a website."

Lukas spun in his chair. "What do you mean we don't have a website?"

"It's down again," Amelia said. "You might want to look into that. And might I remind you—it was your idea to switch to Bloggernaut Lite." She paused. "It's only crashed once this week. Might be a record."

Lukas threw up his hands. "It was free," he said. "And a guy on Reddit said it scaled."

Outside, Washington Street moved slow under the high-summer heat—traffic crawling past open windows, wind chimes faint in the breeze. Bassett's Hardware displayed hand-lettered signs advertising fishing licenses and bulk birdseed. Miller's Barbershop kept its red, white, and blue pole spinning lazily, its owner visible through the plate-glass window, reading a newspaper in his empty chair. Down the block, the local pharmacy—owned by the Forrest family for seventy-seven years—kept its lights on, the front window cluttered with sun-bleached Band-Aid boxes and a handwritten sign listing reduced hours. Cliff, the mailman, sweating through his uniform, exchanged pleasantries with the bank teller on her smoke break. A dog barked from a yard tucked behind the shops, then went quiet. A car door creaked open and slammed shut—out-of-state plates, vacation traffic.

She was halfway through a sentence about how John McMullen's rowing technique had "unexpected kick for a man pushing ninety" when Lukas rolled his chair toward her desk—

—and slammed into it.

"Hey, Sam. You hear anything about a cargo plane almost going down last night at Mount Pocono Airport?"

She looked up. "What?"

Lukas bounced once, steadied himself, and kept talking. He perched on the edge of her desk, unusually still. "My cousin's brother said something," he said. "He was working at the Wawa by the airport. Said a guy came in around midnight, looked like he'd seen a ghost. Said he watched a twin-engine cargo plane barely get off the runway. One of the engines died. Said it didn't look like it was going to clear the trees—but it did." He shook his head. "Swears there were branches stuck in the landing gear and everything." He paused. "Must've been one hell of a pilot."

Sam's heart clenched.

Eric had been home that morning—normal, casual—eating a toasted bagel like it was any other Tuesday. He'd flown all night and acted like it was nothing. Coffee. A kiss on the forehead.

Sam blinked, then looked back at her screen. "You think there's a story there?" she asked.

Lukas shrugged. "Maybe. Could be nothing. But I'm gonna call the airport, see if I can get someone on record." He glanced at her. "Doesn't your husband work out there? See if he heard anything."

Sam nodded slowly.

Lukas stood and drifted away, tossing his phone into the air and catching it one-handed. "Heard it might've been overloaded too," he added, already halfway across the room.

Sam's eyes drifted to the window. Toward the sky. Her screen still read: Lake Harmony Canoe Race Showdown.

She saved her work and stood. A strange wave of nausea rolled through her—sudden and hot. She pressed a hand to her stomach, willing it to pass. The air in the office felt thin.

CHAPTER 17

Navigator's Prayer

Five years earlier

It was mid-October when Sam flew out to see him. Three months since the night they met on July 4th in New York City. Street musicians. A fire escape. Fireworks. They'd talked every day since. Texts. FaceTime. The long-distance blur of it. Eric picked her up at Pittsburgh International Airport just after sunrise, and they headed southeast on the Pennsylvania Turnpike into the hills. Sam watched as the city fell behind—smokestacks and stadiums giving way to farms and fence lines, the thick woods ahead lit with leaves of copper and fire-autumn gold. She rested her elbow against the door, her shoulder angled toward him, close enough to feel the warmth of his arm when he shifted gears.

"Is this where you grew up?" she asked, watching the ridgeline roll like an orange sea.

"Close."

"But I thought we were staying with your parents."

"We are."

"So, you grew up close to—but not—"

He reached over and squeezed her hand. "You'll see."

They pulled into the lot at Somerset County Airport—2G9—a high field with a single paved runway cut into the Laurel Highlands. A few small airplanes sat tied down in front of the terminal, their wings rocking gently in the wind. The hills beyond were alive with October fire.

"You brought me to an airstrip?"

Eric tipped his chin toward the far end of the ramp. "Not just any airstrip."

A hangar sat ahead—corrugated steel, sun-faded and rust-patched, an old U.S. Army Air Force stencil above the sliding doors. Eric pulled the truck to a stop, hopped out, and crossed to the handle, pausing just long enough to glance back at her.

He gave it a tug, then braced and heaved. The big panel screeched reluctantly open, metal grinding on metal. A whiff of musty air rolled out—old oil, old leather, pine, dust, and time. He crossed to a heavy-duty wall switch, wrapped his hand around the metal lever, and pulled.

The overhead lights buzzed to life. Sam followed, blinking as her eyes adjusted.

Inside, the hangar looked nearly untouched since World War II. High rafters ribbed with rusted steel. An old wooden ladder chained to the wall. Tires stacked in a corner. Canvas-covered crates stamped with stenciled numbers. A rusted bicycle leaned against a tool cabinet. Pin-up girls curled on faded calendars. It smelled like old stories.

A weathered leather bomber jacket hung from a nail near the door, its lining torn, the name tag long faded. Above it, a propeller blade—chipped and oil-darkened—was mounted to the hangar. A metal locker stood nearby, its door ajar, revealing a half-empty bottle of Brasso, a pair of scuffed flight boots, and a rolled silk escape map, the edges browned with time. An old flight helmet rested on a stool beneath it; the oxygen mask still clipped to the side.

To the right of the main bay sat a makeshift crew corner—exactly as one might have found it in 1944: a poker table with folding chairs, ashtrays filled with petrified cigarette butts, and a chipped enamel coffee pot still perched on a hot plate. Behind it, a wooden cabinet held a tin of wing polish, a weather log, and a row of yellowed, dog-eared manuals. One lay open to a checklist for the B-24.

On the far wall, an ancient bulletin board displayed curling orders, ration cards, and a hand-drawn map of the European theater. The floor was cracked concrete, stained with grease, cigarette burns, and ghostly tire marks that led nowhere.

Taped to the corner of the bulletin board, half-curled at the edges, was a black-and-white photograph of a B-24 Liberator. Six crewmen stood in front of it, squinting into the sun, uniforms rumpled, arms slung over one another's shoulders.

The Liberator's name was stenciled just beneath the cockpit window: *Troublemaker*. Beside it, painted on the fuselage, was a reclining pin-up girl with dark curls and a strapless dress, one leg bent just so, lips parted in a half-smile. Even in monochrome, Sam could feel the cheek in the World War II nose art—the wink, the swagger. The paint was chipped in places, the metal scuffed and streaked with oil, but the girl was still there.

Bold. Sexy. Something for these crewmen to believe in at the edge of the world.

Eric ducked under a wing and disappeared behind a small airplane, rummaging through a pile of gear. She heard the scrape of metal, the rattle of a tow bar. A moment later, the dull thunk of a chock kicked free.

Sam wandered. She ran her hand along a steel support beam, its paint worn smooth by time. An old clipboard still hung from a nail, its pages brittle and yellow. Against the far wall, a battered workbench sat beneath a row of dusty windows.

Above it hung a bronze plaque. She stepped closer. The lettering was simple, engraved deep into the metal. She read it quietly, her lips barely moving:

NAVIGATOR'S PRAYER

With whispering wings, we fall for endless sky.
There may be storms but still, we climb.
Love does not wait for calm to fly.

It stays, it steadies, it trusts the time.
—2nd Lt. Sheldon Ross
Navigator, B-24 Liberator
8th Air Force, 1944

She read the lines again; simple and raw. Not poetry. Just a scared boy's attempt at hope in a world that seemingly had no room for it. That was what made it beautiful.

Maybe Sheldon had been 19 years old, lying awake on an Army cot somewhere in England, missing a girl whose letters smelled like home. Sam traced the final line with her eyes, then looked around the hangar—at the ribs of steel, the suspended dust, the quiet gravity of history.

Behind her, Eric clipped a tow bar to the tailwheel and began pulling a plane into the sunlight. Out on the ramp—separated from the rusted hangars—sat one so polished it seemed to hold the whole morning in its skin.

High-wing.

All aluminum.

No paint—only metal and shine. The cowling gleamed like chrome. Inside, the red leather seats caught the sun and glowed like hot embers.

Sam stared, eyes wide.

Eric smiled.

"She's a 1944 Luscombe 8A Silvaire," he said. "Built during the war. Taildragger. Bare aluminum. Sixty-five–

horsepower Continental. No starter motor. Hand-propped every time."

"She looks . . . amazing."

"She's not mine," he said. "My buddy's dad keeps her hangared here in Somerset. Said I could borrow her—as long as I don't ding the prop on the grass strip where we're landing. Which means you're on grass-runway spotting duty."

"Grass strip?"

"Yep." He started toward the Luscombe. "I figured if you were going flying for the first time, it should be worth remembering."

The Luscombe 8A Silvaire sat low to the ground. The lines were elegant, not flashy, the door hinges bare. The pedals looked like polished bicycle parts. The instrument panel was a tight cluster of black dials—airspeed, altimeter, oil pressure, compass. No GPS. No nav suite. Only analog breath.

"You picked this plane on purpose," Sam said. "For me?"

"Isn't she beautiful?"

"She is." Sam looked at him. "You didn't say anything about doing something this . . . sexy."

"Then it wouldn't have been a surprise."

"You planned this whole thing for me?"

"I mean . . . yeah."

"I wanted your first flight to be in a cool airplane. Plus, there's a grass strip there—most people never get to land on one—and I wanted—"

Sam leaned in and kissed him.

"Well done."

Eric cleared his throat.

"Okay. That's . . . going to make the preflight take a little longer."

Sam held his gaze, fighting a smile.

He stepped around the nose of the Luscombe and began his walkaround.

She followed him with her eyes as he moved around the taildragger in his broken-in leather flight jacket, T-shirt, and blue jeans, adjusting flaps and checking fuel caps like it was second nature. The jacket pulled tight across his back when he leaned in, sleeves creasing at the elbows. He looked completely in his element—focused, calm, eyes scanning with purpose. He ran his palm along the polished leading edge.

"You look very professional."

He didn't answer. He moved down the wing, checking the surface, eyes intent.

"Like . . . extremely capable."

He crouched by the tire and ran his thumb along the tread.

"Do you always look like that when you're concentrating?"

He straightened and finally met her eyes. "You're not making that easy."

She stepped closer.

"Take your time. I'm not going anywhere."

"I hope not."

She tilted her head. "We'll see how your landing goes."

Eric laughed, shook his head, and pulled off the hinged cowling door. He checked the oil, closed it, and stepped to the nose.

"Stay clear," he called.

Sam backed up, suddenly unsure of what he was about to do.

"Wait. You're going to start it from out there?"

Eric nodded. "No starter motor on this one. I've got to hand-prop it."

He reached into the cockpit, cracked the throttle, mixture rich. Primed the engine. Then stepped to the propeller.

"It's old-school," he said. "Dangerous if you don't know what you're doing." He gripped one blade with both hands. "You're pulling it through compression—trying to get a spark when the magnetos fire."

"Oh, right . . . of course," Sam said, watching his hands.

He swung the prop through in one sharp motion.

The engine coughed once.

He swung again.

This time, the engine caught—a bark, a snarl, then the smooth rumble of old aluminum. The propeller spun into a blur.

Eric walked back to the cockpit, like it was nothing. Like he hadn't just wrestled a spark out of 75-year-old metal.

He climbed into the cockpit and motioned for her to join him.

She did—clumsy with the step, knees folding into the tiny space. The red leather was warm. The glass curved close. The control stick between them felt like an invitation to a different time.

"These old taildraggers are tricky to taxi," Eric said.

"It's beautiful."

Eric nudged the throttle forward, and the Luscombe began to roll—tail low, nose high, engine humming. The tailwheel clattered over the uneven ground as he worked the rudder pedals—left toe, right toe, then back again. Taildraggers didn't taxi like tricycles. They swayed. Wandered. Demanded attention.

He kept his heels off the brakes, tapping the rudder like he was walking a tightrope laid down by the breeze. Wind streamed through the open side vents. The tail swayed as they curved toward the runway threshold.

Then—without losing speed—Eric tapped right brake and swung the tail around in a graceful pivot, lining them up on centerline. The nose settled. The horizon steadied.

The Luscombe waited.

Eric glanced over. "You ready?"

Sam didn't answer.

She leaned across the narrow cockpit and kissed his cheek, quick and warm. Her hand brushed his shoulder as she pulled back, grinning behind her sunglasses.

He slid his sunglasses into place.

"I'll take that as a yes."

He pushed the throttle forward.

The Luscombe surged ahead, quick and light, tail low. The stick eased back under his hand. The tail lifted. The ground fell away, and Sam felt it—the clean, weightless pull of their first flight.

They weren't airborne yet, but the horizon had already shifted.

The nose dipped. The wind pushed harder, louder, and the Luscombe 8A Silvaire skated fast across the October morning, wheels humming on the asphalt.

Then the main wheels left the earth.

The Luscombe lifted into the sky like it had been waiting all autumn to climb. The takeoff was short. Only a few hundred feet—light. No lurch, no hesitation. Just lift. Smooth. Certain.

Sam gripped her seat once then let go.

The Luscombe climbed—light on the controls at first, and even lighter still the higher it rose in the sky. It didn't roar like a new plane; it slipped upward, easy, like flying was still a remembered promise.

The world fell away.

The ridgelines rolled beneath them in a wash of gold and flame. Western Pennsylvania bloomed with color—trees in orange, green, red. Roads narrowed into veins. Dairy farms stitched the hills together like buttons on a patchwork quilt.

Sam leaned toward the window, awestruck. "It's like flying over a postcard."

Eric pointed to the panel. "Airspeed. Altimeter. Oil pressure. Compass."

He tapped each dial in turn. "That stick in your lap—that's flying."

She leaned toward the window, eyes wide.

"You can see forever."

She smiled, as if realizing it wasn't just the flying.

"I love it. I wasn't sure if I would—but I do."

"Phew. It only took two months of planning and one perfectly timed weather forecast."

She leaned over and kissed him again without thinking. Like she couldn't wait any longer.

Along the way, Eric pointed out landmarks—the spine of Laurel Hill, the glint of Quemahoning Reservoir, and then the city of Johnstown below, tucked deep where the hills closed in tight around it.

He nodded toward a cluster of brick buildings near the edge of town. "That's Bishop McCort. That's where I went to high school."

Sam leaned closer to the glass.

Rivers threaded through the town and came together at the valley floor, and the Johnstown Incline Plane cut a straight line up the mountainside, the scale of the climb visible even from this height. Then he pointed toward a dark break in the ridge, the land carved away where it shouldn't have been.

"Do you see where the railroad tracks run through that gap?"

"I see them."

"That's what's left of the old South Fork Dam," he said. "The one that burst in 1889. Caused the Johnstown Flood. Killed over two thousand people."

Sam leaned forward. "I've heard of the Johnstown Flood. I never knew it was caused by a dam breaking."

"It was owned by the South Fork Fishing and Hunting Club," he said. "Andrew Carnegie. Mellon. Henry Clay Frick."

He pointed again. "You can still see some of the old cottages."

Sam raised her phone and snapped a photo as the landscape slid past—the cottages and an old clubhouse briefly centered in the frame.

Eric pointed to a bend in the valley. "And right over there's where we're going."

A tiny farmhouse appeared, tucked among rolling hills and white picket fences. A red barn sat off to one side, and a couple of ponds reflected the sky below it. A herd of Highland cattle wandered near a sloped pasture, their shaggy rust-red coats catching the afternoon light.

"That's the field," Eric said. "Uphill. Short. There's a little bump halfway down."

"Is this the part where I rate your landing?"

He smiled. "Grass-strip duty. Tell me if you see anything like holes or rocks. Or cows."

"Cows?"

"Yeah. We're landing in their pasture."

Sam's eyes widened, full of curious wonder and disbelief.

"Here we go." He circled once, then lined up with the pasture. The Luscombe floated low over the fence line. Wind swirled the fallen autumn leaves across the pasture as he flared. The wheels kissed the field then bounced once. Grass and leaves blurred past. The bump hit. He corrected. They rolled out uphill and stopped near a row of round hay bales by the picket fence.

Sam exhaled. "Okay. That was amazing."

Eric reached for the *Shutdown* checklist, flipping switches, "Sometimes it can be a little tricky to figure out the crosswind in these—"

Eric leaned back. "So how was my landing?"

"I'll give it a 7."

"Only a 7?"

"Okay, maybe 7.5."

She leaned in and kissed him, her tongue brushing his upper lip. "I'm going to need to see another one."

They unlatched the doors as a few of the Highland cattle looked up—fluffy and shaggy, long hair hanging over heavy horns—then, utterly uninterested, went back to grazing.

Eric's parents stood by the fence line, waving.

He turned to her. "Ready to meet my folks?"

Dinner was warm and easy—chicken pot pie, homemade applesauce, and lots of butter in everything. Sam ate gratefully, laughing at stories Eric's mom talked about his childhood. His dad barely said ten words but smiled whenever she looked his way. After the plates were cleared, Sam and Eric sat on the porch swing with mugs of hot cider, the boards creaking beneath them, a few late crickets ticking in the fields. The air was cool, carrying the scent of woodsmoke from a neighboring farm. Above them, the sky had deepened into that velvet blue that meant winter wasn't far.

Sam leaned against him. "They're sweet."

"They are."

"I wasn't expecting the photo of you in Underoos and a Superman cape."

"That one never dies."

They stayed on the porch until the stars came out. At one point, Eric reached for her hand. She let him take it and leaned in, their lips brushing. The kiss deepened, and Sam moved closer.

Then the porch light flicked on. "Y'all turning in?" his mom called.

Eric pulled back, eyes closed for a second. "Apparently."

Inside, his mom handed Sam a folded towel and pointed down the hall. "It's just past the bathroom. Bedroom's across."

Eric looked at Sam, hesitating. "I'll take the couch."

She gave him a small, knowing smile.

They kissed once more in the hallway—just enough to make it hurt a little more when they parted. Sam shut the bedroom door behind her and took in the faded posters and high school wrestling medals hanging from the posts of Eric's old bed frame. She lay down on the narrow twin bed and pulled the quilt to her face. It smelled like cedar and fabric softener. In the living room, Eric stretched out on the couch, one arm behind his head, eyes fixed on the ceiling.

Both were wide awake.

CHAPTER 18

Fly Steady

The next morning, after a simple breakfast of eggs and toast, they walked back through the pasture, boots damp with dew. The Luscombe sat waiting at the edge of the field, its silver skin catching the early light. Eric ran his hand along the leading edge. Sam watched him from behind; her hands tucked into the sleeves of her coat.

"Am I still on grass-spotting duty?"

He looked back at her. "Only if you want the job."

"I want the promotion."

Eric pulled the prop through, and the Luscombe came to life on the second swing. The engine purred, ready and eager. He helped Sam into her seat, then climbed in beside her.

The takeoff was smooth with mist curling off the field behind them as they climbed. His parents waved from the fence line. Sam rested her hand on his knee. They climbed southeast over western Pennsylvania—past creeks, empty roads, and rows of yellow trees lit by the low sun.

"That was fun. I like your parents."

Eric glanced over. "So how am I doing?"

Sam didn't answer. She leaned against the window, watching the ridgelines stretch west, some trees already fading toward winter brown.

"You know, I didn't sleep much."

"Me neither," Eric said without turning.

Sam bent down and tugged off her boots, letting them drop to the floor. Then she peeled off her wool socks, one at a time, and tucked them inside the boots. Her bare feet settled lightly against the cockpit floor.

Then came the zipper of her jacket, sharp against the smooth drone of the engine.

Eric glanced over. "Too warm?"

"Cabin temp's climbing," she said.

He adjusted the vent near her window, though his eyes lingered.

Sam leaned back and unclasped her belt. She slid out of her jeans, easy and unhurried.

"Everything okay?" he asked, his voice a little tighter.

"Everything's perfect."

She leaned forward, reached both hands behind her neck, and drew her sweater up and over her head. She folded it once and tucked it on the floor.

Eric said nothing.

Black lace. Bralette. Panties. That was all.

"You wore that on purpose," he finally said.

"I did." She held his gaze. "But not for long."

Eric swallowed.

For a heartbeat she hesitated—then leaned back, eyes closing, deciding. Her fingers found the clasp at her back. She took her time, long enough for him to feel it, then let the bralette fall into her lap.

She opened her eyes and held his gaze. She lifted just enough, steadying against the doorframe as lace slipped free, brushing past her ankles and over her toes.

Eric looked back to the panel. Outside scan—quick. No traffic. Then to her.

The Luscombe Silvaire leveled at 4,500 feet. Eric dialed back the throttle. Trimmed. Checked heading. His jaw flexed once before he looked at her again.

"You need to climb a little higher," she said.

Eric glanced at the altimeter, then back at her. "What do you mean?"

"Five thousand two hundred and eighty feet, right?"

Eric cleared his throat. "This is not something you put in a . . . flight plan . . . uh—"

"I know."

He stared. "Sam?"

"Yes—?"

She turned toward him in the cockpit, found her footing. He guided her position and she climbed onto him.

"Eric?"

"Are we—?"

"I've never done this before," she breathed, shaking her head. "Any of it. Flying. Trusting. Falling."

He waited.

She reached for his free hand.

"And yeah," she said. "We are. At least, I think we are."

He nodded. "We are."

She kissed the corner of his mouth, her lips brushing the mic. "You promised me a memory."

"I also promised my buddy I wouldn't ding his dad's airplane."

She pressed her lips against his mouth.

"Then you better . . . fly steady."

Eric adjusted the trim lever. His hand hovered on the stick.

The Luscombe held altitude.

He checked the horizon, then the airspeed—steady. No traffic. Smooth air.

"Are you sure?" he asked.

Sam kissed his neck.

"I'm sure."

She was completely naked—he was still fully dressed.

That was the part that undid him.

Her toes brushed his hand—soft, bare, still cold from the floor.

She reached down, unclasped his belt.

The Luscombe nosed up, then sagged—a quick float.

Airspeed bled off.

"Sam—hold still."

He pitched down an inch, fed in power, and caught it.

She froze, reading him. "Eric—"

"I've got it."

His scan tightened—airspeed, attitude, altitude—then back to her eyes.

Jesus.

Don't drop her.

Her foot sliding along his thigh.

The headset cords tangled on Sam's ankle.

The edge of the door handle pressed against her hip.

The ridgelines passed below as the 1944 Luscombe Silvaire rocked gently on the wind.

They held altitude.

They held each other.

On whispering wings—somewhere over the Laurel Highlands, above waking farms and Sunday church bells—they fell and made good on a promise.

CHAPTER 19

Candy Apple Red

Their bedroom was lit by a single lamp on Sam's nightstand. A thin sheet lay loose between them, barely there, tangled around their legs. Above them, the ceiling fan hummed, cooling their skin as the night air moved across them, making every place they touched feel warmer.

Eric lay on his back, one hand behind his head, staring at nothing.

Sam turned toward him, propped on one elbow, the sheet slipping from her shoulder. "Was it your plane?"

His chest rose. Fell.

"Yeah," he said. "It was me."

She watched his face in the half-light. No surprise. No excuses. Just tired.

"Why didn't you tell me?"

"I wanted to. I just . . ."

He didn't finish.

She laid her head on his chest and threaded her fingers lightly through the hair there, feeling his heartbeat under her palm.

"I heard it at the office," she said. "I knew. As soon as they said it."

His hand slid down past her lower back, pressing into the curve there, and she felt the intention in it before the words came. "I figured it would get around."

Her fingers traced a slow line across his chest and down his stomach, stopping there.

"Were you scared?"

"Not during."

"Why not?"

He shifted on the pillow.

"Training."

"And after?"

"Mad." He dragged a hand down his face. "Mostly at myself."

Sam reached up and traced his jawline.

"Was your plane too heavy to fly?"

"Bruce loaded it before I got there."

She slid her hand across his belly, down lower and back again.

"And he told you to fly it anyway."

"Or he'd get another pilot to fly."

"So, you flew."

"I flew."

"And you almost didn't come home."

Eric turned his head. "But I did."

"Don't say that like it makes it okay."

"I'm not." He shook his head. "I'm just . . . trying to figure out what to do next."

"You almost died, Eric."

He shifted just enough to rest his hand across her ribs—not holding, just touching. Making sure she was still there. "You know what I got for that flight?"

He was still staring at the ceiling.

"0.2 hours. That's what it looks like in my logbook." He let out a breath. "Some rich kid racks up five hours at a time flying a brand-new King Air with an autopilot. I bring back an overloaded airplane on one engine—and I only get to log 0.2 hours."

Sam turned her head. Her voice was flat.

"Don't keep talking like this is about hours, Eric. It's not." She pulled her body away, watching the shadows shift across the ceiling. "You almost died, and you didn't even tell me." Her mind drifted—not to what almost didn't happen, but to what almost did. The shape of loss and how it changes everything without asking. Their knees touching beneath the sheet, bare skin to bare skin. She listened for a long time to the sound of his breathing.

He let out a breath. "I should've told you."

She rolled onto her side to face him.

"My dad painted my toenails once. For my sixth birthday."

"Candy-apple red." She smiled.

Eric put his arm around her.

"That morning. Before the . . . He said it was, so I'd always remember how special I was."

She flexed her toes.

"I guess I never got over it. And any time I think I'm safe, I remember how fast it can all be taken away."

"I can't go through that again," Sam said. "I can't do this if I'm going to worry every time you fly. I can't lose you too, Eric."

"I know."

"I need you alive more than I need you flying. Especially now."

He turned to her, searching her face.

Sam rolled onto her back. Her hand drifted to her stomach.

"I think I'm pregnant."

Eric turned toward her.

"I haven't taken a test," she said. "But I know."

He sat up, swinging his legs over the side of the bed, rubbing both hands through his hair.

"From last weekend?"

She nodded.

"Are you sure?"

"No, but I've never been more sure of anything my body's told me before," she said. "I'll schedule something with Dr. Magro in a couple weeks."

He stayed quiet.

"I'll bet you're scared now," Sam said.

"I'm not."

She sat up. "Well, I am."

He turned back toward her. "The Goose will be fixed in a few weeks. We'd be behind a couple months, but I could still apply for airline jobs by the end of the year—maybe early next—"

For a second she just stared at him.

"That's not what I mean, Eric." A tear slid from the corner of her eye. "It's not about the airlines. I don't want you flying for that guy anymore."

"How are we going to pay our rent, Sam?"

"I don't care," she said. "I'll pick up a second job. I'll write during the day, pour coffee at night—whatever it takes."

She looked at him—in the eyes.

He ran the numbers in his head. An extra year at least.

"Just promise me you're done flying for him."

Eric listened, then nodded.

"Okay."

"People are always looking to take flying lessons." As he said it, he knew it wasn't true. "I'll find more students. It won't be multi-time, though."

"Eric."

The silence lengthened until it became uncomfortable.

"Please—promise me."

His eyes went to their clothes scattered in a loose trail toward the bed—his jeans, her white ankle socks, his boots, the black lace panties, the bra with the tiny pink bow, his crumpled T-shirt.

Don't drop her.

"I'm done flying for Bruce."

Sam folded into him.

"I promise."

Eric rested a hand over her stomach. *"My precious love."*

She let out a small, broken laugh and shook her head against his chest.

They held each other in the quiet.

Sam reached over and turned off the lamp.

They lay there in the dark, not quite asleep, watching the fan spin overhead.

CHAPTER 20

Glitter

Eric parked at the edge of the tarmac—away from his usual spot. Bruce hadn't said a word since the flight. Not about the engines. Not about loading the Goose over max gross weight—or how Eric had brought her back in one piece. He walked toward the hangar quickly. He didn't want questions, but he needed to see the Goose.

She sat lopsided inside the maintenance hangar at Mount Pocono Airport. With her cowlings off, she reminded Eric of a stripped down car up on cinderblocks. Rust had bloomed along the rivets on her belly. The right engine was torn open, and her metal guts were exposed. The once-red paint was more ghost than color now, faded to a chalky gray and streaked with oil, rain, and time—*casket gray.*

Inside the hangar, a small, alarm-clock style radio played low on a shelf beneath the clang of tools. Behind the wing, a mechanic towered over a mobile tool cart. Grease on his forearms and in the creases of his neck. His ball cap bore the logo of a regional airline that hadn't flown in decades. *Carlton* was stitched in red script above the pocket of his oil-stained overalls.

"Hey," Eric said.

The mechanic looked up.

"You the guy who flew her last?"

"Yeah."

"I figured." He wiped his hands on a rag. "Been wondering when you'd show."

"How long's she going to be down?"

"Both engines are toast."

He shrugged.

"Three, four weeks. Minimum. Longer if the mounts are bad." He motioned to the open nacelle. "We pulled the right filter—full of glitter."

Eric stepped closer.

The mechanic tipped the can and let it drip into Eric's palm. Oil and metal flecked together, catching the overhead lights. He rubbed it between his fingers.

"Don't know how the hell she ran as long as she did," the mechanic said. "Metal everywhere."

"Left one quit on takeoff."

"Haven't even looked at that one yet." The mechanic tossed Eric a rag. "Were you heavy?"

"I was full, but . . ." He trailed off. "Bruce said we were okay."

The mechanic barked a laugh. "Sure he did."

"He yanked everything out like he didn't want anyone to see."

"You saved her." The mechanic shook his head. "Don't know how, but you did. Cooked this right engine, but you saved her." The mechanic looked at him. "And yourself."

Eric wiped his hand clean. "I didn't really have a choice, ya know."

The mechanic took the rag back.

"Didn't have a choice?" he asked. "Look, kid. I've seen a lot of pilots just like you over there flying for that guy."

Eric didn't respond.

"He pushes people. Shady cargo runs. Pencil-whipped logbooks," the mechanic snapped the rag. "This won't be the last time."

Dylan rasped from the radio behind the wing. A twin lifted off outside. He took one last look at the Goose, then turned to go.

Behind him, the mechanic spoke again—his voice lower.

"There are old pilots . . . and there are bold pilots . . . but there are no old, bold pilots."

Eric turned back.

The mechanic opened his mouth like he was about to say something else.

"Yeah?" Eric asked.

"Nothin', kid." He tossed the rag onto the tool cart. "You must be a hell of a pilot."

Eric nodded once.

He stepped back into the sunlight as a Piper Arrow climbed away from Runway 5.

He watched the windsock twist—like it couldn't decide which way to fall.

CHAPTER 21

Hundred-Dollar Hamburger

Nasser walked around the Cessna 150 with the checklist in hand, ticking through the preflight like a seasoned pilot. He tapped the rudder, drained the fuel sumps, tugged on the ailerons. Thankfully, he hadn't asked about the Goose. Maybe he hadn't heard yet, Eric figured.

It felt like any other preflight—walk-around, fuel check, dipstick. But this time, they were going somewhere.

It was Nasser's first cross-country flight. He'd chosen Gettysburg Airport.

"Left fuel cap secure. Right secure. Oil . . . 7 quarts. We are good."

"Remember the burn rate we planned for?"

"Ten gallons per hour. Plus, a thirty-minute reserve."

"Good." Eric knelt and inspected the landing gear strut. "Did you file our flight plan?"

"I filed the VFR flight plan," Nasser said. "It feels very different to be flying to a different airport."

They finished the walk-around inspection and climbed into the cockpit. The doors clicked shut with that light C-150 click. Nasser adjusted his seat and reached for the checklist.

"Master switch on. Throttle cracked. Mixture rich."

Nasser turned the key. The engine barked, stumbled, then caught—a low rumble settling into a steady 1,000-RPM idle.

"Oil pressure in the green," Nasser said. "Amps good. Suction . . ."

"Sucking . . ." Eric said flatly.

"Sucking?"

"Sorry," Eric said. "That joke never gets old."

They taxied down Alpha at Mount Pocono Airport. Scattered clouds lingered at 5,000 feet, but otherwise it was a perfect VFR day.

At the run-up area, Nasser ran through the checklist again. "Mag check . . . both drops within limits. Suction gauge . . ."

He glanced over. "Sucking."

"Sucking confirmed," Eric said, laughing, and happy to see Nasser settling into himself.

"Engine instruments green. Flight controls free and correct."

"Let's do this."

They lined up on Runway 5. Winds calm.

"Mixture full rich. Lights on. Final check—doors latched?"

"Latched."

Nasser advanced the throttle. The Cessna 150 surged forward, tires humming against the pavement.

"Engine instruments green. Airspeed alive. Gauges in the green . . . rotate at 60 knots."

At fifty-eight knots, he gave a gentle pull.

The nose lifted.

The ground fell away.

"Positive rate of climb," Nasser said. "Clear of obstacles. Flaps up."

They leveled at 4,500 feet and trimmed for cruise. Nasser leaned the mixture and set cruise power at 2,300 RPM.

"The Wright brothers ran a bike shop in Dayton," Eric said, tapping the altimeter as they settled in. "Built wings in a shed. Flew a few hundred feet." He glanced out at the wing. "Now we're cruising over Pennsylvania with GPS and noise-canceling headsets, navigating by satellites."

Nasser set the power and leaned the mixture.

"Just remember," Eric said. "Aviate. Navigate. Communicate. In that order."

"Heading 246 degrees," Nasser said, confirming compass against GPS. "ETA Gettysburg: one hour, seven minutes."

"Don't let the GPS fly for you," Eric said. "Use it to confirm. You fly the chart."

"Yes, Eric," Nasser replied.

Below them, the ridgelines of Pennsylvania rolled out in greens and browns, stitched together with roads and farmland.

"Crossing I-81 . . . next is the Susquehanna, west of Harrisburg."

They hit light bumps over sun-warmed fields. When a skydiving drop zone appeared on the sectional, Nasser adjusted his course east to stay clear.

"Good. Keep scanning outside," Eric said. "Always know where you are. Remember—superior pilots use their superior judgment, so they never have to use their superior skills."

Nasser nodded.

"What's rule number one, Nasser?"

"Always fly the airplane."

"You got it."

Nasser scanned the instruments, then back outside. His eye caught something.

"Traffic one o'clock. Moving right to left."

Eric spotted it—a red Mooney M20B. Moving fast, right where it should be.

"Expensive," he said, as it passed across the nose of their Cessna.

When they reached Gettysburg, Nasser tuned the CTAF.

"Gettysburg traffic, Cessna One Niner Two Niner Six, ten miles northeast, inbound for full stop. Runway 24."

They began descent into the Gettysburg's traffic pattern.

"Runway in sight," Nasser said. "Winds light southwest. I will enter on the 45 for left downwind."

Eric said nothing.

Only watched.

Nasser made his calls, set up for base, dropped flaps, and rolled onto final. He held 70 knots, adjusting power. The VASI lights dipped from red to white.

"Don't chase the VASI," Eric reminded. "Trust your picture."

Nasser held 60 knots down final, adjusting power. At the threshold he eased back on the throttle.

The Cessna 150 settled with a chirp. One small balloon, then a solid landing.

"Cessna One Niner Two Niner Six clear of Runway 24," Nasser called, then looked at Eric.

"Nice work. Congrats on your first cross-country."

They parked on the line next to the other single engine airplanes and shut down. Nasser jumped out and pulled the tie-down ropes from the pad and looped them through the wing rings, walking the slack out to the anchors and cinching it tight. The nylon was sun-bleached and frayed, stiff with age, but it held. Eric tied off the tail, gave the wing a brief shake. They turned and walked toward town, leaving the Cessna 150 resting on the field.

They walked past split-rail fences and open fields, low stone walls threading the hills like old scars that never quite healed. Nasser took a few photos but didn't speak. Eric didn't either. The silence felt appropriate.

At Herr Tavern, they sat beneath a maple tree on the deck. The breeze lifted their napkins and stirred the leaves. The ground sloped away toward the battlefields. Nasser looked down the road. Beyond the hedges and fencing, the land stretched wide and low.

Then he took a bite of his burger. "This is the first time I have flown just for somewhere to eat."

"Welcome to the world of hundred-dollar hamburgers," Eric said. "That's flying. It's the journey and the destination."

"Do you have a favorite place to go, Eric?"

"Latrobe. There's a restaurant in the terminal—DeNunzio's. Trust me, your wife will love it."

"Thank you, Eric. I will remember that."

They ate slowly while Eric had Nasser talk through the flight back to the Poconos—heading, winds, where the terrain rose, what the afternoon thermals might do to the air. He reminded him to lean the mixture once they climbed and to keep an eye on the gauges.

There was nothing formal about it. But Eric knew Nasser would remember his first cross-country flight forever.

On the walk back, Nasser asked, "How long until I can solo?"

"Soon," Eric said. "If your landings stay clean, I'll sign you off next week."

"Next week? Oh no, I am not ready."

"Then I won't sign you off. Not until we both are. The FAA considers me responsible for everything you do as a student. If you mess up, it's on me. So, I won't sign you off until we're both ready."

Back at the airport, the preflight was methodical and unhurried. Nasser climbed into the left seat like it belonged to him now. Engine start. Run-up. Checklist. Takeoff roll.

As the nose lifted from Gettysburg's short runway, Eric looked out over the fields slipping beneath them.

Nasser climbed out at Vy—best rate—and turned toward the Poconos.

Eric cracked the air vent, leaned back, and let the soothing hum of the engine do the talking.

CHAPTER 22

Lou's Dirty Water Dogs

"What about David Roseman?"

Eric looked up from the table. "Who?"

"You know . . . from Lovers' Cove. The guy in the red blazer."

"The Sinatra guy?"

"Yeah. Didn't he say he always wanted to learn to fly?" Sam asked, passing him their tray and sliding onto the bench beside him at a floral-painted picnic table. "It would be more hours."

"The Frank Sinatra guy said a lot of things," Eric unwrapped his hot dog. "I flew almost twenty hours last week."

Sam looked at him, surprised. "Twenty?"

"Give or take."

"Wow. That's actually really good."

Eric bit into his chili dog, grease dripping onto the wax paper.

"Sure—I'll give Sinatra guy some flying lessons."

He took another bite of his hot dog and laughed through the chew, shaking his head.

The hot dog stand—if you could call it that—was an old Airstream trailer converted into a kitchen on wheels. A crooked, hand-painted sign swung from a tree branch:

Lou's Dirty Water Dogs—*a 42nd street tradition.*

The Airstream's aluminum siding was plastered with a handwritten menu and a faded price list, alongside unapologetic warnings like:

No Ketchup After Age 12-Don't Even Ask

Cash Only

Sam was unwrapping hers—mustard and sauerkraut, just like her dad used to make. "It'd be more flying hours," she said. "And more money."

Eric wiped his fingers on a napkin. "Babe, I was kidding. I don't think he was serious. He was just making small talk with his guests." He smirked. "*Lover.*"

Sam shook her head, thinking of the over-the-top weekend at Lovers' Cove.

Eric nudged her with his elbow. "Isn't this great? We're in the woods, eating hot dogs by a stream." He took another bite. "Forget The Bruce Goose. We should just find a couple of big trees and open a taco stand."

Sam sipped from a plastic cup of water. "He said the Steinway's still there. Remember? The Model D. The one that '*hummed in the floorboards.*' It'd make a great story for the paper."

Eric watched the water slip over the stones then looked back at her.

"I really don't think he was serious about flying lessons."

"He was. And I can't stop thinking about that piano," Sam said. "The one that barely fit through the door. I want to see it."

Eric scratched the side of his jaw. "It's probably covered in dust."

"We could use the money," Sam added gently.

Eric sighed. "You really think he wants flying lessons?"

"He's rich. Maybe he's bored." She said.

"Right, and maybe Frank Sinatra and Billy Joel did a dueling piano set up there in '75 too."

Sam stared at him, then said dryly, "Honey, I don't think Frank Sinatra played piano. He was the singer . . . I think?"

They both laughed, the sound carrying a moment longer than it should have, fading into the trees. Somewhere beyond the woods, a Harley hummed on a distant road. A stream rumbled beside them, water slipping over smooth stones. Fifty feet downstream, a wooden footbridge crossed it, faded prayer flags tied to the railing. Beyond it, the forest folded into itself, dense with ferns and rhododendron. Sunlight flickered through the maple canopy, casting gold across the faded tabletop, and the air carried pine needles and distant campfires—childhood summers in the Poconos, back before you realized how quickly they passed.

The Poconos in summer have a way of wrapping around you. Hot dog stands hidden in the forest. Candle shops tucked into log cabins. Coffee joints run by Brooklyn refugees who escaped rent and brought their espresso machines with them. A bookstore run by an old man who claimed he'd once been a roadie for Led Zeppelin—no one could prove him wrong. He gave discounts to teachers, firefighters, police officers, and anyone who brought pot brownies.

"You know that place we pass on Route 390? The one with the big red heart on the gate?"

"Yeah," Eric said. "Honeymoon something."

"Honeymoon Hideaway," Sam said. "I looked it up. That was one of the Roseman family's resorts—the one David mentioned to us. They owned a whole cluster of honeymoon spots. Lovers' Cove, Paradise Pines, Cupid's Secret Palace, and Honeymoon Hideaway. They're all gone now, except for Lovers' Cove. But their very first one is still standing."

Eric looked at her. "Did you just say Cupid's Secret Palace?"

Sam sipped her water. "It was the first Pocono resort to have an archery range."

"Really. Cupid's Secret Palace . . . with an archery range."

"Yep." Sam leaned in a little. "Want to know what their slogan was?"

"I don't know. Do I?"

"Where love never misses the target," Sam said—then burst out laughing. "I'm dead serious."

Eric joined in: "How romantic . . . and strange. Sinatra guy would be perfect for flying lessons."

"Exactly," Sam said. "Romantic. Strange. And perfect."

"That was a joke, my *precious love*."

This time, Sam didn't return laugh. She just looked at him—trusting him to hear what she wasn't saying.

Eric reached for his lemonade, already knowing he was outmatched. He took a sip.

"Alright," he said. "Call him. See if you can get a tour and—if he wants to fly, I'll give him lessons."

"Really?"

"Sure, honey."

"Should I call him now?"

"Now?"

Sam waited.

Eric shook his head. "Why not? We'll find out pretty quick if he's serious."

Sam took out her phone and scrolled to David Roseman's name, her thumb hovering just above the screen.

Eric wiped his hands on a napkin and watched her—curious. Then he noticed it. David Roseman

—already saved. No hesitation. No searching.

Sam glanced at him and gave a wry, unapologetic smile—guilty as charged.

Eric shook his head, amused. "You already had his number saved."

She shrugged. "Didn't want to carry his card around."

"Naturally," Eric said. "So subtle."

She took a sip of her water and smiled as she lifted the phone to her ear. "Ready?"

He leaned back. "You are adorable."

She propped herself on her elbow.

"Hi, Mr. Roseman—this is Sam Young. We met at Lovers' Cove. The writer. Yes—the apostrophe."

She glanced at Eric, lifting her eyebrows.

"Yeah, I wanted to follow up because, well . . . I keep thinking about that Steinway you mentioned. Yes the one where, the one where Frank Sinatra sang."

She nodded as he spoke. "I'd love to see it. Even just for a few photos. I'm working on a piece about the old honeymoon resorts, and that piano feels like the heart of it."

She shot Eric a triumphant look.

"Oh, you will? That would be amazing. Thursday morning? At the gated entrance?" She couldn't help smiling. "Perfect. I really appreciate it, Mr. Roseman. Yes—absolutely. I'll see you there. Thank you so much."

She hung up and let out a squeal before she could stop herself.

"So," Eric said, "we're going to see the Sinatra piano."

"Thursday morning. He didn't even hesitate."

"You are adorable."

She leaned into him and finished her water. "You already said that."

He kissed the top of her head. "I love you."

"I know." She tilted her face up to him. "I love you too."

Sam glanced at her phone again. "I just . . . I have a good feeling about this story." She brushed the screen with her fingers as if replaying the call.

"You think Frank Sinatra really played there?"

"Does it matter? I mean… it's possible."

Eric nodded slowly. "So somewhere between Philly and New York he thought, why not swing by a heart-shaped-bathtub joint in the Poconos."

She smiled. "He's a little before our time. Who knows?"

"Yeah," Eric said, "but now I kind of want to believe it. I want to picture Sinatra in his tux—tie loosened, sleeves rolled up—crooning *Strangers in the Night* under a mirrored ceiling.

"Next to a giant champagne-glass hot tub." Sam added.

"One hand on the mic—pinky ring catching the neon."

"Pinky out," she said. "Pure lounge swagger."

Eric slipped into a passable Sinatra voice. "'Ladies and gentlemen of Cupid's Hideaway . . . somebody tell the guy who did the sign—the apostrophe's in the wrong spot.'"

"You are on a roll, my love." Sam laughed. "That's not legend. That's kitsch."

Eric lifted his lemonade. "To kitsch."

She clinked her water against his. "To Sinatra."

A breeze moved through the trees. A dragonfly skimmed the stream, its wings flashing in the light. Kids with hot dogs in hand splashed in the shallows, shouting, their laughter carrying through the woods.

Sam watched them. "You ever wonder," she asked, "what it would be like to stay here?"

"What do you mean?"

"We always assumed we'd leave after you got your hours in," she said. "But maybe staying isn't the worst thing. Maybe Bruce Payne's broken plane is a blessing."

She looked at him, searching his face. "I'm okay here, Eric. I didn't think I would be—but I am. Take the time you need."

She reached for his hand.

"We're okay."

"I'm starting a taco stand."

She shook her head. "No. You'll run a flying school."

"And you'll write the history of Cupid's Hideaway and Archery Range."

"And Cupid's Chocolate Fondue Sauna & Moonlight Jacuzzi Spa . . ." she added, leaning in.

"Mmm."

She kissed him.

"Exactly."

"We're going to be broke forever," He said.

Sam leaned against him. "I don't care. As long as you'll never have to fly that old Rooster—or whatever you call that plane."

"Rooster?"

"Rooster, turkey . . ." She poked him in the ribs. "Some kind of bird."

"They call her the Goose, my love."

"I'm glad you won't fly that Goose again. Let's find that bookstore—the Zeppelin roadie."

"You just want to smell old books."

"And patchouli," she said.

They walked toward the parking area—a flattened patch of dirt marked by rusted stakes and gardening twine. Eric opened the door to their FJ, then turned. "There's something about this place," he said. "You drive two hours out of the city, and you're in another world."

Sam looked at him.

"It's like someone built a crazy theme park and then just let the forest take it back."

She blinked. Then a slow grin spread across her face.

"That's really good."

"You can use it," he said.

"I will."

"I stole the first part from you, anyway."

"Yeah," she said. "That sounds more like it."

They drove off, the FJ Cruiser kicking up dust as Lou's Dirty Water Dogs—*a 42nd Street tradition*—faded into the trees behind them, waiting for the next pair of hungry lovebirds to find it.

CHAPTER 23

Hearts in the Hills

Sam tapped the space bar with the side of her thumb, starting the grainy YouTube video. The narrator's voice crackled out: "Come to the Poconos—where love blooms and time stands still!" On-screen, a couple grinned too hard in front of a heart-shaped tub. The camera lingered on bubbling water beneath pink light, then cut to a rotating bed turning slow and steady.

Sam leaned back in her desk chair at *The Pocono Classifieds*. Stacks of tourism pamphlets, library books, and a yellow legal pad dense with blue-ink scribbles crowded her workspace. Below her, the drum of footsteps and chatter from Small Mountain Coffee seeped through the floorboards.

Sam slipped her earbuds in and queued up a soft-rock playlist—pure honeymoon-resort cheese. Crooners, piano intros, vows sung in major keys that never left anything unresolved. Research, she told herself.

But the truth was simpler than that.

She liked listening to songs that believed in forever. She'd always liked them. Even after she learned the world didn't always keep its end of the deal.

Her eyes drifted to the corner of her desk where David Roseman's business card leaned against her water bottle—matte ivory, crisp, expensive. His name embossed like it belonged on the door of a private club.

Thursday morning. The gate.

The idea that a place could hold love. That a weekend could make it last. That the right music and the right lights and the right room—heart-shaped tub included—could turn two people into something unbreakable. And if she could write that down in a way that felt true, maybe she could hold onto it, too.

Sam clicked the video off and opened a fresh document.

The blank white screen stared back.

She typed a working title anyway.

Hearts in the Hills

She stared at it until it started to feel corny. Then she let herself keep it. Corny was fine. Corny was honest. It was a honeymoon region. It wasn't supposed to be cool.

Her fingers hovered.

She pictured Eric, at Lou's Dirty Water Dogs, laughing with mustard on his thumb. She pictured him in his flight jacket, those stupid Ray-Bans she loved. She pictured the way he looked at her when she smiled at something small—like he'd been waiting for her to be happy.

She wanted more of that.

She started typing fast, before her brain lost the thread.

Hearts in the Hills

Draft — Sam Young, *The Pocono Classifieds*

The Poconos have always been a place for couples—an easy drive from the city, a quick escape into the woods and quiet roads, where ordinary life can feel far away for a weekend.

She stopped.

That was safe. That was true. That was also . . . bland.

Sam deleted *always* and retyped the sentence without it. Always was a word that tempted fate.

The Poconos have long been a place for couples—

Better.

She hit return twice and added the thing she actually cared about, then immediately tried to sand it down before it got sentimental.

People didn't come here for luxury. They came for permission—permission to be ridiculous about love.

She stared at the word *permission.*

It felt too sharp. Too clever.

She left it anyway. She could fight with it later.

She reached for her legal pad and flipped to the page she'd been building since the night at Lovers' Cove. It looked like a mess, but it was her mess—facts mixed with instinct, history mixed with ache.

Angle: romance as industry / what couples bought

Avoid: brochure voice

Rosemans: multiple resorts — only Lovers' Cove open

Hideaway: first / still standing (per David)

Cupid's Secret Palace: archery / slogan / burned

Sinatra: rumor / no proof / he loves it

Steinway Model D: claim / verify

Question: why people needed this

Sam tapped her pen against the last line.

Because love is hard, she thought.

Because being married is hard.

Because nothing stays effortless forever, and people will pay good money to pretend it does.

Her playlist shifted—soft sax, slow drums, a chorus that sounded like it had never met real life.

Sam turned back to the draft and forced herself into the part Constance would demand: structure, sourcing, restraint.

By the late nineteenth century, city families arrived by rail to spend summers in the mountains. In the early twentieth century, hotels followed.

By the mid-twentieth century, the region began marketing something more specific: the honeymoon.

She paused and added brackets—private honesty.

[Need exact dates + citation for "mid-twentieth century."]

She opened a township archive tab and a scanned tourism-history PDF she'd already downloaded. She wasn't looking for pretty sentences. She was looking for anchors.

The screen filled with grainy images: brochure covers, ballroom photos, a smiling couple in a gazebo that looked staged even back then.

Sam copied a few lines into her notes—not to steal, just to lock down the bones:

1950s: Hideaway expansion mentioned in township materials (verify)

Roseman name appears in property transfer list (verify)

Archery slogan appears in brochure scan (cite)

She opened the brochure scan again and found the line, exactly as she remembered:

WHERE LOVE NEVER MISSES THE TARGET

Sam laughed once—quick, involuntary. Then she felt her throat tighten right after, because it was funny and it was sad at the same time.

Love missed the target all the time.

People still shot anyway.

She typed, careful this time:

One Roseman property leaned into spectacle: Cupid's Secret Palace, which advertised couples' archery as part of the experience.

[Confirm opening year.]

[Confirm fire date + official cause.]

"Where Love Never Misses the Target," one brochure declared. [Cite scan]

She kept moving, keeping everything she couldn't yet prove in brackets so she wouldn't lie to herself just because a sentence sounded good.

Then she hit the part she'd been avoiding.

Frank Sinatra.

Because Sam wanted to believe it. She hated that she wanted to believe it. But she did.

Not because Sinatra mattered.

Because the story mattered.

A famous voice in a lounge in the woods. A moment that felt like proof that romance could be bigger than everyday life. A legend you could pass down.

Sam wrote it the only way she could write it without turning into a brochure:

Local lore insists Frank Sinatra visited Honeymoon Hideaway. There is no public documentation to confirm it.

[Ask David: source of story / who repeats it / any living witnesses?]

Even without proof, the rumor persists—because the Poconos were built on the idea that romance should feel larger than life.

She read that last clause and immediately highlighted it.

Too grand.

Too much like she was arguing.

She deleted the clause and replaced it with something smaller.

. . . because people like stories that make love feel real.

That one stayed.

A chair scraped in the hallway. Footsteps. A shadow at her door.

Constance appeared, holding a red pen and a stack of proofs like she was about to stab the printer into obedience.

"How's the honeymoon thing," Constance said.

"Thursday," Sam said. "At the gate."

Constance's eyes flicked to the business card, then to the screen.

"Good," she said. "Maybe he'll buy an ad."

Sam didn't blink. "Maybe."

Constance leaned in just enough to read the Sinatra line. Her mouth tightened.

"This," Constance said, tapping the screen with the red pen, "is fine. 'Local lore.' 'No documentation.' That's what keeps you alive."

Sam nodded.

Constance's gaze shifted to the earlier line Sam had written—permission to be ridiculous about love.

Constance read it twice. Then she looked at Sam.

"That," Constance said, "is the piece."

Sam's chest warmed and she hated how much she needed that.

Constance straightened. "Just don't let Roseman steer it."

"I know," Sam said.

Constance left without another word, already halfway back into the fight with the proofs.

Sam sat, listening to her playlist and the coffee shop noise.

Then she opened a second document and typed what she'd actually bring Thursday: questions, not poetry.

QUESTIONS FOR DAVID ROSEMAN —THURSDAY

— Confirm dates: Hideaway founding/expansion/closure (what's documented?)

— Sinatra story: where it started, who tells it, why he believes it

— Steinway claim: model, when acquired, why it mattered

— What he wants remembered (and what he refuses to talk about)

She saved both files.

HEARTS_IN_THE_HILLS_DRAFT_1

SINATRA_QUESTIONS_THURSDAY

Then she shut the laptop.

PART III

Weight

CHAPTER 1

Cadillac Escalade

The FJ Cruiser rumbled along Route 390 beneath a canopy of towering Pocono pines. Sunlight flickered through the trees in golden shafts, striping the dashboard like an old film reel. Sam sat barefoot, toes propped on the dash, scrolling through her phone with one hand. The borrowed digital camera from *The Pocono Classifieds* rested in her lap.

She wasn't talking. Just absorbing.

On her screen: grainy YouTube clips, digitized postcards, brochure scans. One ad promised THREE NIGHTS / ONE PRICE / ALL INCLUSIVE ROMANCE. Another bragged that for $199 you got buffet dinners, disco nights, a bottle of champagne—and, if you timed it right, a live performance by a guy who once opened for Barry Manilow.

Sam stared at an old Honeymoon Hideaway brochure. The tagline: Where love never fades.

Eric glanced over. "What are you reading?"

"Did you know," she said, voice distant, "the Poconos had more honeymoon suites per capita than anywhere else in the country? More than Vegas."

Eric considered that. "How proud they must've been," he said. "Putting that on a billboard."

Sam didn't answer. Her eyes stayed on the screen. "I know it was cheesy. But it meant something to people. It gave them a place to believe in… even if just for a weekend."

The forest unfurled ahead—rolling hills dense with evergreens, tangled with wild rhododendron. Here and there, a collapsing sign or a vine-choked stairway to nowhere flickered past between the trees.

Eric downshifted as the road narrowed. "These places—they really get to you, don't they?"

"I just want to see if there's anything left," Sam said. "Something I can write down before it disappears."

They rounded a final bend and slowed to a stop.

A rusted gate leaned off its hinges between two stone pillars, one cracked down the middle. Vines crawled over everything, twisting around the base, climbing the posts like they were reclaiming a promise. A heart-shaped sign dangled crookedly from the fence, its once-bright letters faded to ghost-gray:

HONEYMOON HIDEAWAY

Eric put the FJ in park.

Sam lifted her camera and snapped a photo through the windshield. "It's like it's been waiting for someone to remember it."

They stepped out together, gravel crunching beneath their feet. Sam adjusted the camera strap, her heart thudding harder than she expected.

And then she saw David Roseman.

He stood beside a black Cadillac Escalade off to the side of the road—dove-gray blazer, fine leather gloves in hand, one pocketed as if the woods had dress code. Chestnut suede oxfords, clean on the gravel, untouched by the mud at the edges.

He stared down the washed-out drive where a swollen stream had chewed a trench straight through the earth.

When he heard them, he turned. "Looks as though nature had other plans," he said, gesturing toward the ruin. "The road's gone. I haven't been back here in years. I had no idea."

Sam's steps slowed. "There's no way to get in at all?"

"I should have checked first. My apologies."

Sam looked past him, through the trees. The resort was somewhere beyond. She raised her camera, took a few halfhearted shots, then lowered it. The strap tugged at her shoulder.

"It's like it doesn't want to be found."

Sam stepped closer to the edge of the washout, testing the ground like she already knew the answer.

"Careful, baby," Eric called, stepping toward her.

The gravel gave way immediately. Mud sucked at her shoe and she slid half a step before catching herself.

The camera slipped from her hand and dropped—lens knocking once against a stone before landing face-down in wet grit. She crouched and picked it up, turning it over. Mud smeared the glass and leaf pulp clung to the barrel. She wiped it once with her sleeve, then put the cap on with a soft, final click.

David Roseman looked away, as if he'd learned long ago not to stare at disappointment.

"It was beautiful," he said. Just stating a fact that didn't need proof.

Sam nodded.

In her head, the story had already shifted.

She turned back toward the FJ.

Eric squinted into the trees.

Then he turned to David Roseman.

"Didn't you say your grandfather built a runway here?"

CHAPTER 2

A Walk In The Park

David Roseman clutched the edge of the seat with both hands, knuckles pale, legs locked straight. His blazer was bunched beneath the seatbelt, his sunglasses sat askew, and his scarf—perfectly tucked—had no business being in a small airplane.

From the backseat of the Cessna 172, Sam watched David Roseman—his perfect clothes, his white-knuckled grip. "Everything okay up there?" she asked.

"I'm fine," David Roseman said, his jaw set. "This isn't quite the altitude I'm accustomed to."

A sudden jolt knocked his elbow into the window—his scarf followed, flopping into his mouth. He tugged it out calmly, as though nothing had happened, and exhaled through his nose. David Roseman cleared his throat too quickly, then adjusted it, as if it were the problem. The turbulence wasn't dangerous. But it was undignified.

"Are you certain this is safe?"

"Flying is very safe," Eric joked. "Now crashing—that's a different story. Crashing is dangerous."

David Roseman didn't laugh. He tightened his grip on the seat edge.

"I would appreciate," he said evenly, "if we could avoid the distinction."

Eric glanced over. "You're doing great. We're only at three thousand feet. That's about the height of two Empire State Buildings stacked on top of each other."

David Roseman wasn't sure how he'd ended up here. One day he was offering a polite anecdote about a runway; the next, he was squeezed into a seat designed for someone with much shorter legs.

Buckled in. Far from anything he could control. The seat smelled faintly of sweat and vinyl. The engine whined like a hedge trimmer. This was not how elegant men traveled.

"This is not precisely how I imagined returning to the hideaway," David Roseman said.

Sam leaned forward between the seats, her digital camera already clicking. "The light is perfect! Look at the ridges—this is incredible. The air's so clear, you can see forever."

Below them, the Poconos unfurled in rolling waves a thousand shades of green. Cabins, hidden lakes, and the bones of old resorts peeked through the trees.

"Cold front's over Pittsburgh," Eric said. "We've got maybe an hour before it gets ugly." He banked left, the wingtip dipping toward the ridge. "See it?"

Sam gasped.

Honeymoon Hideaway.

From the air, it looked like a secret palace, slowly reclaimed by the woods. The main lodge stood center—its roof flashing in the sun like a beacon. Beyond it: gazebos, ponds, walking paths, and shapes of tennis courts.

"It's beautiful," Sam said.

"My grandfather designed it," he said. "He wanted it to feel like a piece of Manhattan set down in the wilderness. Crystal chandeliers. Velvet drapes. The Steinway in the lounge—he insisted on the D. And heart-shaped tubs—because a proper honeymoon resort should offer something even the city didn't. In its time, it was the place. Weddings were booked years in advance."

Sam sighed, raising her camera.

Ahead—a narrow black line cutting through the trees: the old runway.

"Looks clear from up here. We'll confirm on the flyby." Eric throttled back and eased lower. The Cessna 172 dipped toward treetop level. "Look for debris, downed trees, branches—anything that wants to ruin our day."

David Roseman glanced over, eyes wide. "In other words," he said, "a crash?"

"Nope. That's why we're gonna check it out first," Eric said, as he pulled the throttle to idle and glided the Cessna 172 lower.

They skimmed the tree line above the runway. Grass pushed through the centerline. A few pine branches scattered near the far end.

"Looks pretty clear to me." Eric pulled up and circled wide, setting up a straight-in approach.

"You're actually planning to land there?" David Roseman asked.

Eric adjusted the flaps and pulled some power out.

"You can land anywhere," he said, then glanced over at David Roseman. "Once."

David Roseman turned back toward Sam. "Is he serious?"

He looked at Eric. "Because I need to know whether that was a joke."

"Just a walk in the park, Kazansky."

David Roseman rolled his eyes.

"*Top Gun* reference," Eric added, with a grin.

"Yes, I'm familiar with the film," David Roseman said.

Sam giggled from the backseat, unable to help herself.

The runway opened ahead.

Flaps down. Throttle back.

Eric lined up with the runway. Sam braced herself as the treetops slid past.

David Roseman gripped his seat.

Landing assured, Eric pulled the power out.

Then—

A deer.

It bolted from the tree line—legs flashing, eyes wide.

"Shit," Eric muttered, yanking the yoke.

The Cessna 172 bounced once, then settled hard.

A blur of a cotton-white tail vanished off the left wingtip.

It bounced again.

The tires met the runway with a bump and a squeak. They were down.

"That . . . almost ruined our day," Eric said.

David Roseman released his grip. "I have always hated deer."

The engine ticked as they rolled toward the rusted hangar.

"Welcome to Honeymoon Hideaway International," Eric said. "Please check the seatback pockets and overhead bins for your belongings. Thanks for flying with us."

David Roseman rolled his eyes. "Spare me."

Sam giggled from the backseat.

CHAPTER 3

Forever Begins Here

"It's beautiful."

Her voice echoed across the abandoned ballroom.

Sam stepped through the threshold, feet bouncing on marble that had buckled with time. The grand ballroom opened before them—two stories tall, vast and breathless, like a forgotten cathedral. Dust hung in the air, sweet with mold and something faintly floral, as if roses had once tried to linger.

The windows were boarded now, beams of light squeezing through slats to stripe the room in fractured gold. Crystal sconces clung to the walls at crooked angles. Most of the round tables still stood, their linens stiff with age. A few napkins still remained—folded into swans, edges curled and yellowed. Above them, a mural stretched across the domed ceiling: a bride and groom drifting among clouds beneath peeling gold letters that still promised: Forever Begins Here.

David Roseman stood just inside the doorway, surveying it.

"This was the ballroom," he said. "Nearly a thousand weddings. They'd dim the lights before dessert. A quartet in that corner—" he pointed toward a shadowed platform— "and the whole room would go quiet."

He smiled.

"But the heart of it was through here."

He didn't look at them when he said it. He was already walking.

Sam followed.

Eric lingered by the fireplace.

A wedding portrait hung crooked above the mantel. The couple inside beamed.

He stepped closer.

There was a faint smear at the corner of the groom's mouth.

Cake.

No one had bothered to wipe it away. Or even notice. Not the bride. Not the photographer. Not anyone, all these years.

David Roseman's voice drifted from the hallway. "The lounge is this way."

Eric glanced once more at the photo, then followed. "Whole ballroom," he muttered. "And nobody ever noticed that."

Thunder rolled faintly beyond the boarded windows.

Sam snapped a photo without turning around. "What, honey."

“Nothing,” he said. “We should keep moving,”

David Roseman turned down a side hallway. The air grew damp. Wallpaper hung in curled sheets, revealing cracked plaster beneath. The crown molding, once elegant, was now caked with black mold.

A brass plaque, tarnished but still legible, was fixed beside a door:

HIDEAWAY LOUNGE

“The lounge,” David Roseman said. “This is why we’re here.”

CHAPTER 4

Cobwebs & Rhinestones

Sam stepped inside first. Her camera stayed at her side—for once.

It took a moment for their eyes to adjust. The lounge was shadowed, half-swallowed by collapse. Part of the ceiling had caved in, letting a shaft of sunlight pour through, illuminating a single corner.

And there—

The piano.

Red.

Not mahogany.

Lipstick red.

David Roseman drew in a breath.

Eric stepped forward slowly.

"You're kidding," he said. "That's the one?"

Sam stopped.

Rhinestones had once rimmed the front. Most were gone now, leaving faint glue halos.

"Frank Sinatra performed here," Eric asked. "At that piano?"

David Roseman moved in slowly.

"You sure it wasn't Elton John?" Eric asked.

Sam followed David Roseman.

"Are those rhinestones?" Eric asked.

David Roseman studied the lacquer, the curled veneer, the missing stones. His brow furrowed. For a long moment, no one spoke. He stepped closer, running his hand along the edge, his fingertips tracing the faint glue halos. His mouth opened slightly, then closed.

"I don't . . ." he said finally. "I don't remember it being red."

"So red," Sam said.

"So red," David Roseman echoed.

Eric pressed his lips together. He knew now was not the time.

"It was a Steinway. Model D. Gloss black. Always."

His thumb hovered near a cigarette burn. "They say he came in late . . ."

Eric glanced at him. "Didn't we already do this?"

"No photographs?" Sam asked.

"None," David Roseman said. "But the good ones . . ." He adjusted a cufflink that didn't need adjusting. "Don't require proof."

Eric shook his head. "Give me a break."

Sam didn't hear him. She raised her camera.

Click.

The skylight creaked overhead. Dust drifted through the beam of light and settled on the lid of the piano.

No one moved.

Then Sam spoke: "What did he sing?"

David Roseman drew in a slow breath. His hand rested flat on the lid, as if feeling for something beneath it. He didn't look at her. "They say he walked up, sang a full set with the pianist, then left."

"I can hear it," Sam said.

"I can hear it, too," David Roseman said. "The music. Laughter. It's faint . . . but still there."

She felt it wash over her then—that sudden, devastating longing. For rooms that once held music. For people who once believed. For moments you didn't know were the last until they were already gone. She swallowed hard, trying to keep it down, but she started to cry.

She reached over and hugged David Roseman, resting her cheek against his shoulder.

He froze. His arms hovered, unsure—elbows bent at odd angles, hands drifting somewhere between her back and not touching her at all. He turned his head to look for help. For a second, his eyes searched her face as if looking for recognition. He looked at Eric.

Eric glanced at the red piano, then back at David Roseman, and he gave a small nod.

David Roseman slowly, awkwardly, put his arms around her. He held her like a man shaking hands with grief. As if her sorrow might wrinkle his lapel.

Sam pressed her face harder into his shoulder, her sobs muffled by expensive fabric.

"There, there," David Roseman said, stiffly.

Then, softer: "There."

After a moment, Sam stepped back, wiping her cheeks.

"Sorry," she said. "I got your jacket wet."

David Roseman looked down at the damp spot on his lapel, then back at her.

"It's only a jacket."

"She gets like that sometimes." Eric said.

Sam let out a short breath that almost passed for a laugh. It didn't quite land.

David Roseman's eyes flicked to him. For a second it felt like Eric had said too much. He brushed at the damp lapel with his handkerchief.

A loose board somewhere in the ceiling tapped once in the wind.

The piano sat between them, red and silent.

Sam wiped her hands on her jeans.

"You think it could ever be saved?"

David Roseman looked at her for a long moment. Then he shook his head.

"No. There are things you only get one chance to fix." He caught himself. "Honeymoon Hideaway was glorious once. That's enough."

They stood like that for a moment longer—no longer strangers, not quite friends—bound by a shared moment in time. It passed between them like a thread—thin and fragile. Impossible to explain.

"Thank you for bringing me, Mr. Roseman."

The wind pushed through the broken windows. The heart-shaped sign knocked against its chain. They stood there a moment longer, listening to the storm gather.

CHAPTER 5

Come Fly With Me

Thunder cracked. A gust of wind swept through the broken windows, lifting a veil of dust from the floor.

"Are you sure it wasn't Lady Gaga?" Eric asked, laughing.

"Oh, you're hilarious," David Roseman said flatly.

Thunder cracked again. Closer still.

"I don't remember it being red." A bewildered laugh escaped him. "Or the rhinestones. Were those always there?"

They ran from the resort toward the runway.

At the Cessna 172, Sam took one final photo bracing against the wind.

David Roseman hesitated at the airplane door.

"Do you think I made a mistake—leaving it behind?"

"Mr. Roseman." Eric slapped a hand on his shoulder. "That's a conversation for another time. Right now, we need to get airborne."

They climbed into the Cessna 172.

Eric ran his hand across the panel, cracked the throttle, mixture rich, and turned the key. The engine caught and settled into a steady idle. He did a quick run-up—mag check, carb heat, gauges in the green—then glanced at the windsock.

David Roseman adjusted his seatbelt carefully, mindful of the pressed seam in his slacks.

"Hurry up and close the door," Eric said, flipping switches. "We've got to get out of here."

David Roseman reached across and pulled it shut. A flash of irritation crossed his face before he smoothed it away.

The latch caught.

Something clattered loose.

"The door handle's come off." He held it at arm's length. "It's in my hand."

"Is it latched?" Eric asked, without looking.

"How would I know if it's latched? Do I look like an airplane door latch expert? The handle just broke off."

"You'll be fine," Sam said from the back. "It's probably fine."

"Is the door going to open in the air?"

Eric eased the throttle forward, eyes on the runway. "No. The airflow will keep it shut."

"Forgive me if confidence isn't my dominant emotion right now," David Roseman said, still holding the broken handle as if it might bite him.

Eric taxied, angling the nose away from the dark, building clouds. He eased the throttle forward and rolled them toward the end of the runway.

"Are we going to have enough speed to lift off?" David Roseman asked, peering through the windshield.

"We're turning around," Eric said. "Need to take off into the wind. Can't launch with that much tailwind."

David Roseman let the door handle drop to the floor.

At the end of the runway, Eric made a smooth 180-degree turn. They now faced the storm head-on. Lightning forked across the sky.

David Roseman adjusted his scarf. Then adjusted it again, his hand lingering briefly at his throat.

"Are we actually doing this?"

Eric said nothing.

David Roseman turned in his seat and glanced back at Sam. "Are you all right with this?"

Sam met David Roseman's eyes.

Then she leaned forward and kissed Eric on the cheek.

"Wait a moment—this is a terrible idea."

Eric adjusted his sunglasses and shoved the throttle full forward.

The engine roared. The Cessna surged down the runway toward the blackened sky. Tires hammered uneven asphalt. Rain began to slap the windshield as airspeed built. Leaves and small branches skittered sideways across the pavement, driven by the wind, as the nose charged toward the storm.

Lightning split the air ahead and struck the runway.

David Roseman gripped his seat with both hands.

The wheels lifted. Sheets of rain battered the plane.

Then David Roseman's door blew open with a violent bang—wind and rain tearing into the cockpit.

David Roseman screamed.

Sharp. Involuntary. Wholly unflattering, that seemed to surprise even him.

He looked down as the runway dropped away, nothing between him and the ground but air.

Sam moved before the sound had finished leaving his mouth. She leaned forward, braced a knee against the seat, and grabbed the door with both hands. The wind fought her, shrieking through the opening, but she hauled it back and slammed it shut.

Eric glanced over, then returned to the yoke, holding them steady as the sky bucked around them.

David Roseman cleared his throat, smoothed his scarf, and behaved as though nothing had happened.

The Cessna 172 jolted, the nose twitching in the headwind. Eric gripped the yoke, eyes locked on the thunderstorm ahead.

Off the left wingtip, Honeymoon Hideaway blurred—its red roof swallowed by gray mist, the lodge dissolving into the storm.

The wings rocked. A gust hit hard. Eric banked—sharp, quick.

Sam's fingers tightened around her seatbelt.

David Roseman said nothing, eyes wide.

Another flash lit the clouds as the Cessna turned away. Thunder cracked beside them. They climbed, the wind now pushing them clear of the worst of it.

And then Honeymoon Hideaway was gone.

At 2,500 feet, the air smoothed. Eric leveled the wings and scanned the panel. "We're clear," he said, voice tight with leftover adrenaline. "Storm's behind us."

Sam let out a long breath and sank into her seat. "Jesus. That was . . . intense."

David Roseman blinked at the windshield. "That was the single most terrifying experience of my life."

"I noticed," Eric said.

David Roseman cleared his throat.

Sam giggled from the backseat.

The mood shifted. The jagged underbelly of the storm began to break apart ahead of them. Ten minutes later, they were skimming a couple hundred feet beneath a softening overcast.

Eric adjusted the trim and glanced back. "Wanna see something?"

"See what?" David Roseman answered automatically.

Eric pushed the throttle forward and eased the nose up. The Cessna climbed into the cloud layer—a dense, glowing wall of white. Blue vanished. They were inside it now. Surrounded. Floating.

Sam inhaled sharply. "It's like flying through a dream."

David Roseman said nothing, eyes locked on the vapor curling past the wingtips.

And then—

They burst through the top.

Sunlight flooded the cockpit. Above them stretched endless blue. Below, a vast ocean of white cloud tops, gold at the edges.

Sam gasped. "Oh my God . . ."

"I never get tired of this," Eric said as the airplane skimmed the cloud deck.

"Is it always sunny up here?" Sam asked.

"It is, if you climb high enough."

Sam smiled. "It's always sunny if you climb high enough." She reached for her phone. "Hang on."

A crackle. Then brass.

Then that voice.

Sinatra.

Come Fly With Me.

David Roseman laughed. "You've got to be kidding."

Eric dipped a wing and carved a smooth arc across the sky, banking gently as Sinatra crooned about getting "up there."

David Roseman was still wide-eyed—but now he was smiling. "This is . . . extraordinary."

Eric pushed the nose down and let them fall back into the mist. The world turned white again—only instruments anchoring them—then they punched up through into blue once more.

Sam whooped, laughter ringing over the music.

Eric leveled off and paralleled the cloud tops, sunlight gleaming across the cowling.

"Not quite," he said as Sinatra sang about perfect weather, "but close enough."

Mount Pocono appeared ahead, runway cutting through broken clouds.

"You ready?" Eric asked.

"Sure. Why not?"

Eric pulled back, kicked rudder, and rolled hard left. The airplane snapped into a spin, spiraling through the cloud deck. The world blurred. Sam grabbed the seat.

David Roseman cursed.

Sinatra carried them through it.

The spin unwound and they leveled beneath the cloud base. The runway rose to meet them.

Flaps down. Power back. A quiet glide.

The wheels kissed asphalt like a memory coming home.

They taxied toward the hangar as the last bars of *Come Fly With Me* drifted from Sam's phone.

David Roseman didn't move. Then he exhaled. "That was not what I was expecting."

He unclipped his seatbelt and climbed down carefully from the Cessna 172. A small puddle was near the tire, rainwater shimmering with a thin film of oil.

He paused.

Looked at it.

Adjusted his footing.

Stepped wide.

Another puddle waited just beyond it. He pivoted, threading a narrow path between them, landing finally on dry pavement with visible relief.

He checked his loafers.

"Puddles."

He brushed the toes lightly with his hand and adjusted his scarf back into perfect alignment.

The engine ticked as it cooled.

Sam leaned forward, her voice soft in Eric's ear. "That's the most beautiful thing I've ever seen."

"You should see it from my side," he said.

CHAPTER 6

Ghosts of the Hideaway

The sun sank behind the hills, washing their apartment in warm light. Eric lay slouched on the couch, a forgotten cup of coffee cooling on stacked milk crates beside him. Sam curled against his side, laptop balanced on her knees, one bare foot resting across his lap as he rubbed it absently while she typed.

He watched her frown at the screen, chewing her lip in concentration.

"You're hot," he said.

"I'm trying to concentrate." She smiled anyway.

A moment later, she leaned back against him. "Finished."

"Can I read it?"

She hesitated, biting her thumbnail. Then she turned the laptop toward him. "Be gentle," she said, aiming for a joke but missing it.

Eric took the computer and settled it in his lap. At the top of the document was headline.

He began to read:

GHOSTS OF THE HIDEAWAY

By Sam Young, Staff Writer
The Pocono Classifieds

There's a kind of silence that only exists in places where people used to laugh.

I heard it last week, standing in the ruined ballroom of the old Honeymoon Hideaway just outside Mount Pocono. The velvet curtains hung limp and moth-eaten. Some of the round tables still stood. A few napkins remained—folded into swans, their edges yellowed and curling inward. Above them, a mural stretched across the domed ceiling: a bride and groom drifting through painted clouds beneath peeling gold letters that still promised:

Forever Begins Here.

It should have been just another forgotten ruin. But it wasn't. Because this place had been loved.

Built in 1954 by a man named Elias Roseman, Honeymoon Hideaway was once one of the crown jewels of the Poconos—a wonderland of heart-shaped tubs, champagne-glass whirlpools, and mirrored ceilings. At its peak, hundreds of newlyweds poured in each weekend, flooding the halls with the scent of perfume, pressed silk, and polished expectation.

They came in Cadillacs and Oldsmobiles, posing for Polaroids in front of the swan-boats. They believed in things.

In love.

In honeymoons that never ended.

In forever.

And then—slowly, like a long kiss goodnight—it was over.

David Roseman, the founder's grandson, flew us into the resort's runway—once reserved for just the wealthy, now overgrown with weeds and a cracked tarmac. My husband Eric was at the controls, with Mr. Roseman in the right seat. I was in the back, with camera and notebook in hand. It was a stormy day, with flashes of sunlight breaking through.

"Frank Sinatra sang here once," Mr. Roseman told me, gesturing toward the piano in the corner of the Hideaway Lounge. "One summer night in the '60s."

I asked politely. "Have you ever seen any photos?"

He shook his head. "No. But I swear, sometimes late at night, when the place was still full . . . you could hear Frank Sinatra's voice, echoing through the halls."

I'm not sure I believe that. But I believe he believes it.

The resort's downfall reads like the obituary of an era: cheap airfare, the rise of Las Vegas, then Atlantic City, changing tastes, aging infrastructure.

Time passed, love faded—and so did the wallpaper. No one wanted mirrored ceilings anymore. They wanted spas and Wi-Fi. The old magic simply didn't scale with modern expectations.

And yet . . . the old magic still lingers.

> There's something about walking through a place like Honeymoon Hideaway—where nostalgia lingers like perfume on the collar of a lover's worn shirt. Something that catches in your throat. I don't know why.
>
> I was six years old when I lost my parents. I don't remember most of it.

Eric swallowed, reading that line twice before he could make himself move on.

> But here, in this ruin of velvet and ghosted laughter—I felt something familiar. Something breathtaking and aching. As if the walls were grieving too.
>
> I don't believe in hauntings.
>
> But I do believe in residue.
>
> We stood outside near an old fountain, now dry and cracked. The swan sculpture was chipped and missing one wing.
>
> Mr. Roseman stepped closer to it. He brushed a bit of moss from the stone, his fingers lingering along the broken edge.

"I used to think I'd reopen it someday," he said.

He kept his eyes on the statue.

"I always thought I'd go back."

"Go back?" I asked.

He gestured toward the main lodge behind us.

"To fix it?"

He nodded once. "Something like that."

"What changed?"

He looked at me, and for just a second, something flickered behind his eyes.

Then it was gone.

"Time," he said. "It takes everything eventually."

Maybe it does. But for now, Honeymoon Hideaway is still standing, holding on to what it can. Waiting for someone to remember. Or forgive.

Maybe both.

Sam pulled her knees up, waiting.

When Eric finished reading, he paused, thumb resting on the trackpad. Eric put the laptop aside and pulled her into him. "It's beautiful," he said.

"Do you think so?"

"Absolutely," he said. "It's amazing. You're an amazing writer."

She shook her head. "I don't know if it's that good."

"Babe . . . he didn't exactly hand you Pulitzer material."

CHAPTER 7

Lover's Cove

By midafternoon, David Roseman had already dealt with three minor crises. The pump in Suite 436 had gone out again—one of the older heart-shaped tubs, temperamental in the heat. Maintenance swore it was fixed. David Roseman asked them to replace it anyway. No guest celebrating their honeymoon wanted to hear the word *temperamental.*

Out on the lake, one of the swan-boats had taken on water and started sinking. He radioed for an attendant.

The radio crackled once. Then nothing.

A couple in a neighboring swan-boat paddled over, hauled the first pair aboard, then made a slow, triumphant return to the dock—four adults balanced awkwardly on one plastic bird, waving like they'd just rescued survivors from the Titanic.

David Roseman stood at the water's edge and watched the abandoned swan-boat continue to settle, its white neck tilting lower, water sloshing visibly inside the hull. He calculated how long it would take to sink completely, and which attendant he could plausibly ask to wade in after it without turning the afternoon into a story guests would tell later. He flagged a dockhand and pointed—casually enough to suggest it was already handled.

Then the delivery truck arrived late with the afternoon alcohol order. David Roseman checked the invoice—peach schnapps, chocolate liqueur, and several cases of pink sparkling wine—signed anyway and slid the clipboard back through the window. It wasn't quite champagne, but there wasn't time and the couples probably wouldn't know the difference.

He walked two steps away from the dock—out of earshot of guests, out of range of phones—and called the number on the invoice.

The owner picked up on the second ring.

"Tom. It's David Roseman."

A pause. A cheerful voice on the other end.

"This order is wrong."

Another pause—excuses warming up.

"No," David Roseman said. "Don't explain it to me. Fix it."

He watched a couple nearby point at the sinking swan-boat and laugh like it was part of the entertainment.

"You're confusing me with someone who negotiates after being disrespected."

He ended the call, slid the phone back into his pocket

Inside the main building, music floated down the corridor—*Endless Love.*

Check-in music.

He was making a mental note to line up a about the delivery order when the music changed.

He stopped.

The opening acoustic guitar drifted through the hall—patient and unmistakable, moving downward in a careful descent, notes stepping away from each other instead of reaching. Beautiful in the way resignation can be beautiful. It was a sound meant for letting go, not arrival.

Landslide.

David Roseman looked up at the nearest speaker, then down the corridor toward the front desk, where one of the younger attendants was straightening a stack of "Candle Use and Fire Safety" pamphlets.

He walked over.

"Amanda," he said. "May I have a moment?"

"Yes, Mr. Roseman?"

"That song—Fleetwood Mac. We don't play that here."

"Oh. Sorry."

"That's quite all right," David Roseman said. "An easy mistake." Then added—because he always did— "They're a good band. It's just . . . their songs aren't really love songs."

She nodded.

"They're breakup songs," he said. "They sound romantic until you listen closely. Regret. Resentment. People realizing too late what they've already ruined. Not exactly honeymoon material."

Amanda stared.

"Lionel Richie works because his songs mean what they say. They don't circle back and undo themselves at the end."

"I see," Amanda said.

"I would love to play *Every Rose Has Its Thorn*," he said. "It has a great melody. Strong chorus." He shook his head. "But it ends with them moving on."

Her eyebrows lifted.

The console clicked.

Endless Love returned, exactly where it had left off.

"Thank you, Amanda."

As he turned away, he knew it was an upstairs issue only. DJ Romeo knew the rules. He didn't need to worry about DJ Romeo. He never did.

"Mr. Roseman?" Amanda said, a step behind him. "There's actually one more quick thing."

He stopped and turned back.

"We had . . . a situation last night. Some guests in the Lovebird wing. Running in the hallway." She cleared her throat. "Wet."

"And naked?" David Roseman asked because it saved time.

Her cheeks colored. "Yes."

"Thank you, Amanda. Please have Daniel in housekeeping check the carpets."

She nodded, relieved to have something normal to do. "And you're on the cover of *The Pocono Classifieds* today." She reached beneath the counter and held out a folded newspaper. "A lady named Constance dropped off a stack this morning."

"Also," she added, "she said to call if you wanted to buy ad space."

David Roseman took the paper. "Thank you."

He walked toward the elevators, unfolding it as he went. The resort moved as it always did—controlled, efficient. Guests drifted between dinner reservations and hot tubs. Music floated up from the lounge. Laughter rose and faded along carpets whose patterns had softened with time.

By the time he reached his suite, the paper was open in his hands.

Ghosts of the Hideaway

He read the article once.

Then again.

It did not accuse. It did not blame. It did not turn Honeymoon Hideaway into a punchline. It described the ballroom. The mural. The history. It treated the place—and him—with a tenderness he hadn't anticipated.

He reached the final line and folded the newspaper carefully, aligning the corners, smoothing the crease with his palm. He set it aside.

Outside, a woman slipped from a swan-boat with a splash. Her husband jumped in after her. Applause drifted across the courtyard.

David Roseman did not look up.

CHAPTER 8

Red-Handled Scissors

A pair of red-handled scissors lay beside a portable transceiver tuned to CTAF. Eric sat on the edge of the picnic table outside the FBO at Mount Pocono Airport, elbows on his knees, eyes fixed on the far end of Runway 23. Summer heat shimmered off the tarmac. The Cessna 150 idled at the threshold.

He raised the binoculars again.

Nasser was still out there—engine running, propeller turning lazily, the Cessna 150 creeping forward a few feet at a time—only to stop short again. It had been fifteen minutes.

Eric lowered the binoculars.

He had used the same, red-handled pair on dozens of shirt tails over the years, and today he planned to use them again—cutting Nasser's shirt after his first solo flight.

First solos were sacred. They marked one of the biggest moments in a pilot's life—maybe the biggest.

Eric keyed the mic on the transceiver. "Nasser, Mount Pocono UNICOM. You okay out there?"

Static. Then a click.

"*Yes,*" came the crackly reply. "*Just . . . waiting for the wind to die down, Eric.*"

Eric looked up. The windsock sagged at half-mast, unmoving.

He watched the Cessna 150 sit there, engine idling, prop turning, the nose pointed straight down Runway 23.

"You've got this, Nasser," he said. "You've done the pattern a dozen times with me. Same as the three this morning. This is no different. You can do it."

No response.

Eric keyed the mic again but stopped.

He waited another two minutes, watching as the Cessna 150 inched forward again. For a second, it looked like Nasser was going to do it. The airplane lined up straight, nose pointed down the runway, brakes squeaking as it rolled to the numbers.

Then it stopped.

And stayed stopped.

Eric took his sunglasses off.

"Come on, brother."

A black Cadillac Escalade rolled up and parked beside the FBO, tires crunching over the gravel.

Eric glanced up, then back to the binoculars trained on Nasser from the picnic table. Until it registered—black Escalade.

The engine shut off. A door opened.

David Roseman stepped out. Linen shirt. Pressed chinos. Sunglasses that probably cost more than Eric's FJ. He moved with the easy assurance of a man who'd never once had to do something he didn't want to do.

"Morning," David Roseman said, extending a hand.

"Hi, Mr. Roseman. Nice to see you."

"Call me David," he said easily. "After all, you did nearly kill me a couple of weeks ago." He looked at the picnic table. "What are the scissors for?"

Eric followed his gaze. "My student out there. First solo."

"And the scissors?"

"Flight-school tradition. When a pilot solos for the first time, the instructor cuts off their shirt tail."

David Roseman waited.

"In the early days," Eric went on, "instructors sat behind students in open-cockpit biplanes. No headsets. No radios. If the student screwed up, you tugged their shirt tail to get their attention."

He looked out toward the runway. "First solo means they don't need you anymore."

"Is he going to do it?"

"He's ready," Eric said. "He just doesn't know it yet."

David Roseman watched the distant Cessna 150. Then he turned back. "I read the article your wife wrote," he said. "I gave it some thought. I want flying lessons."

"That's . . . great." Another student. More hours. More pay. Sam had been right.

"When can we start?" David Roseman asked.

"Next week," Eric said. "We'll get the paperwork going. Medical. The basics."

"How about tomorrow morning at eight?"

"I've got Nasser then."

"Tomorrow morning is really what works for me." He looked toward the Cessna 150, then back at Eric. "Maybe he can reschedule."

"I can check," he said. "But Nasser's already on the schedule."

David Roseman looked back at the airplane.

"I don't think he's going to do it."

Eric kept his eyes on the runway.

The Cessna 150 began to roll again, then it eased into a slow left turn, taxiing back toward the ramp.

The radio crackled.

"Eric, I am coming back. Sorry. I—I cannot do it."

Eric keyed the mic. "Copy that. Come on back."

He put the radio down beside the scissors.

The Cessna rolled to a stop at the tie-downs. The engine cut. The propeller slowed, then stopped.

Nasser stepped out, head down.

Eric walked toward him. David Roseman followed.

"I am sorry, Eric," Nasser said. "I really thought I could."

"It's better to be on the ground wishing you were flying, than the other way around."

"Just performance anxiety," David Roseman said, like he was being helpful.

Eric laughed and shook his head.

Nasser looked at Eric. "I do not know what performance anxiety means."

"Nothing," Eric said quickly. "He's joking."

David Roseman smiled. "Don't take this the wrong way, but you made a mistake: you let it become a performance."

Nasser looked up.

David Roseman continued, voice smooth. "When you're being watched, you freeze. It happens. The solution is simple: no audience next time. No scissors. No ceremony. Just do it quietly—like an adult."

Nasser's face flushed. "You don't know me."

"I run a business—" David started.

Nasser stepped closer. "Who are you?"

Eric stepped between them. "This is David Roseman. He owns Lovers' Cove."

Nasser's voice rose. "Then stand over there, David Roseman. You are not my instructor."

Eric lifted a hand. "Nasser—"

"Go give your advice to someone else," Nasser snapped. "And stop joking. I do not think it's funny."

David Roseman's smile held—then thinned. "That's unnecessary."

"Yeah?" Nasser said. "Go talk about performance anxiety in your . . . love resort."

David Roseman's eyes narrowed.

"Middle Eastern," David Roseman said lightly, like it explained everything. "Of course. Always so dramatic."

Eric's voice cut in. "David."

Nasser went still. "What did you say?"

David Roseman's smile sharpened. "Relax," he said. "It's a . . . joke. The first one was, anyway."

His eyes locked on Nasser.

He turned to Eric. "See you tomorrow at eight." Then, to Nasser with a mock salute: "Better luck next time."

And then he was gone.

Nasser stood staring at the tarmac.

"What the hell just happened," Eric said quietly. "Pardon my language."

"I don't belong here, do I?"

Eric shook his head. "Don't say that. You belong here. You're going to solo."

Nasser sighed.

Eric rested a hand on his shoulder. "Ever hear of Bessie Coleman?"

Nasser shook his head.

"First Black woman to earn a pilot's license," Eric said. "She went to France because nobody here would teach her. Then came back and barnstormed across the country."

Nasser looked out toward the runway.

"She flew anyway," Eric said.

"I thought I could do it, Eric."

They walked back toward the FBO together.

The red-handled scissors lay untouched on the picnic table.

CHAPTER 9

No Show

Mount Pocono Airport was clear and cool. Visibility better than ten. Winds light and variable. The windsock barely moved. No convective junk on the horizon. VFR.

Eric arrived ten minutes early.

He always did.

He parked in his usual spot, slung his flight bag over his shoulder, and crossed the ramp toward the Cessna 172. The airplane sat on the tie-down line in the sunlight.

Two good hours, he thought.

He checked his watch.

7:52 a.m.

He'd tried to move Nasser to ten.

Nasser couldn't.

"Family appointment," he'd said. "I cannot change it, Eric."

So, Eric had cancelled him.

Just this once.

Eric leaned against the wing strut and took a sip of his coffee.

7:59.

He glanced toward the parking lot.

Nothing but a few cars and the Mount Pocono Airport maintenance van.

8:05.

Still nothing.

He checked his phone.

No message.

No missed call.

He stared down the access road again, expecting the black Escalade to appear at any second.

8:11.

The coffee was gone.

He shifted his weight and looked at the sky instead. Calm air. Clear sky.

Two clean hours in the pattern.

Some ground reference maneuvers.

Maybe slow flight.

8:17.

He pulled out his phone and typed:

Hes late..Maybe not coming?

He stared at the screen.

Then deleted it.

Sam would feel bad. It wasn't her fault.

8:23.

The FBO door swung open behind him and another instructor's student walked out laughing, headset in hand. Eric watched them taxi away.

Another airplane taking off.

Another hour not his.

8:31.

He looked at the parking lot again.

Then finally turned and walked inside.

The terminal building always smelled like stale coffee. A corkboard near the counter held weather printouts and a faded flyer for a Father's Day pancake breakfast that had already passed.

Mount Pocono Aviation ran from the back corner of the terminal — a simple counter, a scheduling computer, and a wall of shirt tails signed in black marker.

"Morning," the line girl said without looking up.

"Morning," Eric replied. "David Roseman still on the schedule for eight?"

She clicked the mouse twice.

"Yep. Eight to ten. With you."

"Did he call? Say he'd be late?"

She shook her head.

"Nope."

Eric stood there a moment.

"Alright," he said.

He walked back outside. The Cessna 172 sat exactly as it had thirty minutes earlier. Sun glinting. Calm air. Perfect conditions. He stood beside it and did the math.

Two hours.

Two hours of pay.

Two logged hours.

Gone.

He thought of Nasser.

Of the way Nasser had stood on the ramp yesterday after the comment.

Of the way he hadn't said anything.

And now David Roseman wasn't even there.

Eric checked his watch one last time.

8:42.

Then he picked up his flight bag, walked to the FJ, and drove home.

Two hours lost.

Sam lounged on the couch, laptop open, one foot tucked beneath her. *We Can Work It Out* played low from her speakers—bright and deceptively upbeat, Paul's voice carrying through the small living room.

"You're home early."

"He didn't show."

Sam looked up. "David?"

Eric put his flight bag down harder than he meant to.

"Did he call?"

"No."

Sam exhaled. "Oh."

Eric crossed to the desk drawer automatically. Pulled it open. Took out his logbook.

It was habit now. Sit. Log. Total them up.

He flipped to the next blank line.

Sam watched him. "So, he just . . . didn't come?"

"Eight to ten," Eric said. "Perfect VFR. Lost the block."

He wrote the date.

Aircraft: C172.

He paused.

"Two hours," he muttered.

Sam leaned back against the couch arm. "That's frustrating."

"Frustrating?" He gave a short laugh. "That's groceries. That's electric. That's—"

He stopped.

He wrote something down.

Sam frowned. "What are you logging?"

Eric didn't look up. "I should log the two hours anyway. I was there."

She stared at him.

"You weren't flying."

"I was scheduled. Airplane was reserved. I showed up."

"You didn't fly."

He erased something.

Rewrote it.

2.0

"It's not like I was sitting at home," he said. "I was on the ramp. Preflighted. Ready to go."

"Eric."

He capped the pen. Uncapped it again.

"Honey, you can't log hours you didn't fly."

He kept his eyes on the page.

"It's just two hours."

"That's not how it works."

He sat back. The chair creaked.

"It's not like I'm inventing time," he said. "It was booked time."

She didn't soften.

"If you didn't take off, you didn't fly."

Silence.

The refrigerator kicked on.

In the background, The Beatles.

He looked at the total time at the bottom of the page.

Close.

Not close enough.

He leaned forward again and wrote something—quickly this time.

Sam watched the movement of his hand.

"Did you?" she asked.

He closed the logbook.

"What are you working on?" he said instead.

She held his gaze a moment longer.

Then she turned back to her laptop.

"Wayne the commuter," she said. "He times his bathroom breaks at Delaware Water Gap."

Eric nodded absently.

"Smart."

CHAPTER 10

Touch and Go

Eric stood near the tie-down row at Mount Pocono Airport, sipping lukewarm coffee. Clear skies. Light wind. The air on the ramp smelled of jet fuel, pine trees and campfire smoke.

His phone buzzed in his pocket.

BRUCE PAYNE: 600SE good to go *Lots of shit to haul* lets do this

Eric stared at the screen. Bruce Payne in pure form—but it hit like a punch to the gut. He locked the screen and shoved the phone back in his flight jacket, remembering the promise he made to Sam.

Not tonight.

A black Escalade curved into the lot and rolled to a smooth stop beside the terminal.

David Roseman stepped out, dressed in a crisp white shirt with the sleeves neatly rolled, Cartier sunglasses perched on his nose, every line of him pressed and polished. He adjusted his collar and walked toward Eric like a man arriving for brunch, not a lesson he'd already missed once.

"Emergency at the property the other morning," David Roseman said, approaching. "It simply slipped my mind. But here I am."

Eric glanced past him toward the empty parking lot, then back at him. "Yeah. I noticed."

David Roseman offered a small, controlled smile. "Unfortunate timing."

"Nasser couldn't reschedule. So I lost the hours."

David Roseman absorbed that without flinching. "Then I'll make a point of being worth the time."

"I guess, we'll see."

David Roseman hesitated. "About the remark I made to your student . . . it was in poor taste."

"Yeah. It cut him pretty deep. You should take that up with him. Not me."

"Fair enough."

Silence stretched between them. Eric thought of the counter inside the terminal, the wall of signed shirt tails—names and dates in black marker, proof that someone had once taken the runway alone.

Eric broke the quiet. "Politics and religion," he said, glancing toward the airplane. "You ready?"

They walked over to the Cessna 172.

"This one's ours," Eric said. "Four seats. High wing. It's forgiving—and honest."

David Roseman looked it over. "Same one from last time?"

"It is."

"I had hoped I remembered it incorrectly—being that small."

"You'll get used to it," Eric said, handing him the checklist. "Let's start with the preflight. Fuel, oil, control surfaces, tires—everything. Always."

They walked around the Cessna together. Eric moved through the preflight inspection with practiced rhythm; David Roseman followed closely, peering into the open hatches and access panels with theatrical suspicion—but asking sharp questions.

"So, blue fuel is good?"

"Blue means one hundred low-lead aviation gas," Eric said. "Clear or pink—that's bad."

"Good to know," David Roseman said, peering into the wing's inspection panel.

They climbed into the cockpit. David Roseman paused before closing the door.

"Snug," he said, settling into the left seat. "Though I suppose one shouldn't expect much elbow room in a sky-bound sardine tin."

"Welcome to general aviation," Eric said, flipping on the master switch.

Eric talked David Roseman through the *Before Start* checklist. The engine caught on the first crank. Sunlight streamed through the windscreen as the propeller spun, and the instrument panel came to life.

"Mount Pocono Traffic, Cessna Seven Five Two Delta Romeo taxiing to Runway Two Three," Eric called on the radio, then turned to David Roseman. "Toes on the rudder pedals, heels on the floor. Just follow along on the pedals and yoke for now."

They taxied toward the runway, wheels humming over the pavement.

"Remember how this goes?" Eric asked.

"Not precisely," David Roseman said. "Last time, a thunderstorm was bearing down on us."

Eric lined up on the centerline. "I've got the controls. Just relax."

He pushed the throttle in. The Cessna surged forward, the engine rising in pitch. Within seconds, the runway sank behind them, and the earth dropped away.

David Roseman's jaw loosened. "Not as bad as last time."

"You're getting used to it."

They leveled off at 3,000 feet. Good VFR day.

"Your airplane."

David Roseman gripped the yoke.

"Straight and level first. Then a shallow left turn."

David Roseman eased the Cessna 172 into a bank. The horizon tilted; he corrected with small, deliberate rudder inputs.

"Feels heavy," he said. "Like it wants to fall through the turn."

"That's your trim," Eric said. "Take the pressure out. Two fingers."

David Roseman adjusted the wheel. The control pressure eased. The airplane settled.

"Better," Eric said. "Let's do it again. Same bank. Same altitude. Don't chase it."

Eric demonstrated first—rolled into a shallow turn, held the pitch, nudged the rudder, eyes moving through the scan.

"Watch the nose," he said. "Not the wing."

David Roseman nodded.

"Your airplane."

He matched it almost exactly. Bank angle. Rudder input. Altitude within twenty feet.

Eric didn't touch the controls.

They leveled out on heading.

"You've got a feel for it," Eric said. "Your scan's tight. Corrections are clean."

David Roseman glanced over briefly.

"I'm not doing anything special," he said. "I'm just doing exactly what you told me to do."

Eric smirked. "That's your secret?"

"That's my philosophy," David Roseman said. "If someone knows more than I do, I listen. I do precisely what they say. Nothing more."

He returned his eyes to the horizon.

"And it works," he added.

"If only all my students listened that well."

They worked through turns, climbs, descents, and straight-and-level flight. David Roseman absorbed every correction, his focus sharp, his questions thoughtful.

Eric took the controls back and entered the pattern. "I'll land this one. You follow along. Watch the sight picture, the power setting, the airspeeds."

The Cessna 172 settled onto the runway with a chirp. Eric mashed the throttle. "This is called a touch-and-go. Next landing is yours."

They lifted off again. David Roseman flew the pattern cleanly, with Eric following lightly on the controls. The second landing was smooth—nearly perfect. Eric didn't touch the yoke.

"That was pretty good," he said. "You're a natural."

David Roseman kept his hands on the yoke.

"I could do this," he said. "On my own."

Eric didn't smile.

"I like your confidence," he said. "But you don't know what you don't know."

David Roseman met his eyes. No hesitation.

"I can do this."

"Good."

Eric reached forward and pulled the throttle back to idle.

"That's why you're not going to," he said.

As they taxied off, David Roseman unbuckled and exhaled. "That was . . . rather extraordinary," he said. "I don't often feel small. But up there . . ." He trailed off, eyes on the sky.

Eric killed the engine.

"Good, again," he said. "Because we can log that. And maybe do it again."

"Yes," he said. "I believe we will."

CHAPTER 11

Campfire Lattes

July moved on, hot and slow. Sam picked up a part-time job at Small Mountain Coffee—early mornings, clanging tampers, broke ESU students paying with pocket change. Steam. Milk. The register opening and closing. Over and over. A few shifts a week.

She was still writing every day. A notebook stayed tucked in her apron, where she scribbled ideas between orders. Her hand drifted to her stomach, then dropped back to the counter. She hadn't told anyone. It was still too soon.

Eric stood on the sidewalk, watching her through the coffee shop windows. She moved with ease behind the counter, handing a latte to a customer with a smile. She looked beautiful, but she also looked tired—a smear of espresso foam on her wrist, dark circles under her eyes just barely visible under the soft café lights.

From the sidewalk, he could hear a college kid near the back, perched on a stool with an acoustic guitar, halfway through *Wonderwall*, as Sam steamed milk and called out orders without missing a beat. His hands stayed buried in his flight jacket pockets. Bruce Payne's text still sat on his phone like a live wire.

He opened the café door. The bell chimed. The place smelled like espresso and cinnamon—and underneath that, the fake sweetness of Campfire Latte syrup. Smoky. Not quite right.

She looked up and smiled.

CHAPTER 12

Cold Garlic Bread

The TV flickered, washing the living room walls in pale blue light. A box fan hummed in the open window, partially drowning out the sound of a sitcom laugh track. On the floor, Sam and Eric sat cross-legged around two bowls of spaghetti and a foil-wrapped bundle of garlic bread. Eric twirled a forkful and slurped it into his mouth. Sam lightly dabbed at the marinara sauce with a piece of garlic bread, her toes tucked beneath her.

"Okay," she said, dropping her garlic bread and wiping her hands with a paper towel. "Promise you won't make a big deal?"

Eric looked up. "You're pregnant with twins."

"No," she said. "Though . . ."

His eyes widened.

She shook her head. "No. It's not that."

He exhaled. "Okay. What?"

She handed him a paper towel.

"Constance is shutting the paper down. End of the month."

"What do you mean, shutting it down?"

"Two more issues. That's it."

He put his fork down. "Just like that?"

"That's what she told us."

He wiped his hands. "You gonna be okay?"

"I mean . . . yeah." She leaned back on one elbow.

"It's fine." She looked away when she said it.

Eric didn't answer.

Sam rubbed her stomach. "My head's somewhere else lately. You know?"

He reached over and brushed a crumb from her knee. "Still sucks. You worked hard for that paper."

"It's just a job," she said quietly. "It's just—I'll look for another one."

They ate in silence. The sitcom laugh track swelled from the television, canned and relentless. The window fan hummed against the heat.

Eric cleared his throat. "So, listen . . . David Roseman is going to keep flying. Probably one or two lessons a week. That'll help. But not enough to cover everything. I've been thinking—"

"Thinking what?"

He looked over. "Bruce texted me. Said the airplane's fixed."

Sam lowered her fork.

"I didn't text him back yet," Eric said. "But . . . I could fly a couple nights a week. It'd be multi-engine time. What the airlines look for. It's—"

"Eric." Sam didn't raise her voice.

"Sam, but—"

"You promised me. Not him. Not that plane."

"I know. I did. But I can't just sit around."

"Hours aren't worth your life," she said. "You almost crashed. And you didn't even tell me."

He pushed his plate aside.

"I'm way behind. Guys I trained with are already in jets."

She nudged his knee with her toes.

"You're not," she said. "You're just not there yet."

"I don't get there sitting on the ground."

"I know." She held his gaze. "But I can't do that again, Eric."

He didn't answer.

She sighed. "I get it. It's multi-time. Just not for him."

The laugh track from the TV swelled.

She held his gaze, one hand resting over her stomach. Then she leaned her head against his shoulder.

He put his arm around her, resting his cheek against her hair.

"You promised," she said.

He glanced at the foil on the floor between them.

"The garlic bread's cold."

She looked up.

"We'll survive."

CHAPTER 13

Five Clicks

Outside the cockpit, the world had flattened into blackness. Blue taxiway lights traced a line between hangars and pine trees that felt closer than they were. The airport sat quiet beneath a low, heavy sky, the last of the evening bleeding into the tree line while a few stars pressed through the thinning overcast.

Inside a parked Cessna 150, Nasser sat alone. The instrument panel cast a dim green wash across his face. Tomorrow night, he would take his first night flight with Eric. Tonight, he practiced—running the checklist from memory.

"Battery on. Mixture rich."

He moved his hands across the panels. Battery switch. Mixture. Throttle. Magnetos. His lips barely formed the words. Normal procedures. Memory items. Flow patterns.

He imagined the engine catching.

Mixture. Crack throttle. Engage starter.

He could almost feel the vibration.

The UNICOM hissed.

"Mount Pocono Radio, any aircraft in the area . . . I need help landing. I can't find the runway."

Nasser stared at the mic hanging off the instrument panel. He looked out toward the approach end of the runway and saw the red beacon of an aircraft circling.

"Mount Pocono Radio, any aircraft or ground station. Do you copy? I do not see any lights on the runway. Cannot find the airport"

Nasser glanced at the empty FBO. He keyed up. "Aircraft calling Mount Pocono UNICOM, key your mic five times. That will activate the runway lights. Repeat: key your mic five times to turn on the runway lights."

Silence. Then static.

"Five times. Okay."

Nasser leaned forward, peering into the dark. A second later, the clicks came—rapid, and the runway came alive. Two parallel strings of lights bloomed to life along the pavement, white and amber cutting a straight line through the black.

Above him, the airplane turned back toward the runway—still too high.

"You are too high," Nasser called over the frequency. "Go around. Set it up again."

The aircraft climbed out and circled wide in the dark.

"When you come back," Nasser said, voice steady now, "do not chase the lights. At night the runway will look lower than it is. Trust your descent. Aim for the first third. Hold your picture."

The red beacon swung through another turn.

"You will not see the ground the way you do in the daytime," Nasser added. "Keep a little power in. Fly it down."

The aircraft rolled out on final again, descending slower this time.

"Better," Nasser said into the mic. "Hold that."

It crossed the threshold and touched down with a hard bounce, then another. A skid, an ugly correction, then a final thud.

But it stayed down.

Nasser exhaled. He jogged toward the airplane. The landing lights swept across him as he approached. The cockpit door opened.

Nasser stopped.

CHAPTER 14

Runway Lights

David Roseman stepped out. A second man followed—a gray-haired Black man in a light jacket, face unreadable in the dark, hands tucked into his pockets as if this kind of thing didn't scare him anymore.

"Thank you," David Roseman said. "I wasn't aware that the runway lights were on a timer."

Nasser said nothing.

"I'd appreciate it if you kept this between us," David Roseman added.

He took a step away, then stopped. Turned back.

"About the other day," he said. "That comment. It was out of line."

Nasser met his eyes. "You are not even checked out to solo. Why are you flying with a passenger?"

David Roseman's jaw tightened. "I apologized. Let's leave it there."

"Performance anxiety," Nasser said. "Why did you say that? I know what it means, now."

David Roseman let out a short breath through his nose. "I'll meet you at the car, Randall."

The man nodded and walked toward the lot.

David Roseman faced Nasser again.

"I took the plane up to show my partner the area," he said. "That was a mistake. I'd appreciate your discretion."

He held out his hand.

Nasser looked at it.

Then at him.

"Partner?"

"Yes," David Roseman said evenly. "Problem?"

Nasser's jaw tightened. "I'm not shaking hands with a يطول," he said—the Arabic word his uncles always spat like a curse.

The air shifted.

"Of course you're not," David Roseman said quietly. He lowered his hand.

His smile thinned.

"We clearly have cultural differences." He nodded toward the airplane. "And here's a fact in America: be careful where you point that thing. People get nervous when they hear your accent on the radio and see an airplane circling."

The words landed clean.

He turned and walked toward the Escalade parked under a lone pool of light.

At the door, he stopped.

Leaned in.

An embrace.

Then a kiss.

Not hidden. Not hurried.

Two men in silhouette, touching like it required no explanation.

David Roseman straightened, then turned once more.

He held Nasser's gaze.

Then climbed into the Escalade.

Nasser's shoulders drew inward. He shifted his weight. Breathed out sharply through his nose. A muscle pulsed in his cheek.

The Escalade started, headlights sweeping across the ramp before vanishing into the dark.

Nasser stood alone on the tarmac while the pilot-controlled lights hummed behind him.

Fifteen minutes.

Then the runway lights blinked off.

Mount Pocono Airport slipped back into darkness.

CHAPTER 15

Multi-Time

She was at Small Mountain Coffee, pulling a double shift. Eight hours on her feet, then staying late to close out the register. He pictured her wrist wrapped in that beige brace she sometimes wore, her hair tied up, her hand pressing against her lower back during break.

Eric sat on the couch, his flight bag open at his feet. In the kitchen, the sink dripped. Outside the window, a brown UPS truck idled at the stoplight.

His logbook lay across his lap, pages smudged at the corners, dog-eared from use. A pen clicked in his hand as he totaled the most recent entries again.

He stared at the number.

It wasn't rounding anymore.

It was falsifying.

He knew it.

He added the column again.

1.4

1.9

2.3

1.7

He paused, carried the number, recalculated.

Nobody flies fifty hours in a week at Mount Pocono. Barely twenty. On a good week.

He flipped back a page and erased one of the entries. The pencil's rubber hissed, leaving a pale smudge where the number had been. He wrote the new number carefully, then froze.

It looked worse. Too neat.

He erased it again, until the paper began to thin.

He turned back another page.

He didn't touch the totals this time. Just adjusted the legs. A 1.1 became a 1.4. A .9 became a 1.9. Small enough to disappear inside the column. Nothing anyone would question. Nothing that would jump off the page.

He added the column again.

Still not enough.

Some of his friends from flight school had reached it already.

Eric flipped back through the logbook. He'd done a lot — flight instruction, sightseeing legs, night cargo runs, a few charter gigs. They all added to his total flight time.

Just not fast enough.

He put the logbook down and picked up his iPad.

Regional airline hiring minimums.

He scrolled past banner ads.

1,500 hours required.

Multi-engine preferred.

In rare cases, applicants with high-quality multi-engine time below 1,500 hours may be considered.

He stared at that sentence.

High-quality multi-engine time.

He put the iPad down.

The apartment creaked as the UPS truck outside drove off.

He flipped back to last December. Empty lines. Snow months.

He leaned back into the couch and stared at the ceiling.

I promised her I was done with Bruce.

He picked up his phone.

Opened his messages.

Just a few trips until I find something else.

His thumb hovered.

He heard her voice in his head.

To: BRUCE PAYNE

He stared at the empty text field.

He'd only do a few trips. Just until—

He typed:

When do you need me to fly?

He read it once.

His thumb drifted toward Delete.

He pictured Sam behind the counter at Small Mountain Coffee, wrist brace showing under her sleeve.

He hit Send.

CHAPTER 16

Double-Booked

The morning at Mount Pocono Airport was heavy with humidity, the sky a pale, washed-out blue, hinting at storms lurking to the west. Eric chugged an extra-large coffee outside the FBO. He had a cross-country leg with Nasser planned for Newark Liberty and was hoping the thunderstorms would hold off. He spotted David Roseman's Escalade pulling into the lot—then Nasser's Honda rattled in a minute later. Eric checked his phone. 7:45 a.m. Right.

He had double-booked them for 8 a.m. David Roseman stepped out first—white linen shirt, Cartier sunglasses, sleeves rolled. He glanced at the Honda, then slid the sunglasses up onto his head. Nasser emerged behind him in his usual bomber jacket and scarf, his expression already sour. They both stopped and stared, then looked at Eric. Eric sighed. "My bad. I double-booked."

David Roseman sniffed. "Great."

Nasser crossed his arms. "Yeah, come back later, guy."

David Roseman fired back. "How about you come back later, guy."

Eric raised his hands. "Am I missing something here?" Silence. "Well," Eric said, "that's on me. I've only got time for lesson today. We'll go together—David takes the first leg, Nasser, you fly us back." Both men stiffened.

David Roseman squinted toward the Cessna 172. "As long as we don't go anywhere near Lower Manhattan."

Nasser shot back, "As long as we aren't stealing airplanes and kissing our boyfriends in the parking lot."

Eric stepped forward. "What is going on?"

David Roseman didn't look at him. "No idea what *Top Gun* here's talking about."

"I'm not flying with a يطول," Nasser snapped.

David Roseman took off his sunglasses.

"What was that?"

"You took your boyfriend up in an airplane without a license," Nasser said.

David Roseman scoffed. "Get a load of this guy."

Eric held up a hand. "You're not signed off to solo. Much less carry passengers. Is that true?"

"No one stole anything," David Roseman said.

Eric's voice rose. "If something had happened to you up there, it's my ass. Do you get that?"

"I understand your concern, Eric."

David Roseman met his eyes. "You need not worry about me."

Eric stared at him a moment, then turned to Nasser. "What do you want me to say?"

Nasser's glare didn't move. "He's disgusting."

David Roseman said, calm and cold, "Careful with that temper—very Middle Eastern of you."

Both men stepped forward.

"Enough!" Eric barked. "I don't care who's more offended—you're both out of line."

Nasser muttered in Arabic.

David Roseman narrowed his eyes. "What was that?"

Nasser didn't hesitate. "Kiss your boyfriend."

Eric pointed to the Cessna 172. "Okay. That's it. I've already filed a flight plan to Newark. David flies out. Nasser flies back."

Neither moved.

Eric lowered his voice. "You don't have to like each other. I've only got time for one lesson. Get in—or go home."

The tension hung there.

Eric broke the silence. "We're going." He turned and walked to the airplane.

CHAPTER 17

Statue of Liberty

David Roseman climbed into the left seat without a word. Nasser slid into the back. Eric settled in beside David Roseman and plugged in. The sky was clear. Calm winds. But the dew point was rising, and the forecast called for thunderstorms by mid-afternoon. They taxied. Took off. David Roseman held heading and altitude while Eric offered minor corrections. They navigated the familiar checkpoints toward Newark using pilotage and dead reckoning, the ridgelines and highways slipping beneath them. A river came into view—wide, silver-blue, shimmering in the late morning light. It unspooled from upstate, winding past towns and forest before straightening toward the city. Bridges arched over it, stitching New Jersey to New York. Barges moved slowly along the current. On either side, the city pressed closer—rows of rooftops, piers, and windows flashing in sun.

Eric pointed. "There's the Hudson River."

David Roseman followed his finger.

"Ever hear about US Airways Flight 1549?" Eric asked.

David Roseman glanced back. "Sully?"

"Yeah," Eric said. "Bird strike took out both engines right after takeoff out of LaGuardia. He ditched an Airbus A320 right there."

David Roseman looked down again.

"People think water's a good place to land in an emergency," Eric went on. "It's not. Catch an engine—the airplane cartwheels. Comes apart."

"Then why did it work for Sully?" Nasser asked from the back.

"It shouldn't have," Eric said. "That's why it's called the Miracle on the Hudson."

He keyed the mic and called New York Approach Control for clearance into the airspace.

Ahead of them, the Hudson River curved toward Lower Manhattan.

The Statue of Liberty rose into view—torch lifted.

"Cessna Six Niner Two November Delta, descend to One Thousand Two Hundred and Circle the Lady. We'll squeeze you in on Runway Two Nine when there's a gap."

David Roseman answered.

"Descend to Onc Thousand Two Hundred Feet. Cessna Six Niner Two November Delta."

He eased the Cessna into a gentle right bank. Then he glanced at Eric.

"Circle the Lady?" He paused. "What does that mean?"

"It means we're going to practice turns around a point," Eric said.

"The statue's the point."

David Roseman didn't answer.

"Make your turn to the left," Eric instructed. "Don't rush it."

David Roseman eased the yoke into a steady left bank.

The horizon tilted.

"Watch your radius. The wind's gonna push you on the backside," Eric said. "You'll need more bank there. Then less as you come around."

David Roseman adjusted—slightly steeper bank, little left rudder, a touch of throttle. The turn smoothed. Below them, the Statue of Liberty remained perfectly centered on their left wingtip—arm raised, still offering what she always had.

"Nice," Eric said. "Don't fight the wind. Work with it."

The turn tightened.

"It's not about perfection," Eric added. "It's about correction. The winds are always changing, so you've got to adjust. Make your corrections and stay with it."

Ferries cut white trails across the harbor as they came around again.

"Every turn's a little different," Eric said. "Even when it feels the same."

David Roseman glanced over—then nodded.

"Watch how you're drifting and correct it."

On the third pass, Eric just watched.

The left wingtip remained perfect while The Statue of Liberty stood steady in the sun.

"Good," Eric said. "Now ease out the bank."

"Wind is pushing you wide," Nasser said. "Add about five degrees of bank, David."

David Roseman corrected.

The turn tightened back up.

"There you go," Eric said.

From the back seat, Nasser spoke. "Good job, David, I hope mine look like that."

David Roseman didn't turn around. He cleared his throat.

"Thank you."

The radio crackled.

"Cessna Six Niner Two November Delta, make a left base for Runway Two Niner. You're number two for the runway, following the United Triple Seven on five-mile final. Caution wake turbulence."

David Roseman looked at Eric. "Caution what?"

Eric jumped in. "Roger that, Newark Tower. Cessna Six Nine Two November Delta will make left base for Runway Two Niner."

He looked at David Roseman. "Caution wake turbulence means we're landing behind a heavy jet, and if you land too close, they can flip a little airplane like us."

David Roseman glanced over.

Eric looked at him. "So, be careful."

"Cessna Two November Delta, cleared to land on Runway Two Niner."

"Cleared to land. Runway Two Niner."

CHAPTER 18

Thunderstorms Don't Care

After they ate at the pizza place Eric liked—the one just off the ramp with the cracked Formica tables—they walked back toward the Cessna.

David Roseman glanced up and met Nasser's eye.

Nasser looked away.

Back at the airplane, they swapped seats.

Nasser flew the return leg.

"Nasser, I have to cancel tonight's lesson."

"Okay, Eric. Why?"

"The Goose is fixed. Quick trip to Albany and back."

"The Goose?" David Roseman said.

"A junky cargo plane," Nasser said. "Looks like it should be in a junkyard."

He caught himself. "Sorry, Eric."

"Scrapyard," Eric said. "It pays the bills and I need multi time."

David Roseman leaned forward. “I wouldn’t do it.”

“Your wife does not like the Goose. Does she Eric?”

“No. Which is why I’m not telling her.”

The words sounded worse out loud than they had in his head.

“That’s going to bite you in the ass.” David Roseman said, leaning back in his seat.

Outside the cockpit window, thunderheads brewed in the distance, lit off by flashes of lightning.

Eric pointed. “There. Thread that gap.”

Nasser adjusted course.

They slid between towers of rising clouds—sunlight on one side, blackness on the other—then broke through into clear air.

“You ever flown into one?” David Roseman asked.

“Into what?”

“A thunderstorm.”

“No.” Eric said. “You don’t fly into thunderstorms.”

He looked toward a towering anvil to the west.

David Roseman followed his gaze.

“That’s severe turbulence and hail,” Eric said. “Dressed up like a nice puffy cloud.”

“Scott Crossfield,” Eric said, “First guy to fly at twice the speed of sound. Flew the X-15.”

David Roseman glanced at the towering cloud. “And?”

"Killed in a Cessna 210. Thunderstorm over Georgia in 2006. He tried to punch through it. The airplane broke apart in flight."

David Roseman leaned back in his seat.

"Crossfield flew rocket planes in pressure suits. Thunderstorms don't care who you are," Eric said. "You either respect them, or they kill you."

A flash lit the horizon ahead.

"See that?" Eric said. "Come right a few degrees. Stay under the base. It'll be smoother."

Nasser corrected, easing the yoke and adding a touch of power.

The bumps faded.

As they descended, the ridgelines came back into view. Fields. Pine. Mount Pocono Airport ahead.

The Cessna 172 cooled on the ramp. Its engine ticked in the falling light. Inside the FBO, the vending machine buzzed. A faded poster of the Wright brothers curled at the corners above a dented coffee pot. Nasser poured himself a cup. David Roseman stood by the window, arms folded, watching the daylight fade over the taxiway.

Nasser glanced over. "You held altitude well."

David Roseman looked over, surprised. "That's unusually kind of you. Thank you."

The coffee machine hissed.

"I used to panic in slow flight," Nasser said. "I hated the stall horn. Thought it meant I did something wrong.

Took me a while to learn—it just means you are close to the edge. Not over it."

David Roseman nodded slowly.

"It's about attention." Then, after a moment: "And about respect."

Without looking up, Nasser said, "I am sorry, David. About what I said this morning. About your partner."

David Roseman inhaled—

then stopped.

"His name is Randall."

Nasser looked up. "My father would never approve of saying that."

Outside, the last flight-school airplane of the day climbed into the sky.

Its rumble faded, then vanished.

David Roseman smoothed the cuff of his shirt.

"Your landings have improved."

"Yours too, David."

David Roseman considered that.

"I shouldn't have made that tasteless joke, Nasser. I apologize as well—but to be fair—my landings have always been rather good."

He didn't reach for his cuff this time.

Nasser shook his head and laughed.

Then, he extended his hand.

David Roseman looked at it—then reached out, elegant as ever, and shook it.

CHAPTER 19

ALB

5:12 PM—Sam:

You on your way home?

(No response.)

5:38 PM—Sam:

Everything okay?

5:44 PM—Eric:

Yeah. Still working.

5:44 PM—Sam:

Okay. Just checking.

(Forty minutes pass.)

6:26 PM—Sam:
You still at the site?

(Three dots appear. Disappear.)

6:31 PM—Eric:
In ALB.

(Pause.)

6:32 PM — Sam:
How'd you get to Albany?

(Long pause. Eric reads it twice.)

6:35 PM — Eric:
What do you mean?

6:36 PM — Sam:
I mean
How did you get there

(Eric stares at the screen. The ramp is dark. The Goose sits with her cowlings open. He types. Deletes.)

6:39 PM — Eric:
I flew here.
What do you think.

(Pause.)

6:41 PM — Sam:
How.

(He knows what she's asking. He pretends he doesn't.)

6:43 PM — Eric:
Sam.

6:44 PM — Sam:
I'm asking a question.

(He types. Stops. Deletes. Types again.)
6:46 PM — Eric:
No, Sam.
Not the Goose.
I flew a 172 up.

(Silence.)

6:49 PM — Sam:
K.

(He stares at the K.)

6:49 PM — Eric:
What does that mean?

(No response.)

6:53 PM — Eric:
Sam?

6:57 PM — Sam:
It means okay.

6:58 PM — Eric:
Doesn't sound like okay.

(Long pause. Sam is standing in the kitchen. Phone in hand. She's not angry. She's trying to read tone.)

7:04 PM — Sam:
I wasn't accusing you.

7:05 PM — Eric:

Felt like it.

7:06 PM — Sam:
I literally asked how you got there.

7:08 PM — Eric:
You asked how like you already knew the answer.

(Pause.)

7:12 PM — Sam:
I asked how because you said you were "working."

(He reads that three times.)

7:14 PM — Eric:
Flying is working.

(Long pause.)

7:19 PM — Sam:
Just wondered how you got to Albany. That's kind of a long flight. That's all.

(His jaw tightens.)

7:22 PM — Eric:
Ok.

(He looks at the Goose through the hangar door. N600SE.)

7:23 PM — Sam:
Okay.

(He hates that word.)

7:24 PM — Eric:
You don't believe me.

(She types. Deletes. Types again.)

7:28 PM — Sam:
Eric, yes I believe you.

(He stares at that.)

7:45 PM — Sam:

Did you eat?
7:46 PM — Eric:
Yeah.

He didn't.

7:46 PM

Sam doesn't answer right away.

She opens his contact.

Taps his name.

The little blue location arrow spins.

Eric — Albany International Airport

Not the rental car lot.

Not the highway.

Right on the edge of the cargo ramp.

She zooms in.

A small gray hangar.

She stares at it for five full seconds.

Then she presses the side buttons on her phone.

Click.

The screenshot flashes white.

She doesn't send it.

She just saves it.

7:50 PM — Sam:

Have a good flight.

He almost types something soft. Something honest.

He types:

"Love you."

Deletes it.

Types again.

Deletes it.

7:53 PM — Eric:

Heading out soon.

No reply.

8:11 PM — Sam:

Text me when you land.

He stares at that one.

8:12 PM — Eric:

I will.

He locks his phone.

The Goose sits quiet in the Albany cargo hangar, oil stains dark under the nacelles.

He walks across the concrete, headset in hand.

He thinks:

She thinks I'm in a 172.

He climbs the ladder.

Straps in.

Battery master — ON.

Boost pump — ON.

Mixture rich.

He hesitates.

Then—

Left engine coughs to life.

The hangar fills with vibration.

His phone buzzes.

He doesn't look at it.

Right engine.

Both props spinning.

He keys the mic.

"Albany Ground, N600SE, ready to taxi."

CHAPTER 20

Fate is the Hunter

The Goose rumbled awake—old metal shaking, panel lights flickering. The cockpit smelled of oil and dust, with a sweetness of burnt insulation that never went away. The seat belt bit into his hip as he cinched it tight; the shoulder harness stiff across his collarbone, rough with years of sweat and grime.

The instrument panel glowed unevenly—needles jittering. Dust on the switches, and the yoke dulled where palms gripped it over time. The attitude indicator was seized, and Eric tapped it once with his knuckle until it aligned.

Another midnight cargo run.

More logbook hours.

He shouldn't be here.

Throttles forward.

The engines roared—uneven, angry.

The Goose lumbered down the runway and heaved into the dark.

He knew her habits: the left lean, the heavy yaw when she was full.

She didn't forgive mistakes.

As the wheels left the earth, he lied to himself.

A few more flights. She won't know.

Rent. Groceries. *Goddamn diapers.*

Logbooks don't lie.

The airlines didn't care. Just the time. That's all they wanted.

Below, Route 611 vanished.

Clouds ahead. Thick and rising.

He keyed up ATIS.

"Northeast Philadelphia Airport. Wind two seven zero degrees at one zero knots. Gusting two zero. Thunderstorms in the vicinity."

Shit.

He climbed higher.

Threaded a gap between storm cells.

Lightning forked to the east.

The Goose rocked—hard.

She heaved, dropped, yawed hard left—shoulder harness tore into his collarbone.

Rudder in.

Trim up.

The yoke jumped in his hands.

He scanned the panel. Breathed.

Then—rain. Hard, blinding.

Loud.

Thunderstorms don't care.

He flicked on the lights.

Nothing but mist and blur.

Downdraft. VSI pinned.

Fuck.

Another jolt.

The Goose bucked like she wanted out.

A flash.

Then dark.

The windscreen lit up.

St. Elmo's fire crawled like a spiderweb.

Licked the edges of the panel in blue-violet fingers.

About to take a hit.

"Not tonight."

Drop to 5,000.

Wings level.

Another gust.

The nose pitched down. VSI dropped fast.

He firewalled the throttles.

Too much. They'll burn up.

Trim.

Feel it.

Balance it.

Left foot—more. More.

Fly the damn airplane.

Now he understood.

The Goose lurched as a bolt of lightning cracked into the nose—white and instantaneous.

The flash lit cockpit.

The panel blinked. One radio went dead. A sharp crack through the headset.

Smell the ozone,

and burnt insulation.

It was survival.

Why am I doing this?

Sam's face flickered through his mind.

Her laugh.

Her smile

—behind the counter at her second job.

Their baby.

Jesus.

Not even born yet. But already everything.

Don't drop her.

He stared into the darkness.

"Fate is the hunter," he whispered.

The sky didn't care what he'd promised.

No denial.

Only choice.

Not tonight.

He mashed the throttles and flew straight into it.

The Goose roared through the storm—howling, leaking, pissed off.

Lightning lit the sky again.

Hold the heading.

Just survive.

Then—through the rain—airport lights: Northeast Philly.

A thread of light through the mist.

Winds 290 at 12, gusting 20.

Cleared to land. Runway 33.

He dropped flaps.

Pulled power.

The Goose jolted sideways.

A gut-punch gust slammed them off the glideslope.

Stay with it.

The wheels hit hard.

Bounced.

Shit.

Another.

Come on, Goose.

Nose down—contact.

She rolled.

Still on the runway.

Done.

Another hour in the logbook.

CHAPTER 21

Boeing 737

Rain fell straight down on Mount Pocono Airport. Water ran off the edge of the roof in a steady line. Eric sat under the awning outside the FBO with his flight bag open at his feet. His boots were wet from the ramp. The ceiling sat low on the ridge on the radar and the band of rain did not move. A Cessna 172 sat tied down on the ramp. Water beaded on the wing and dropped off the trailing edge. The runway was empty. The windsock barely moved.

He checked the schedule on his phone.

CANCELLED — Nasser (reschedule)

CANCELLED — Intro Flight

CANCELLED — Scenic Ride

CANCELLED — David R. (reschedule)

He took out his logbook and opened it to the current page.

One-hour blocks. Out and back. Pattern work. Taxi in.

1.2

0.9

1.1

0.8

0.7

1.3

He looked at them.

He turned to the totals page and added the last week again. He knew what it would be. He added it anyway. The pencil moved. The airport did not.

When he finished, he wrote the new total. He stared at it.

A line guy stepped out onto the ramp, looked up once, and went back inside. The door shut. It was quiet again except for the rain.

Eric thought about the friends he knew from flight school. Some had gone to the regionals when it was still easy. Some had parents who paid for multi time. Their hours piled up because nothing broke and nothing got canceled and they did not sit under awnings waiting.

Then he thought about Sam.

He had told her he was done flying for Bruce. He had said it out loud. He had meant it. The weather did not care.

He closed the logbook and opened it again. He looked at the blank line for today.

He let his mind go where it always went when he stared at that page too long.

Denver.

A base. A schedule that had lines on it. A building with a front desk and a badge scanner and pilots in the same shirts carrying the same black roller bags. They walked like they belonged there.

A simulator bay.

A 737 that moved under you and did what it was told. A clean panel. Working radios. Working autopilot. Nothing held together with tape. Nothing loose that made you wonder what would come off next.

"Engine failure at V1," the instructor says. And it is training. It is not a threat.

He saw the trips the way he had seen them a hundred times.

Denver to Cabo. Cabo back to Denver. Denver to Hawaii.

Long enough to eat two meals in cruise. Hotels on the beach or in city centers. Dispatchers. Maintenance that fixed things. Excited passengers in the back.

Then the paycheck.

A nice car for Sam. A kitchen with counter space, that did not have bikes hanging from the ceiling. A washer and dryer that weren't stacked in a closet. A second bedroom. Sam at a desk that was just a desk. Writing because she wanted to. He looked out at the runway again. Rain washed the pavement clean and kept it empty. He was ready to fly.

The airplane was right there.

He could see the month already. He could see winter. The schedule thinning. The cancellations. He had watched it happen before. It always got tight. Then tighter.

The airplane was right there.

He flipped back to today's date and looked at the blank line again.

Sam's voice came clear in his head. If you didn't take off, you didn't fly.

Bruce's voice came right after. They don't care how you got the hours. They care about one number.

Eric ran the numbers without writing them. Rent. Groceries. The next repair the FJ would demand. How many hours he needed. How many he could get before winter shut the place down.

The rain kept falling.

No one walked out with a headset.

Fuckin' weather.

He waited with his bag open and his headset ready.

He knew what that was.

A story.

He looked down at the logbook. Then he stood up. The rain stung his face crossing the ramp. The 172 sat there, tied down and useless. He untied it anyway. The engine started on the first crank. He taxied slow through the puddles to the self-serve pump and topped the tanks like it meant something. The rain drummed on the windshield. The runway stayed empty. He shut it down and walked back under the awning with his headset in his hand. The logbook was still open.

He wrote 2.0.

CHAPTER 22

Sticky Baklava

Eric sat on the edge of the picnic table outside the FBO, elbows on his knees, eyes locked on the far end of Runway 23. He peered through a pair of binoculars. The summer heat shimmered off the pavement, distorting the Cessna 150 where it sat, engine idling, prop spinning, waiting.

Nasser hadn't moved in five minutes.

Beside Eric: the red-handled scissors, and a black magic marker—ready to mark the occasion of ceremoniously cutting off Nasser's shirt tail. If it happened.

Eric shifted on the bench and glanced toward the FBO door. A poster flapped against the corkboard beside it, held up by a single blue thumbtack:

MOUNT POCONO FLY-IN PANCAKE BREAKFAST

Next Saturday—8 AM

Kids Run the Runway. Static Displays. Discovery Flights

Someone had drawn a smiling pancake in the corner wearing aviator sunglasses.

The bottom edge of the flyer curled in the heat.

Eric looked at it for half a second, then back down the runway.

He keyed the radio. "Nasser, you got this. Just like we practiced."

Static. Then Nasser's voice crackled through, low and unsure. "I know. Just . . . give me a second."

Eric remembered that moment inside the cockpit before his first solo. The nerves. The silence. That strange mix of fear and certainty. The realization that no one else would be there to take the controls. And the deeper truth beneath it: You were ready. You'd trained for this. You could do it.

A door slammed behind him. Eric turned.

David Roseman strolled up in pressed khakis and a short-sleeved button-down, sunglasses perched perfectly on his nose.

"I don't think you're on the schedule today, Mr. Roseman."

"Please, call me David," he said. "I'm not on the schedule." He tipped his chin toward the Cessna 150.

"You came to watch Nasser solo?"

"Couldn't resist a little pageantry," he said. "I believe he may actually do it this time."

David Roseman took a seat beside him on the picnic table. They watched Nasser in his Cessna 150 at the far end of the runway like they were waiting for a Broadway curtain about to rise.

"So, what do you think?"

"He's close. Just nerves."

Another car rolled into the lot.

Two children stepped out first. A girl, maybe ten, in a pale-yellow sundress and silver sandals, gripped a small bouquet of wildflowers loosely in one hand. Her brother, a little younger, wore a pressed white polo and tan shorts, his dark curls still damp from being carefully combed. They stood beside the open door, wide-eyed and quiet, as if they understood the weight of the moment without needing it explained.

Then their mother stepped out. She balanced a foil-covered cake tray in her arms, her long lavender dress catching the sun. A sky-blue hijab, edged in delicate silver thread, framed her face with effortless grace.

The children drifted toward her sides, close but composed, and together they crossed the lot.

The boy looked at the Cessna as they approached, glanced up at the sky, then at his mother.

"Is baba flying yet?"

The woman leaned down. "Soon, habibi."

The three of them walked toward the picnic table, a quiet procession of love and hope.

"Hello," she said softly. "I believe one of you is Eric?"

Eric stood. "That's me."

"I am Aaliyah," she said. "Nasser's wife. I came to watch his first solo flight."

"Nice to meet you, Aaliyah."

David Roseman stood as well.

"But he hasn't gone yet?"

"Not yet," Eric said, eyes back on the runway. "He's still working something out."

She looked out toward the Cessna 150 in position at the runway threshold—engine idling. The red beacon blinked.

"Do you believe he is ready to solo, Eric?" Aaliyah asked.

"I do. As his instructor, I wouldn't send him up if I didn't believe he was ready."

Aaliyah bowed her head lightly to Eric. "May I speak to him?" she asked. "Through your radio?"

Eric handed her the transceiver. "Sure. Just press the button on the side. And then let go when you want to listen."

She lifted it to her lips and pressed the button. Her voice came in Arabic—soft, melodic, filled with tenderness:

"رصان اي كب نمؤأ انأ."

There was a moment of radio silence. Then Nasser's reply, clear and certain:

"ايلاع اي كبحأ انأو."

Neither Eric nor David Roseman understood the words that were spoken through the transceiver. But they didn't need to. The resonance between them carried more lift than the wings overhead.

And then—the engine roared.

Nasser, in his gleaming Cessna 150, surged down the runway. The wheels lifted, the wings caught—and he was airborne.

David Roseman stood. "And we have liftoff."

The children squealed.

Eric exhaled.

David Roseman stepped down from the picnic table. He then smoothed his slacks, horrified. "Oh, for Christ's sake—splinters? I've snagged a brand new pair of Brunello Cucinelli slacks on this damned picnic table?" He pulled at the fabric, furious, trying to smooth it out. He noticed the children, and looked at Aaliyah, "I'm terribly sorry. I beg your pardon."

Eric glanced at him sideways, then at Aaliyah—who turned slightly, one hand raised to her lips, her eyes shining with discrete amusement.

Nasser flew a clean pattern. Radio calls calm. Turns easy. Airplane steady and on speed all the way to touchdown. When the wheels touched the pavement, Nasser's first solo was complete.

He taxied in, shut down, and stepped out to applause. Aaliyah hurried forward. Eric followed with the red-handled scissors.

Eric turned him around and snipped the tail of his shirt. "Tradition," he said. "First solo." He handed the cloth to Nasser. "Next stop: private pilot license."

Nasser took the fabric and stared at it, then looked at Aaliyah. "I did it," he said, holding up his cut shirt-tail like it was a gold medal.

David Roseman reached out. "Congratulations."

"Thank you, David."

Eric handed Nasser a black Sharpie. "Now sign it and I'll put it on our 'First Solo' wall."

Nasser crouched over the picnic table and carefully wrote:

First Solo

Cessna 150 — N19296

Aaliyah peeled back the foil from the cake tray, revealing a golden sheet of pistachio baklava. The smell of honey and spice drifted into the afternoon air. The children were already picking at the edges—fingers sticky, smiles wide.

At the picnic table, David Roseman stood talking with Nasser and Aaliyah. Their conversation was animated, punctuated by glances toward the kids, who beamed.

"Baba, you flew so good!" the little girl shouted, mouth full, cheeks flushed with sugar and excitement.

Nasser scooped her up with both arms. "Thank you, sweetie."

The boy held out two fingers coated in honey. "Mama said you were scared."

"Did she, Zaid?"

Aaliyah frowned, "No. Mama said Baba was *brave*," then stepped closer, resting her hand on Nasser's back.

Eric watched them all for a long moment—a knot in his chest catching, then twisting. He stepped away and carried the Nasser's shirttail into the FBO. The First Solo wall was near the back, by the coffee pot and vending machines. Dozens of faded, bright, mismatched shirttails hung there—names, dates, tail numbers layered in Sharpie.

He stood in front of the wall for a while, then found a spot and pinned Nasser's among the rest.

CHAPTER 23

Elegant Maneuvers

The Cessna 172 climbed smoothly through 2,300 feet, engine humming at 2,400 RPM. Outside, the Pocono ridge line rolled away in green waves beneath a sky streaked with cirrus. Eric adjusted his headset.

"Jimmy Doolittle proved you could fly an airplane without seeing the ground at all," he said. "But he proved something else too—when you stop trusting the instruments and start trusting your gut, the sky kills you."

David Roseman nodded.

"Let's start with clearing turns," Eric said. "Pick a heading and give me a standard-rate left turn, then right. Standard rate."

David Roseman, dressed in a navy cashmere sweater over a pale lavender Oxford, nodded with theatrical confidence. He adjusted the Cartier aviators on his nose, then said, "Yes. I'm familiar with a standard-rate turn."

"Show me, then."

David Roseman banked to the left, eyes flicking to the turn coordinator. "Ball centered," he said, as if narrating for an audience. "Maintaining altitude."

They rolled out precisely 180 degrees later.

"Right turn," Eric said.

David Roseman complied—hands light on the yoke, wrists slightly lifted, as though touching the controls might smudge them.

When the clearing turns were complete, Eric said, "Good. Let's go into slow flight. Carb heat on. Power to fifteen hundred."

David Roseman's movements were precise. "Flaps ten." Then: "Twenty. Thirty. Airspeed coming down . . ."

As the stall horn began to whine, David Roseman peered straight ahead. "She makes her displeasure known."

Eric glanced at the pedals. "Hold altitude. Right rudder. Nose up just a touch more."

The Cessna 172 floated at the edge of lift—horn blaring, controls sluggish.

"Nice job," Eric said. "Now climb out—clean up the flaps on speed."

David Roseman recovered like a pro. No ballooning, no abrupt pitch changes.

"You've done this before," Eric said.

"I did watch the John and Martha King's YouTube channel," David Roseman said. "Last Sunday. With a bottle of Chablis."

Eric looked over. "Okay. Next: power-on stall."

David Roseman set it up smoothly. Full power. Nose up. He narrated with a flourish: "And now, for the drama." Buffet. Yoke in his lap. Horn screaming again. The airplane stalled and David Roseman immediately lowered the nose, held right rudder, and got the wing flying again losing minimal altitude.

Eric checked his altimeter again. "That was textbook."

"Textbook?" David Roseman sniffed. "That was *GQ*."

"Alright. Let's try some steep turns. Pick a visual reference off the nose."

David Roseman chose a shimmering lake in the distance. "Lake Naomi. I once took a date there. Let's try a 360 and see if I get sick again."

They entered the turn—45 degrees bank. David Roseman added power and held back pressure.

"Altitude within 50," Eric said. "Roll out on your heading. Don't let it drift."

They rolled out within 5 degrees.

"Again, to the right."

David Roseman rolled into the turn and adjusted the trim wheel.

By the end of the second turn, Eric leaned back. "Impressive."

"It certainly was," David Roseman replied.

"Let's see how you handle a chandelle."

David Roseman smirked. "Ah. The elegant maneuver."

They entered from level flight: full power, coordinated turn, nose smoothly rising through the horizon. Halfway through, David Roseman adjusted elevator and bank angle with airline-pilot-like finesse. As they rolled out, the airspeed was low, the pitch held high.

"Honestly? That was better than mine."

David Roseman looked sideways. "Eric, you're too kind."

Eric scanned the area. "We'll finish with a lazy-eight."

David Roseman tilted his head. "Or," he said lightly, "we could do something a bit more interesting."

Eric didn't look at him. "Lazy-eight."

"An aileron roll would be quicker."

"No."

David Roseman's hand moved before the word finished leaving Eric's mouth. He pulled the nose up ten degrees, voice smooth and theatrical. "Pitch up slightly. Gain a little energy. Ailerons full deflection—"

The horizon began to tilt.

Eric grabbed the yoke and stopped the roll cold.

The wings snapped level.

"What are you doing?"

David Roseman blinked. "Demonstrating an aileron roll."

"We don't do aerobatics in a Cessna."

David Roseman settled back in the seat. "Of course."

Eric held the yoke another second, then released it.

"There's a big difference," he said. "An aileron roll snaps the airplane around its longitudinal axis. You need higher speed to roll it. Mess it up, you could break the airplane. Ruin your day."

David Roseman's mouth twitched. "Yes. That would be… unfortunate."

"A barrel roll," Eric continued, "is different. You make a corkscrew around an imaginary point in front of the nose. It's a climbing, coordinated roll. You stay positive G the whole time. It's safer than an aileron roll."

David Roseman arched an eyebrow. "Safer."

"In this airplane? Yes."

David Roseman watched him a beat longer, then said, mild as a man ordering wine, "So we don't do aerobatics in a Cessna . . . unless we do *the safer kind*."

Eric didn't answer right away. He checked the area again. No traffic. No clouds. Nothing to witness stupidity but the sky.

He took the controls.

"Watch."

David Roseman's grin spread slow. "Ah. So this is the part where you tell me not to do something—"

Eric pitched the nose up into a climbing turn, adding a smooth roll as the horizon began to arc.

"—and then you do it anyway," David finished.

Eric heard it and hated how true it sounded.

The sky rotated around them. The airplane flew a wide corkscrew, never going light or dropping.

They came out on the same heading.

Level.

"That's a barrel roll," Eric said.

David Roseman stared at him like he'd just learned a priest smoked. "That was aerobatics."

"That was a demonstration," Eric said. "Once."

David's grin returned. "Of course it was."

"My turn," David Roseman said.

Eric hesitated.

"Okay, Jimmy Doolittle. Your airplane."

David Roseman set it up carefully this time. Pitch. Roll. Coordinated rudder. The horizon rotated around them again—clean.

They leveled.

"Not bad," Eric said. "But listen—" He glanced at the panel, then at David Roseman. "We're not allowed to do those without parachutes . . . so don't do it again."

David Roseman didn't look at him.

"I don't recall wearing parachutes when you flew us home from the Hideaway."

Eric gave a tight smile.

"But there's a difference," Eric said, "between knowing how to do something and knowing when not to."

David Roseman adjusted his sunglasses. "Well, Eric. Maybe we're all just trying to look good."

CHAPTER 24

Dirty Dancing

Eric glanced at the clock on the panel.

"Alright. Let's head back. I've got a flight tonight."

David Roseman adjusted his scarf and glanced toward the horizon. "Very well." He dialed up the ASOS and began a slow descent to pattern altitude.

"So where are you flying that piece of junk tonight?"

"Stewart Airport and back."

David Roseman scoffed.

"Ah. The Catskills." He adjusted his sunglasses. "Home of the Jackie Mason matinee and waiters named Irv."

"What do you mean?"

"They were major competition for my family, back in the day."

"For Honeymoon Hideaway?"

"For the Poconos. Period."

He smoothed his scarf.

"The Catskills always carried themselves as though they were the crown jewel of the American vacation scene. 'Oh, we've got Fyvush Finkel doing two sets and a brisket carving station.'"

Eric glanced over.

"The Borscht Belt gave you heartburn," David Roseman said evenly. "The Poconos gave you hickeys."

"I had no idea there was a rivalry."

"There was," David Roseman said. "They had their highbrow comedy."

He leaned back slightly.

"We had glow in the dark Twister. Midnight limbo contests that would've made a rabbi faint."

"And I'll bet they didn't even have swan boats."

"Not a chance."

"And God help you if you tried to dance after nine. You'd get a look like you'd elbowed a Torah." A faint smile. "Meanwhile, here? Disco until three. Regret by breakfast."

"So, you're saying the Poconos were better?"

David Roseman adjusted his sunglasses.

"They sold tradition. We sold fantasy."

Eric reached down and dialed in the ASOS frequency again. "Sam loves Dirty Dancing."

David's hand paused on the trim wheel.

"Yes," he said.

"29.94, on the altimeter."

David Roseman set the altimeter without looking down, eyes fixed on the horizon.

"Of course she does. Everybody loves that movie."

He checked the attitude indicator, then eased the nose up a degree and fed in a touch of power.

"My parents took me to Grossinger's once. Linen blazer. Roy Rogers with extra cherry juice. A pianist playing *Moon River* like it was sacred."

He rolled his shoulders back slightly, as if settling into an old memory.

"Charming. Well-run. Impeccably mannered."

A faint smile.

"Everybody loves that movie."

He kept the wings level, hands light on the yoke.

"But I promise you—nobody ever got laid in a place like that."

He didn't grin. He just turned his head slightly and looked at Eric.

"And that was rather the point."

Eric snorted, then keyed the mic. "Mount Pocono Traffic, Cessna Seven Niner Golf Quebec entering left downwind for Two Three."

CHAPTER 25

You Stink

The Cessna 172's engine ticked as it cooled.

Across the ramp, two warbirds rolled in from the north end of the field — one sleek and silver, the other broad-shouldered and heavy.

A P-51 Mustang taxied past first, its polished skin flashing in the sun, tail low, nose proud.

Behind it lumbered Doc, the B-29 Superfortress — four radial engines rumbling deep enough to shake the hangar doors.

Ground crew jogged out with orange wands.

Eric climbed out of the 172 and pulled off his headset. He watched the B-29 turn onto the transient row.

"Guess next weekend's fly-in is officially happening," he said.

David Roseman followed his gaze. "That's . . . excessive."

Eric smirked. "You should see it when the pancakes start."

David adjusted his sunglasses, still looking at the warbirds. Then he tapped Eric's arm.

"Is that the Goose?"

"That's her. Twin Chieftain."

N600SE sat crooked on the ramp, its faded paint streaked with dirt and grease in patches along the fuselage.

"Looks fast. And dangerous," David Roseman said.

"Actually, slow and stubborn best describes her, in my experience."

"May I take a look inside?"

"Sure."

They walked across the ramp toward Bruce Payne's hangar. The Goose sat half in shadow, her nose angled toward the taxiway like she was already tired of waiting.

Before they reached her, a sharp bark rang out from the hangar.

Wilbur.

The little terrier-schnauzer mutt came charging out from beneath the wing, nails ticking across the concrete, stopping ten feet short of them. He planted his feet and barked again—short, suspicious bursts.

"Easy," Eric said, crouching. He scratched behind Wilbur's ears. "It's just me."

Wilbur's tail started up, but he didn't take his eyes off David Roseman.

David Roseman looked down at him. "Security?"

"Better than the TSA."

Wilbur circled once around David Roseman's polished shoes, sniffed them thoroughly, then trotted back toward the open hangar door—barking again, louder this time.

Inside the hangar, something clanged.

They walked the rest of the way to the Goose. Eric opened the large clamshell air stairs door behind the wing. They climbed inside. The cockpit was spacious and worn; the seats were torn. Eric took the right seat.

David Roseman climbed into the left seat behind him.

"How does she start?"

Eric flipped a switch. "Boost pump on. Throttle cracked. Mixture full rich. Then mags. She'll start. Eventually."

"That's all?" David Roseman asked. "I expected something more . . . temperamental."

"Well, don't forget to start the other one. There are two."

"Funny," David Roseman said. "You know what I meant."

From outside, Wilbur barked again.

A loud knock from behind rattled the fuselage.

"You stealing my airplane?"

Bruce stood outside the cockpit in oil-stained coveralls, his forehead streaked with grease where he'd wiped it with the back of his hand. Wilbur stood at his heel, still keyed up, tail stiff.

Eric leaned out. "Hey, Bruce. Just showing my student the Goo—uh, Chieftain. Bigger. Two engines."

"Didn't know we were giving tours now," Bruce Payne said. "I should charge admission. Make some extra money off her. That'll be twenty bucks."

David Roseman looked at Eric. "I was wondering what that smell was."

Bruce Payne stepped forward. "Say again?"

"Oh, nothing at all," David Roseman replied breezily as he and Eric climbed down from the Goose.

Wilbur gave one last bark as if registering a formal complaint.

Bruce Payne turned back to Eric. "You're on for tonight. Get here early to miss the storms. Unless you want to fly through them—Either way. Can't cancel. This load's time sensitive."

"Okay, Bruce."

"Wow," Bruce said, eyeing David Roseman's polished loafers. "Nice shoes. Maybe I should charge you twenty-five bucks."

David Roseman started to say something—then stopped, reconsidered. He leaned in. "Bruce, was it?" He sniffed once. "You stink."

Bruce looked at David Roseman. Then at Eric. He jerked a thumb toward David Roseman. "What's with this guy?"

Another cargo plane fired up behind him. Without another word, Bruce marched off toward it—yelling over the roar, ducking under a wing. Wilbur followed halfway, then stopped, turning once to look back at David Roseman before disappearing into the hangar.

Eric watched him go.

"Did you just *Top Gun* Bruce Payne?"

David Roseman pulled out a handkerchief and dusted his loafers.

"Maverick. These are John Lobbs. Chestnut museum calf. Two thousand dollars a pair." He glanced at Bruce Payne and shook his head. "Twenty-five dollars is an insult."

CHAPTER 26

Brilliant

The air over Mount Pocono was off.

The ground crew that had just marshaled the Mustang and Doc walked past with tow bars over their shoulders, laughing, unaware of the sky building behind them.

To the west, the ridgelines were already hazed over, their outlines dulled by rising moisture. Over the field itself, the sky still looked harmless—thin, high clouds, nothing organized yet.

The windsock lifted once.

Then sagged.

Dew points were climbing.

David Roseman pulled off his sunglasses.

"I'd like to ask you something," he said. "Why are you flying an old cargo plane for that guy?"

"I need the hours. And the money."

"You're good at this. Teaching. Flying." He paused. "That flight—that was the first time in years I felt like I knew what I was doing."

Eric met his gaze, and for a flicker of a second, honesty passed between them—no sarcasm, no bravado. It stung because part of him knew David Roseman was right.

"Well, first off. There's not a lot of money in flight instructing," Eric explained. "I'm building hours as fast as I can so I can apply for a job as an airline pilot. Sam's working double shifts, and it's hard to make both ends meet." He added. "Plus, we might be having a baby."

"She's pregnant?"

David Roseman went still.

"Then you have no business taking chances like that," he said.

He looked out at the horizon. Then back at Eric.

"Listen to me," he said. "You don't get many people in this world who are all in on you. When you find one—when she's carrying your child, when she's betting her life on you—you don't gamble with that. Not for flight hours."

"I hear you, David. But all I've got is this logbook." Eric said. "I appreciate the advice. But I have to fly tonight."

"Brilliant," David Roseman said. "Make Sam a widow."

Eric gave a dry laugh. "Give me a break David. You've had security your whole life. Money. Hotels. You could afford to take the high road. I have to build my career from scratch."

David Roseman opened his mouth, but Eric kept going, the heat rising in his voice.

"You think I want to fly that piece of junk? You think I don't know the risk? But I have to pay our rent. And the airlines are hiring now. Throw in another pandemic or another 9-11, and they might not hire for years." He shook his head. "So, pardon me for being *brilliant* right now. Who asked you anyway?"

"Nobody," David Roseman said. "Some things deserve to be saved, even when no one's asking." He glanced once toward the Goose, then shook his head.

"What's that supposed to mean?" Eric asked.

But David Roseman was already walking away, his coat flaring in the wind, scarf twisting in the last light.

Behind him, volunteers wrestled with pop-up tents and a banner for the upcoming fly-in pancake breakfast snapped once against its folding table.

He didn't look back.

CHAPTER 27

Pancake Breakfast

7:32 a.m. The first pancake hits the griddle. Steam lifts. Maple syrup and jet fuel braid together in the air. The sun clears the ridge and slides along aluminum wings lined up across the grass—Cessnas, a Cherokee, a Cub with a spinner bright as chrome.

Through the viewfinder—

Pickup trucks and minivans roll onto the grass one after another, doors swinging open as families spill out into the morning air. Kids run ahead toward the airplanes, sneakers damp with dew, while parents unfold lawn chairs and follow the smell of coffee and syrup drifting across the ramp. Over by the fuel drum, a hand-painted sign leans in the breeze:

FLY-IN PANCAKE BREAKFAST

All Welcome.

Click.

Volunteers unfold metal tables and line them up along the hangar wall. Paper plates fan across the surface like playing cards. Plastic forks slide into neat stacks. Between two fuel trucks, a banner snaps in the breeze—AIRPLANE RIDES—one corner sagging.

"Got the banner straight?"

"Looks good."

Click.

Eric crosses the ramp with a stack of waiver forms tucked under his arm, sunglasses pushed up into his hair. He hands off a clipboard without breaking stride.

"Discovery flights at nine."

"Copy."

Click.

The P-51 Mustang comes in low and fast, a silver blade just above the treetops. The Merlin engine screams once across the runway, sunlight flashing off polished aluminum before it pulls up and banks steep into the blue. The sound rolls across the field like distant thunder.

Click.

Bruce Payne stands at three propane griddles. Spatula in one hand. Coffee in the other. Pancakes flip in a steady rhythm.

His T-shirt is already streaked with grease. Wilbur weaves between folding chairs, nose down, already sticky.

Click.

More trucks fill the lot. A minivan door slides open. Three kids tumble out and sprint toward the flight line. A scout troop sets up foam gliders. Orange cones are dragged into place.

Click.

A father lifts his son into the right seat of a Cessna 172. Small hands wrap around the yoke.

"Where does this go?"

The boy doesn't wait for an answer.

Click.

Two hundred and fifty kids line up across the threshold, jittering in neon sneakers and oversized T-shirts, their laughter skipping ahead of them down the centerline. Parents crowd the fence with phones raised. When the whistle blows, they surge forward in a bright, chaotic wave—sneakers slapping white stripes, one girl breaking stride just long enough to wave at her grandmother before sprinting again. Eric waits at the far end with a box of medals, catching them one by one as they cross into his arms, breathless and grinning.

Click.

B-29 Superfortress "Doc" sits heavy on the ramp, four radial engines quiet at last, aluminum skin flashing in the sun. A line of people curves along her wing, hands shading their eyes as they wait to climb the narrow ladder into her belly. Up close, she looks less like a war machine and more like a cathedral with propellers.

Click.

The Goose sits in shadow inside the hangar, tail number half-hidden in the dim light. Eric stands near the wing, talking with Bruce Payne. Too far to hear. Bruce's hand rests on Eric's shoulder a second too long.

Click.

Sam lowers her camera.

Clouds build to the west by the time the griddles cool and the folding chairs begin to stack. Syrup bottles are capped. Trash bags tied off. A yellow Cub lifts east over the ridge, its shadow sliding across the empty runway.

The orange cones still mark the path of the children's race. A dark syrup stain lingers on the asphalt like proof of something sweet and brief.

"Good turnout," one of the instructors says to Sam, glancing at the sky. "Glad we got it all in."

"Yeah," Sam answers. "Storms later?"

"Yeah."

Across the ramp, unconcerned with weather or memory, trots Wilbur.

CHAPTER 28

NOOSE

The apartment held the quiet it always did before a storm.

The windows were cracked. Wind pressed at the blinds. Somewhere nearby, someone had a fire going; the smoke slipped in and settled.

Sam stood barefoot on the bathroom tile.

The plastic test trembled in her hand.

Two pink lines.

Thunder rolled through the walls. Lightning filled the room for a second, bright enough to bleach the mirror, then it was gone.

She rested her left hand over her stomach.

The gold band on her finger caught the bathroom light.

For a moment she watched the ring rise and fall with her breath.

"Okay," she said.

She carried the test into the living room.

Fridge? No.

Pillow? No.

Eric's logbook lay open on the table.

She smiled.

Perfect.

She flipped to the last page.

N600S

3.3 night

Mount Pocono to Philadelphia

Two days ago.

She blinked.

Read it again.

3.3 night.

She didn't move.

The test tilted in her hand. A drop of water from her hair hit the page and spread into the paper.

He told her he was done.

Her phone buzzed.

She didn't look at it.

It buzzed again.

She swiped it open.

LUKAS: Crash at Mount Pocono twin cargo bird Heard anything????

Thunder cracked overhead.

Lightning blew the room white.

The phone slipped from her hand.

The test fell onto the open logbook.

She stared at the words.

Crash at Mount Pocono.

Twin cargo.

Her throat closed.

She grabbed her keys without looking where they were.

The door hit the frame hard behind her.

Rain hammered the windshield as she drove.

She didn't remember turning onto 611.

She didn't remember the stoplight.

Only runway lights in her head.

And one thought that wouldn't stay down:

Not again.

CHAPTER 29

Ooo Wah Ooo Wah

July 4th

Steam curled from the wrecked Subaru, folded around a tree. She cried out for her parents, but the sirens swallowed her voice. She knew by then they wouldn't answer. They never would.

In the darkening sky above, fireworks bloomed—too bright, too cheerful, all wrong.

Strong arms lifted her away from the Subaru.

"It's okay, sweetheart," someone said.

But, it wasn't.

It never would be again.

CHAPTER 30

Cool Cool Kitty

Steam curled from the wreckage. It had folded around a tree, the front end wrinkled—from the nose straight back through the cabin. The airplane lay twisted, the fuselage split open. She heard it again—the radio still playing beneath the hiss of rain and steam, that same bright, bouncy doo-wop chorus about a boy from New York City still going as if nothing had gone wrong at all.

The tail number—N600SE—was half-buried in mud and trees.

Lightning stitched the sky like fireworks. Thunder followed, low and rolling, all wrong.

Blue lights flashed against the hangars.

Sam stepped forward, her clothes soaked.

"Eric . . ." she called out, but the rain carried it away.

She was six again.

She called out.

No answer.

Of course there wouldn't be.

The plane was folded around the tree like paper. Nothing could have lived through that. Nothing.

She called out.

Her knees buckled, rain soaking through her jeans.

She tried to picture him inside the cockpit and couldn't. Her mind refused it. It gave her something worse instead: empty sky. A falling shape. Silence on the other end of a call that would never be answered.

No.

Planes looked worse than they were. People survived worse than this. They did.

They did.

Smoke dragged low across the grass.

Still heard radio again playing from inside the wreckage—bright, stupidly cheerful.

Stop.

People shouted near the twisted fuselage.

Someone would come out.

They would.

They had to.

Her pulse roared in her ears, drowning everything else.

She took another step.

If she saw him—

If she didn't—

She didn't know which was worse.

And then—

Footsteps.

A voice.

"Sam!"

She lifted her head. A figure ran toward her from the terminal building—slipping, recovering, coming fast.

Eric.

He dropped beside her and pulled her in. "It's okay, Sam," he gasped. "I'm here."

CHAPTER 31

The Boy From New York City

Eric's arm was locked around her waist, holding her upright.

She hadn't realized she was leaning that hard until he shifted and she nearly folded again.

"I tried to call you," he said, breath still uneven. "Over and over."

"I don't—" Her voice felt distant. "I don't know where my phone is."

She could still see the two pink lines. The bathroom light on her ring. Her hands shaking then, too—but for a different reason.

Now everything inside her felt hollowed out.

Eric brushed wet hair from her face. "Let's go inside."

He turned her toward the terminal, one hand on her back. She moved because he moved. The rain blurred the runway lights into streaks of white and blue. The wreckage hissed behind them.

She had already imagined telling him.

Now she imagined telling him alone.

Someone shouted from the tree line—

"They got him!"

Eric stopped.

So did she.

Firefighters rushed from the fuselage, reflective stripes flashing in the storm. A stretcher rolled through the mud, wheels catching, men steadying it as they hurried toward the ambulance.

Just a body. Strapped down. Covered in a thermal blanket darkened by rain.

The blanket slipped from the man's shoulder.

Eric's hand tightened at her back.

The face was blood-slick and pale beneath the flashing lights.

David Roseman.

"David?" The name barely made it out.

He stirred as they lifted the stretcher higher. An oxygen mask was pressed to his mouth. Rain streamed over his temples, into his eyes.

Eric stepped forward without meaning to.

David Roseman's eyes opened.

They drifted, unfocused.

Then fixed on Eric.

Then shifted.

To her.

Rain ran off his lashes. His mouth worked like it hurt to move it.

"I'm sorry," he mouthed.

Behind him, the Goose groaned—low, metal in the wind.

The EMTs shoved the doors closed. Sirens rose, and David Roseman was carried away into the storm.

Eric stood frozen, rain pounding his shoulders.

Beside him, Sam heard herself repeat it, rain on her lips.

"I'm sorry."

CHAPTER 32

Orange Juice

"Local businessman David Roseman, owner of the Lovers' Cove honeymoon resort, has been confirmed as the only fatality." Behind the reporter, firetrucks surrounded the twisted wreckage of a twin-engine Piper Chieftain at the end of the runway. "The aircraft attempted takeoff during severe thunderstorm conditions around eleven-thirty p.m. Witnesses say it briefly became airborne before crashing into the trees beyond the runway."

The camera showed torn metal at the tree line. Grainy security footage captured the plane lifting into the rain before disappearing beyond the runway lights.

"Emergency crews reached the wreckage once conditions improved and worked through the night to recover Mr. Roseman's body from the cockpit."

The broadcast cut to Bruce standing near the ramp, the Goose behind him, one wing blackened.

"I caught them in my airplane earlier," Bruce said. "That guy wasn't authorized." He looked toward the trees. "My dog was in there. Wilbur. He always rides with me."

The clip ended.

Back on camera, the reporter glanced at her notes. "Authorities have not confirmed whether anyone—or anything—else was aboard the aircraft. The FAA has opened an investigation into airport security procedures and overall operational oversight. Officials also confirmed that a formal community noise complaint was filed regarding late-night aircraft activity during the storm."

She paused, just long enough to look back toward the wreckage.

"The investigation remains ongoing."

Eric sat on the couch in the same clothes he'd worn the night before, elbows on his knees. On the coffee table sat his logbook. Open. On top of it: the pregnancy test.

Positive.

N600SE — Philadelphia and back.

At some point during the night, she got up, opened the fridge, drank orange juice straight from the carton, and went back to bed without looking at him.

Eric hadn't slept. Bruce Payne's name still hovered in the message thread: unread. He leaned forward and stared at the logbook—tail numbers, dates, hours—and right there in the middle of it all, that plastic stick.

The apartment smelled like wet clothes.

The news aired more security camera footage from a nearby hangar—blurred by rain—N600SE hurtling down the runway, pitching violently nose-up before slamming down.

Back on camera, the reporter glanced at her notes. "Authorities have not confirmed whether anyone—or anything—else was aboard the aircraft. Investigators are examining whether either of the plane's two jet engines malfunctioned during takeoff."

Eric stared at the screen.

"Jet engines," he muttered. "Sure."

Click.

Sam was standing in the kitchen, fully dressed now—jeans, boots, arms folded. Her hair was pulled back; her face was pale, eyes shadowed with exhaustion.

"The feeling that you're completely alone in the world," she said. "It never leaves you, Eric."

Eric didn't move.

"And the worst part? It's the relief," she said. "That relief you feel when the worst finally happens—and you stop having to imagine it. You've never felt that, have you?"

Eric shook his head.

"Well, I have."

Eric opened his mouth—but nothing came out.

She looked away, her eyes drifting toward the logbook. "I was standing in the bathroom, holding that stupid little stick . . ." She nodded. "I should've tested sooner. Then you would've known."

She laughed, once, and it didn't sound like laughter.

"And I'm here, pregnant, and alone, and I don't even know how to breathe."

Eric rose. "Sam—"

"You lied to me, Eric."

He opened his mouth—but she raised a hand, quick. "You promised me."

"I know. I—"

"You're out flying for him." She took a step closer. "Behind my back."

"I know." Eric's face tightened. "I was doing it for us. Building hours."

"You promised me you were done flying for that man," she said. "You looked me in the eye . . . and I believed you."

He took a step toward her, then stopped.

"We only need a couple hundred hours," he said. "I thought—"

"*We* decided together," she said, "that you wouldn't fly for him anymore."

"I wasn't planning to keep doing it."

"You shouldn't have been doing it. Period."

He ran a hand through his hair. "I didn't think you'd find out."

"What?" She stared at him. "You didn't think I'd find out?"

He didn't answer.

"That's worse, Eric."

"I didn't want to scare you."

She grabbed her keys from the counter.

The door shut behind her.

CHAPTER 33

FAA

"Did you bring your logbook and training/endorsement records today, Mr. Young? Paper is fine. If you keep it electronically, we'll need the export or screenshots," the older FAA inspector said. "Whenever there's a fatal accident involving a student pilot, we review the instructor's endorsements and training records. Standard procedure. Did you bring it?"

"I did," Eric's foot tapped against the bench. He pulled the collar of his flight jacket higher.

"Mind if we take a look at it?"

Eric took it from his flight bag slid the logbook across the table. Neither man looked at him.

"Is your full name Eric Andrew Young?" the man asked, though he clearly already knew.

"Yes, sir."

The younger inspector pats his jacket.

Nothing.

Checks the other pocket.

Still nothing.

He looks at the older inspector.

"Do you have a pen?"

The older inspector slides one across the table without looking up.

The younger one clicks it three times before it works.

"Continue."

Eric looked at him.

"Uh. Yes, sir. My full name is Eric Young."

Two men sat across from him in dark FAA windbreakers, the gold seal stamped on their chests. They had arrived without notice in a plain sedan and parked where no one would notice. NTSB agents walked the tree line where the aircraft had left the runway. A state trooper photographed the debris. Yellow evidence flags marked twisted metal in the grass. Oil stains were circled in chalk.

"We're investigating the unauthorized operation of aircraft N600SE," the older inspector said. His voice was steady, almost conversational. "We're just trying to establish a timeline. Start from when you arrived at the hangar."

Eric nodded once. "It was raining pretty hard. I pulled into the lot and the airplane wasn't on the ramp."

"You expected it to be?"

"Yes, sir."

"What did you do next?"

"I checked the hangar."

"And?"

"The door was already cracked open," Eric said. "Bruce keeps it closed."

The younger inspector looked up from his notepad. "Was that unusual?"

"Yes, sir."

Eric hesitated a second. "Wilbur wasn't there either."

The older inspector glanced up. "Wilbur?"

"Bruce's dog. He lives in the hangar. He's always there. If the door's open and he's not around, something's off."

The inspector made a note.

"Go on."

"I stepped inside. The airplane wasn't there. I was in the hangar maybe thirty seconds when I heard an engine spool up. I walked back out and saw the Goose rolling."

"You saw who was in the aircraft?"

"No, sir. Not at that point. It was already moving."

"What happened next?"

"It lifted. Then it didn't climb right." Eric swallowed. "It went off the end."

"Did you know Mr. Roseman had access to the aircraft?"

"No, sir."

"Had you ever authorized him to operate it?"

"No."

"Was he multi-engine rated?"

"No."

"Was he signed off to solo in that aircraft?"

"No."

The younger inspector nodded slowly, writing.

"Did you have any prior indication he intended to fly that night?"

"No, sir."

"Anything else about the sequence?"

Eric shook his head. "After the crash, I tried calling my wife. It was storming pretty hard."

The older inspector closed the notebook halfway. "We're not assigning conclusions here, Mr. Young. We're establishing facts."

"Yes, sir."

"We may have additional questions once we review maintenance records from Mr. Payne."

CHAPTER 34

Constance arrived just after ten, carrying a brown paper bag and wearing her usual lipstick—crimson and unapologetic. She set the bag on Sam's desk and opened it. "Doughnuts," she said. "Didn't want our last week to feel like a funeral. So, we're doing carbs instead of flowers."

"Thanks."

Constance lingered. "I heard about the crash," she said finally. "That was Eric's student, right? The Roseman guy?"

Sam nodded.

"Have you heard anything?" Constance asked. "About why he'd do something like that?"

Sam shook her head.

"Just seems . . . strange." She paused. "He had money. A business. Why take off in a storm?"

Sam didn't answer.

Constance studied her. "You okay?"

Sam nodded. "I'll be okay."

Constance let it go. "I want you to have this." She reached into her tote and pulled out a weather-beaten leather backpack. "Open it." Inside was the old newsroom camera—a battered DSLR, black plastic worn smooth around the grip, corners dulled from years of quick grabs and good use. The mode dial had faded. The lens cap dangled from a frayed string. A thin cloth strap was looped through the side, knotted where it had come loose.

"Wait . . . this is the one I borrowed for the hideaway piece."

"That one, yeah." She glanced at the camera. "Still works. Mostly."

Sam turned it over in her hands. "I thought I broke it." The zoom lens was still attached—heavy, chipped at the edge of the barrel, a faint ring of dried mud around the glass.

"No, you always took the best photos."

Sam smiled. "I always liked the sound the shutter made."

"Figured you might find a few things worth remembering with it."

Sam held the camera, finger resting lightly on the shutter button.

Constance looked around the room—at the mismatched chairs, the half-dead ficus in the corner, the bulletin board pinned with faded headlines and takeout menus. "I'm going to miss this place," she said. Her voice was softer than usual. "Gonna miss all you guys."

Sam looked up. "Even Lukas?"

Constance groaned. "Maybe, but don't tell him that." She shook her head. "He'd never shut up about it."

Sam laughed. "Probably not."

Constance glanced around once more, then added, "Places like this don't come around very often. Not with this kind of heart."

Sam wasn't ready to respond to that, so she didn't. Constance stepped forward and wrapped an arm around her—quick, firm, one shoulder pressed tight. Then she let go.

The phone didn't ring once after Constance left. No new emails. No ad calls. The printer—finally not jammed—had nothing to do. Sam sat alone at her desk after Constance left.

She looked at her phone.

Nothing from Eric.

She unlocked the screen.

Her thumb hovered.

She opened the browser.

divorce lawyer pocono pa

She stared at the words.

The cursor blinked.

She locked the phone and put it face down.

The newsroom felt smaller without voices. She slipped the memory card into the camera and powered it on. The screen flickered to life. Image after image filled the display.

The red rhinestone piano.

David Roseman gesturing toward the lounge ceiling, explaining how Sinatra once stood right there.

Eric looking at David, half-turned, jaw tight, a flicker of annoyance in his eyes.

Everything looked the way she remembered it.

Nothing out of place.

No strange expression.

No hidden glance.

No sign that anything was already in motion.

She paused on one wide shot taken near the edge of the property.

The resort in the foreground.

The lake catching late light.

And in the far corner of the frame, barely visible—

the access road.

Smooth.

Tree-lined.

She zoomed in.

The image blurred as the pixels broke apart.

It was just a road.

She lowered the camera.

Outside the window, a truck downshifted on Washington Street.

CHAPTER 35

Socks

Sam pushed the apartment door open.

It was unlocked.

Of course.

The air was still. Blinds half-drawn.

Eric was asleep on the couch.

Boots kicked off near the coffee table. Socks on the floor beneath him. Bare feet against the cushion.

One arm hanging off the side. His phone dark on his chest.

She stood there longer than she meant to.

He looked younger asleep. The lines around his mouth gone. No edge to him.

Her body reacted before her brain did — a small exhale.

Relief.

He was here.

Still here.

She stepped into the kitchen and opened a drawer. Closed it. Let it slide harder this time.

Waited.

Nothing.

She opened it again. Closed it.

He didn't wake.

Of course he didn't.

She walked back into the living room and sat beside him. Close enough to feel his heat, but not touching. She watched his chest rise and fall. Alive.

The word felt breakable.

When she was six, her father had been alive in the front seat.

Then he wasn't.

There had been no warning. Just music.

Then red.

Her toes curled inside her shoes.

She studied Eric's face.

You love him.

That wasn't the problem.

The problem was that he always believed he'd land it.

She glanced at the logbook.

He had promised.

Not casually.

Not vaguely.

He had promised.

Her hand drifted to her stomach before she noticed.

She had told him she might be pregnant hoping it would slow him down.

Not to leverage him.

To make him choose.

He knew what losing people did to her.

And still—

He slept.

He always slept after.

She leaned forward and studied his hands. Small scars. Grease under one nail he hadn't scrubbed out. The hands that held her. The hands that gripped throttles and made decisions in seconds. She imagined them slipping. The image came fast. Violent. Metal tearing.

She swallowed.

If he dies, you go on.

You already know how.

That was the worst part.

She did know how.

His mouth twitched in sleep. A boy's twitch. A boy who believed he was indestructible.

She hated that it softened her. She hated that if he opened his eyes right now and smiled at her, she would fold. Because love wasn't the question anymore. She wasn't afraid he didn't love her.

She closed her eyes for a second. If she left, she could build something steady. Small. Predictable. A life without waiting for sirens. But she didn't want small. She wanted him.

She looked at his socks on the floor—the gray pair she'd bought him for Christmas, tiny propellers stitched at the ankles.

Then she crouched quietly. Picked them up.

One went into the hamper.

The other went into the trash, under some wadded up paper towels.

She shut the lid.

He shifted.

His eyes opened slowly. "Sam." Relief in his voice.

She didn't answer.

He pushed himself upright, still warm from sleep.

"Sam."

She stayed beside him. Close enough that he couldn't pretend this was distance.

"How long have you been home?" he asked.

Shrug.

"Tell me what to do."

She looked at him.

"I won't fall apart if you die."

He blinked. "What?"

He stared at her.

"That's not funny," he said.

"I'm not joking." She held his eyes.

"I don't want to have to learn how to live without you," she said.

"But I can."

CHAPTER 36

Hole Punched

"Mr. Bruce Payne says he has security footage of you instructing Mr. Roseman on how to start the aircraft."

"What?" Eric shook his head. "That's not true. David just wanted to see the cockpit. That's all."

"Mr. Roseman had a history of unauthorized flights," the younger agent said. "Including one at night with a passenger. You were aware of that?"

"No."

The older FAA inspector flipped a page in his notebook. "A Mr. Nasser Abou Khalil says otherwise."

Eric exhaled, shook his head.

"So you did know."

"Nasser mentioned something once. David denied it."

"So, you knew," the older inspector said. "And didn't report it."

Eric stared at the table. "I didn't know for sure."

The older inspector opened a briefcase and took out Eric's logbook.

Eric's heel started bouncing under the table before he realized he was doing it. He pressed it flat to the ground.

"Let's talk about this."

He flipped to an entry. "Philadelphia. You logged 2.3 hours."

"Okay?"

The younger one laid a dispatch log on the table.

"Mr. Payne also provided Hobbs meter readings from N600SE. It shows 1.3 hours on the same date as the flight you logged to Philadelphia."

"1.3 hours on the Hobbs meter. 2.3 hours in your logbook."

"How do you explain that?" the younger agent asked.

"Maybe I included taxi—"

"And Hagerstown," the older inspector continued. "You logged 2.7. Hobbs shows 1.9."

"Sometimes I round up if—"

"Mr. Young," the younger agent cut in. "Rounding is for tax returns."

The older inspector made a small sound in his throat.

"Let's stick to aviation," he said quietly.

Then, to Eric:

"A pattern," the older one said. "It appears you've been rounding up consistently."

Eric stared at the pages as if seeing them for the first time.

"Under federal regulation," the younger agent said, "falsification of flight time carries no discretion."

He reached into a briefcase and slid an envelope across the table.

"This is a Notice of Investigation," the older inspector said. "Based on the entries in your logbook, a Temporary Suspension is being issued."

Eric didn't touch it.

"Maybe I logged a little more than I flew. I knew it was wrong."

The younger agent's voice hardened. "It's disqualifying."

Eric argued. "It was a few extra minutes."

"Under federal regulation," the older inspector said, "falsification of flight time is disqualifying."

"Your license."

Eric froze.

"Mr. Young. Now."

Eric reached into his flight bag and took out his pilot's license.

The older inspector held out his hand. Then, as if remembering something important, he withdrew it and opened a side pocket of the briefcase. He produced a single sheet of paper. "Before you hand that over," he said, "I need you to initial here acknowledging that you are voluntarily surrendering it."

Eric stared. "Voluntarily?"

The inspector tapped the line with his pen. "It's just the language."

"If I don't?"

The older inspector paused.

The younger one blinked, then looked at him like this was a trick question on a checkride.

"He can . . . do that?" the younger inspector asked.

The older inspector opened his mouth, closed it, and glanced down at the form again. He flipped it over as if the back might have better instructions.

"Yes," he said finally. "You can refuse to sign."

"So I keep it?"

The younger inspector started to nod—then stopped when the older inspector's eyes cut to him.

"No," the older inspector said. "You don't get to keep flying." He tapped the envelope on the table. "This order is what matters."

"But if I don't sign—"

"You'll be requested to return the certificate. If you don't, we escalate."

The younger inspector cleared his throat. "We can . . . mail you a prepaid envelope."

He glanced down at his briefcase, then admitted, "I don't have one with me."

The older inspector didn't look up. "We'll get you one."

He held out his hand again. "Mr. Young. Don't make this harder than it needs to be."

Eric initialed. The older inspector nodded, satisfied—like his initials were the plan all along.

"I'm not the one who stole a plane?" Eric said, more to himself.

The younger agent took out a hole punch.

He tested it once on a blank sheet of paper. CHUNK.

"Works," he said to no one.

Then he reached for Eric's license.

One click. A neat hole. Like it was nothing.

The sound was sharp and final.

The license disappeared into a folder. The agents stood, already done.

"Any questions should be directed to the number on the card," the older inspector said.

They turned toward the sedan.

The younger agent stopped and looked back at Eric.

"Oh. And the dog didn't die."

Eric blinked. "What?"

"The Fire department said the cabin blew open on impact. Dog must've been thrown clear. They found him in a drainage ditch near the runway. Covered in mud. Very much alive."

The agent paused.

"Bit someone."

He shook his head and walked away.

CHAPTER 37

Probably Just Dust

The afternoon passed in pieces. Sam dragged a cardboard box out from under her desk and put it beside her chair. She stared at it longer than she needed to. Her desk was already half empty but the cardboard box made it feel final. She folded the flaps once, then opened them again. Finally, she slid what remained into the box and taped it shut. Outside the window, rain streaked down the glass.

A woman came in briefly to say thank you. She said the story Sam wrote about her grandfather's hardware store "*meant something.*" Sam didn't know what to say. She just nodded and smiled.

Lukas urgently rolled over in his chair and crashed into her desk. "I got something," he said. "You ready?" Before she could answer, he was already up. "It's called *Seen in the Poconos.* I go around the Poconos—like, everywhere—back roads, haunted parking meters, chainsaw-bears, weird gas stations, dogs in truck beds, all of it. And I take pictures. But not like influencer stuff. Real stuff. Local stuff. And then I post it. But here's my twist"—he pointed— "other people can post too. They can add their own photos. Little captions, stories. You know—life stuff."

Sam pressed her lips together and looked down at her hands.

"It's like a living record of the Poconos," Lukas said. "And we just . . . keep adding to it."

"Lukas . . . that's actually a great idea."

"I know, right?" he said. "You in?"

"You know they already have that."

He blinked. "Have what?"

She held up her phone. "Instagram."

He waved her off. "Yeah, but it's not local. Not like this. Nobody on Instagram cares about *Wally Ice Fest* or the garlic festival." He made a face. "Or whatever else we're doing out here."

"Lukas . . ." she said, and her voice came out softer than she intended.

"That's actually a great—"

"Or the *Festival of Wood*," he cut in.

He leaned in, lowering his voice like he was about to share classified intel.

"And you know what else nobody cares about?"

"What?"

"The Poconos has a whole festival built around pickles." He threw a hand up, like he couldn't believe he had to explain it. "*Pickle Me Poconos.* Pickle foods. Pickle drinks. Pickle vendors. Just . . . pickles."

He sat back. "But on *Seen in the Poconos*? That would matter."

His voice dropped as he glanced around the nearly empty room, like he could see it already.

"*Pickle Me Poconos* would matter."

Then he nodded once. "I'd make it matter."

"Lukas," she said, blinking fast, "that might be the best idea you've ever had."

"Right?" His face lit up. "You in?"

She turned away and wiped the corner of her eye with her sleeve.

Dust. Probably just dust.

CHAPTER 38

The Logbook

An NTSB generator clattered near the hangars, feeding temporary power to the ramp lights and the mobile command trailer. Beyond the runway, the Goose remained in the tree line. A crane sat staged nearby, its boom lowered.

Eric hadn't moved since the FAA inspectors left. The picnic table was already wet under a low ceiling that stretched to the ridges beyond the departure end of the runway.

The logbook lay open.

A few drops landed on the page. The paper darkened in small, uneven circles.

Rain came harder. The pages buckled, lifting at the corners.

He didn't hear Sam arrive.

A gust flipped a page. She reached for the logbook, pressing her palm flat against it, trying to close it before the rain did more damage. The cover was swollen and warped. Water spilled from the spine and ran across the table.

She stopped, staring at the pages. Then she took her hand away.

"They took my license."

She sat beside him. Rain boots. Jacket pulled tight. Her hair already wild from the mist, strands clinging to her cheek.

"I'm done," he said.

The rain hammered the table.

She slipped her arm through his.

With her free hand, she pulled the logbook out of the rain.

She leaned in and rested her head against his shoulder.

CHAPTER 39

Betsy Ross

BETSY ROSS

By Staff Writers
The Pocono Classifieds

This week's edition of *The Pocono Classifieds* will be our last. After thirteen years and more than six hundred weekly issues, the paper will close at the end of the month.

For the final cover story, we spent the morning with Betsy Ross at the corner of Prospect and Main.

It was a clear morning with leftover cool in the air, the kind that makes breath visible for a minute before the sun burns it off. The traffic light clicked through its cycle on an empty street. A delivery truck downshifted at the intersection. Farther up the hill, a school bus hissed to a stop.

Every weekday at 7:18 a.m., Ross arrives at the crosswalk and unlocks the chain that keeps the corner closed until it's time. She unfolds a metal chair beside the curb and sets it so she can see both directions. She adjusts the reflective sash over her cardigan and checks the batteries in her hand-held stop sign.

Ross has worked the same crosswalk for thirty-two years. She knows the patterns without looking at a clock: which mornings the kids come running, or which days they drag their feet. She recognizes backpacks more than faces. She keeps extra mittens in her coat pocket in winter, tissues in September for first-day tears, and a spare poncho folded into a sandwich bag for mornings when the forecast changes its mind.

The corner fills in waves. A parent double-parks for ten seconds, door open, a quick reminder to hurry.

A kid hops down from the curb too early and gets redirected. A cyclist rolls through and waits, one foot on the ground, checking a phone.

Once, Ross stopped traffic for a Labrador that slipped its leash and wandered into the street. The dog crossed with the same stubborn confidence as a fourth grader, oblivious to horns and brakes.

At 8:02 a.m., the final bell rings. The sidewalk empties. The last stragglers sprint across on late sneakers, and the bus doors close one by one. Ross folds her chair, locks the chain again, and walks home along the edge of the curb where the gravel collects.

One mother, watching from the opposite side of the street, said, "If she's not there, something feels off."

This issue will be delivered the same way the others have been—folded, stacked, and left by the door.

And then it will be done.

Thank you for reading.

CHAPTER 40

Oklahoma City

Eric had been on the phone since seven that morning, transferred from the local Flight Standards office to the FAA's Airman Certification Branch at headquarters in Oklahoma City.

Every call ended the same way: the investigation remained open. The last call had been the worst. A supervisor in Oklahoma City, speaking in the careful monotone of someone reading from a checklist, explained that the review now included "all relevant operational factors."

"Security procedures. Instructor oversight. Ramp access control," the man said.

Eric leaned against the counter.

"Okay."

"What kind of complaint?"

"A formal noise complaint was filed the night of the accident."

Eric blinked. "A noise complaint."

"Yes, sir. The caller reported 'excessive late-night engine noise and low-altitude maneuvering during inclement weather.' It has been logged as part of the record."

He stared at the kitchen wall.

"Someone complained about the noise."

"All reports connected to airport operations are documented, Mr. Young."

Silence.

"Mr. Young," the supervisor added, sympathy dialed in to regulation level, "I understand your frustration. But there is nothing more I can do for you at this time."

The line went dead.

Eric set the phone on the counter and watched the call timer freeze. 47:24

CHAPTER 41

Tuesday Morning in Tannersville

The chrome-edged 1950s diner in Tannersville was loud. Waitresses in pale pink dresses, their names stitched in red script, called out orders as plates clattered and customers waited for booths. Sunlight slanted through the windows, catching the shine on ketchup bottles and half-filled coffee cups.

Eric had been on the phone with the FAA since seven that morning—transferred, placed on hold, transferred again. The last call had ended ten minutes earlier. He still felt it sitting in his chest.

Sam watched him scroll through his phone. Just dragging his thumb up the screen.

"What did they say?"

He didn't look up. "They're not giving it back."

Her body went still. "What does that mean?"

"They're reviewing everything."

"For what?"

He hesitated.

"Because David was my student," he said. "They're saying instructors are responsible for what their students do. If you sign someone off to solo and something happens later, even if you're not in the airplane, it comes back on you."

She stared at him. "He stole the plane."

"I know."

"So how are you responsible?"

"It's not about stealing," Eric said quickly. "If I signed him off at any point and they think I missed something, they say I shouldn't have endorsed him."

"But you didn't sign him off that day."

"No." He added quickly. "But it doesn't matter. Instructors are responsible for the actions of their students in an airplane. That's the rule."

She frowned. "So if any student you've ever taught does something stupid years later, that's on you?"

"It depends," he said too fast. "Documentation. Whether the instructor exercised proper judgement. If the FAA thinks you were negligent, they can suspend your license while they investigate."

She leaned back, trying to line it up in her head. "But he broke into the plane."

"They're saying the airport failed on security," Eric said. "Bruce is suing them too. He's suing the Roseman estate. Anyone he can drag in. Once lawyers get involved, the FAA—"

He hesitated.

"There was a noise complaint too."

Sam frowned. "A what?"

He waved it off. "Nothing. Doesn't matter."

"This is your career."

He stared at the table. "Yeah."

A server paused to top off their water glasses—*Karissa* stitched neatly across her chest. She overfilled Eric's, water sloshing over the rim and spreading across the table before she noticed.

"Sorry," she said, pressing a napkin down once—more gesture than cleanup—her eyes already drifting past them.

Sam leaned closer, her voice tightening. "You are not responsible for David taking that plane. *Stealing* that plane. Don't let them put that on you."

He almost corrected her.

The logbook flashed in his mind. The erased numbers. The thin paper. The totals that didn't add up.

"I was careless," he said instead.

She searched his face. "Careless how?"

"I should've reported him when Nasser mentioned something was off. I should've documented it. Asked more questions. That's what they're going to say." He shrugged. "That I didn't maintain judgement."

She studied him, still trying to connect the logic. "So because you didn't file a report, they take your license?"

"It is what it is," he said. "Once there's an accident, they go backward. They look at everything, I guess."

She held his gaze another second longer than usual.

Then she exhaled. "This is unbelievable."

She sat back, her anger draining into something heavier.

"Okay," she said quietly. "So this isn't just a delay."

He didn't answer.

She watched him for a long moment.

This was his life.

She reached across the table and took his hand.

"We'll figure it out," she said. "Whatever that looks like."

He nodded once, but he didn't look convinced.

He picked up his phone.

"What are you looking at?" she asked.

"Home Depot's hiring stockers."

"You're gonna get your license back."

"Here's one," he said, scrolling. "Construction. Laborer needed. No experience necessary."

"You would look good in a tool belt."

That earned a half-chuckle. "Yeah. Might help clear my head."

"Of what?"

He exhaled. "Why would David try to take that airplane up? Why didn't I take Nasser more serious when David did it the first time?"

She shrugged.

"But David called him a liar," he went on. "They were already sniping at each other about something. I don't even remember what. I just didn't want to get in the middle of it." He put his phone down. "Honestly, I just wanted to fly. Log the hours."

Karissa dropped their check without breaking stride, laughing at something the man in the backward ball cap said in the next booth. "Oh, you are so funny, Bill," she said, her hand lingering on his shoulder longer than necessary.

"Da Vinci used to lie on his back and watch gulls ride the summer updrafts," Eric said. "He built flying machines nobody understood for centuries. People thought he was crazy." He looked outside. "Same thing with Saint-Exupéry. Flying mail through sandstorms at night because he couldn't not fly. Crashed, broke bones, went back up anyway."

Sam frowned. "What do you mean?"

Eric blinked, the noise of the diner fading as he heard himself. "I get it."

"Okay. But I don't."

A tray crashed somewhere behind them and half the diner burst into laughter. Sam didn't flinch.

"I don't know who I am if I can't fly."

"You're still you." She reached for his hand. "And we're still us."

CHAPTER 42

Fragile

The sun was low when Sam stepped onto the sidewalk, cardboard box in her hands, leather backpack slung over her shoulder.

Eric was there, standing beside a parking meter, hands tucked into his flight jacket.

"Hey. I didn't know you were out here. You could've come up."

Eric looked at the box. "Need a hand?"

"It's really not much."

He took it. "I'll carry it to the car."

Sam followed him across the lot.

At the car, he opened the trunk and set the box inside.

"I'll meet you at home," he said.

She turned back to the fading sign, the dusty windows and the front door that never quite closed. The tears came, quietly, as if they'd been waiting behind her eyes for weeks.

Eric stepped beside her.

She leaned into him.

"I'm really going to miss this place."

He rubbed her back until she steadied.

"I know."

"Thanks for coming."

Sam took one last look at *The Pocono Classifieds*—the tiny office above a coffee shop where they wrote about canoe races. Then she got into her car, followed Eric out of the lot, and drove home.

PART IV

Lift

CHAPTER 1

Extra Gloves

The construction site buzzed as Eric stepped onto the gravel, morning air thick with the clang of metal and the scrape of trowels dragging mortar across cinder block. Scaffolding climbed the half-built wall, yellow rails freckled with concrete splatter, planks gray and splintered underfoot. Dust hung low and settled on everything.

He had a borrowed hard hat and stiff canvas gloves.

A large man in a faded orange safety vest turned as Eric approached.

"You Eric?"

Eric nodded.

"Good. You're tending today." He jerked his chin toward towering stacks of cinder block. "East wall. Keep 'em tight. Keep 'em coming."

Eric rolled up his sleeves and lifted the first block. The edge bit into his palms. He shifted his grip halfway across the gravel and set it down beside the mason. When he turned back for another, the stack didn't look any smaller.

A length of rebar jutted near the pallet, capped with a battered orange mushroom. He clipped it once with his boot and muttered. The next trip, he cleared it by an inch without looking.

The sun climbed. Sweat ran down his spine and darkened the back of his shirt. Dust glued itself to his forearms. He carried two at a time for a while, then went back to one. The pallet dropped lower. The wall climbed higher. By the time he reached the plank, he had to step up onto it to hand the next block across.

"You stack 'em like that, they'll walk by noon," someone called.

"I said tight, not pretty," another voice muttered.

His gloves thinned fast. The rough faces of the blocks chewed through canvas. When he set one down too quickly, a line opened across his fingertip. He wiped it on his jeans and reached for the next.

At lunch, Eric slid into the shade of the scaffold and set his hard hat on the plank beside him. It made a light plastic knock against the wood. He wiped a thumb across the brim, leaving a gray streak where the mortar dust clung.

Across from him, a man with sunburned arms lowered himself onto a split-face jamb and let his own hard hat fall between his boots. It hit, rolled once. Settled upside down.

A strip of black electrical tape held a crack near the crown. A faded UNION LOCAL 1552 sticker clung to the side.

Eric's eyes flicked to it.

Then back to his.

The other man flipped open a metal lunch box, the latch snapping back with a metallic click. Paint had worn off the corners. A faded American flag decal curled at one edge. He unscrewed a green thermos and poured coffee into the cap. Steam rose into the grit-thick air.

"First day?"

"Yeah."

"Jackson." He offered his hand. "You're doing good. Gets easier."

Eric shook it. Jackson's grip was strong, callused.

Eric drained his water bottle and crushed it flat.

"It's a workout," he said.

Jackson barked a laugh. "That's one way to put it."

Eric flexed his hands. Dust flaked from his knuckles. The tips of his fingers were split open, red pushing through the gray.

Jackson noticed. He reached behind him, dug into the back pocket of his work pants, and pulled out a pair of creased, dusty gloves.

"Here's some advice, kid," he said, tossing them over. "Always bring an extra pair of gloves."

Eric caught them.

"You'll burn through the first pair before lunch."

Jackson stood, poured another cup from the thermos, and screwed the lid back on. "Keep 'em. I got more in the truck."

Behind them, an engine revved too hard.

There was a dull plastic crack and a hollow thud.

Jackson turned.

The blue porta-john near the edge of the lot lay on its side, door hanging open, rocking twice before settling.

A forklift idled a few feet away.

Jackson took a sip of coffee and looked at it for a long second.

"Strittmatter! That ain't a parking space!"

CHAPTER 2

#born2fly

Eric sat on an overturned five-gallon bucket near the back of the job site, gloves off, hands raw and gray with dust. His knuckles were scraped from tying wire. Fine powder clung to the sweat on his forearms.

The bricklayers were finishing the grout on the south wall after Eric had spent the morning setting rebar—hauling twenty-foot lengths off the flat-bed, dragging them up the scaffold, cutting and bending them to fit the block cores. He wired the vertical bars in place, dropped horizontals between courses, checked spacing, then did it again. The work left rust streaks on his pants and metal splinters in his palms. When the grout pump started, it filled the cavities around the steel with a wet, gray slurry that splashed and ran and hardened.

He went on lunch break. A radio played low country music beneath the scaffold.

He had two peanut butter sandwiches, chips, and an iced tea. He pulled out his phone.

Instagram.

He hadn't opened it in a while.

The algorithm fed him what it always fed him: airplanes, sunsets, cockpit shots, someone's perfectly framed wing over a perfectly blue ocean.

Then he saw it.

@born2fly_nick

Profile photo: Ray-Bans. Headset. Cockpit selfie. Teeth too white.

Bio:

ATP Track. Seminole Life. God First. Grind Never Stops.

Eric stared at the "Follow" button.

He pressed it.

Instant regret.

He locked his phone.

It buzzed almost immediately.

Nick.

Of course.

12:05 PM—Nick:

No way 😂

You alive bro?

Eric stared at the message.

He typed. Deleted. Typed again.

12:08 PM—Eric:

Yo man. Alive

Three dots appeared.

12:08 PM—Nick:

Dude I haven't heard from you in a while

Saw the follow. Thought maybe you got hacked.

Eric leaned back against the scaffolding. Dust and mortar coated the thighs of his jeans. Rust stains bled across the fabric where rebar had rested all morning. His Timberlands were caked in drying mud, laces stiff with grit.

He took the last swallow of iced tea and chucked it toward the cement mixer. It bounced off a stack of empty mortar bags and disappeared into the pile.

12:09 PM—Eric:

Nah Just laying low

12:09 PM—Nick:

You still flying? Or did you get a real job? 😆

Eric watched a forklift roll past.

He didn't lie.

12:11 PM—Eric:

Building.

Three dots.

12:11 PM—Nick:

Nice. I just crossed 1,380 hrs yesterday.

Dad says if I keep pushing I'll hit 1500 by spring.

Trying to time it with hiring waves.

Eric looked at his hands.

Cracked. Split. Concrete under the nails.

12:11 PM—Nick:

Yeah man. Seminole all week.

Took it down to Myrtle Tuesday to build cross country multi.

Logged like 4.5 in one leg.

Kinda exhausted tbh.

Eric looked up, thinking.

4.5 on one flight.

He used to celebrate 1.1.

12:13 PM—Eric:

Damn man. that's awesome

Nick sent a photo.

Cockpit. Perfect horizon. Clean panel.

Caption: "Another day in the office."

12:13 PM—Nick:

You gotta come down sometime.

We'll split time.

Eric almost laughed.

Split what.

12:14 PM—Eric:

Yeah dude.

12:14 PM—Nick:

Yo random but how's Sam?

Haven't seen her since NYC.

Remember that?

You disappeared for like 40 mins 😂

Eric stared at the screen.

Bleecker Street. Fireworks.

12:16 PM—Eric:

Yeah. That was the night.

She came to PIT a couple times.

12:16 PM—Nick:

Oh yeah. That's right. Man. Crazy.

You always were the ladys man.

Eric didn't respond to that.

12:16 PM—Nick:

She good?

Eric hesitated.

Then typed.

12:18 PM—Eric:

Yeah. She's good.

12:18 PM—Nick:

You guys married yet?

Or still doing the starving novelist thing?

Or is she supporting your broke pilot ass? 😆

Eric wiped his hands on his jeans.

12:20 PM—Eric:

Married.

12:20 PM—Nick:

Oh shit.

For real??

12:23 PM—Nick:

Congrats man.

Another message immediately after.

12:23 PM—Nick:

Guess you better hurry up and get that airline seniority number. 😂

Get her a big house for some kids

Eric looked up at the half-built wall in front of him.

Row by row.

Block by block.

12:25 PM—Eric:

Working on it.

Nick sent another photo.

Him in front of the Seminole. Sunset. Caption: "Closer every day."

12:25 PM—Nick:

Anyway bro I gotta preflight.

Wheels up in 20.

Hit me up

Eric stared at the screen.

He typed.

Stopped.

Deleted.

Typed again.

12:29 PM—Eric:

Fly safe.

The typing bubble appeared.

Then disappeared.

Eric stared at his reflection in the dark screen.

He opened Instagram.

Nick's latest post filled the screen.

Sunset. Seminole. Caption: "Closer every day."

Eric held his thumb over the icon.

Then he deleted the app.

The screen shifted. Empty space where it had been.

He locked the phone.

Pulled his gloves back on.

Picked up a length of rebar and went back to work.

12:33 PM—Nick:

Always do.

The automatic doors slid open. Eric stepped inside, boots leaving gray crescents of dried cement on the tile. He went straight to the counter and filled a large coffee cup, watching it rise to the brim. His hands were still rough from the day. Concrete dust clung to the creases in his knuckles. He rubbed his thumb across his palm and left a streak.

"Eric?"

He turned.

Isabella stood near the refrigerated drinks, a canvas duffel slung over her shoulder. Air Force Academy hoodie. Hair pulled back tight.

"Isabella?"

She crossed the floor in three quick steps and hugged him before he could adjust the coffee. He stiffened for half a second—then hugged her back. She stepped back, still smiling.

"I'm home for break."

"Didn't know you were back," he said.

"Surprise."

"How's it going out there?"

She shifted the strap on her duffel higher on her shoulder.

"It's intense," she said. "Four a.m. wake-ups. Formation drills. Everyone thinks they're hot stuff until they're not."

He nodded once.

"They had me talk through a power-off stall in front of the class," she went on. "No warning. I didn't freeze."

"No?" he said, a hint of a smile breaking through.

"I just heard you in my head. 'Fly the airplane.'"

He looked down at the coffee lid.

"They talk about primacy all the time," she said. "First thing you hear sticks."

He smiled.

"You used to call it something," she said, squinting a little. "Brain . . . brain . . ."

She shook her head. "I can't remember."

"Close enough," he said.

"You wouldn't let me guess," she added. "Ever. That's saving me right now."

He took a sip of coffee.

"They say I'm doing well," she said, quieter now. "But that's because of you."

He didn't answer that.

"So how are you?" she asked brightly. "I thought you'd be chief pilot of United Airlines by now."

He shrugged.

"Workin' on it."

She glanced down then.

At the boots.

The dust along his jeans.

"Why are you covered in dirt?" she laughed. "Your FJ break down again?"

He laughed.

"No, not this time," he said. "Doing some construction."

"Oh."

"Well," she said, forcing the brightness back in, "whoever you're working for is lucky."

He looked at her.

"You changed my life."

He didn't know what to say to that.

"I've got to get going," she said. "We're going into the city tonight to catch a show."

"Oh yeah?" he said. "Watch your altitude in Manhattan."

She smiled politely.

"Keep your scan tight," he added. "Plenty of obstacles down there."

She laughed, but it was softer now. "I'll try not to bust Class Bravo."

"Good," he said. "And if things get bumpy, just—"

He stopped himself.

"Have fun," he said instead.

She stepped in and hugged him again, tighter this time.

"Keep the blue side up," she said quietly.

He held her for a second.

He didn't answer.

She pulled away and walked out through the automatic doors.

They slid shut.

Eric stood there a while longer, then stepped outside into the cold. Cars moved through the lot. A truck door slammed near the pumps.

He kicked one heel against the curb and watched the concrete flake off.

"Sticky brain glue," he said quietly.

CHAPTER 3

Flecks of Concrete

The heater in the FJ clunked and whined as Eric drove home. His forearms throbbed from hauling block and shoveling mortar all day. Sand, cement, water—cut with a hoe until it turned the right shade of gray. Too wet and it slumped. Too dry and the bricklayers swore.

By noon he was carrying block two at a time. Keep the boards loaded. Keep the joints full. Keep out of the way.

Lime from the mortar had dried his knuckles white. Grit lived in the creases of his palms no matter how many times he dunked them in the water barrel.

He pulled into the lot as the streetlights flickered on.

Sam met him at the door, wrapped in a heavy cardigan, her hair loose from the dry air. She stepped closer, touched his face, and picked a fleck of dried concrete from his whiskers.

He kissed her cheek.

"You're late," she said.

"Yeah," he said. "Long day."

He unlaced his boots, then hung his heavy Carhartt jacket by the door. Flecks of concrete clung to his jeans—dusty gray shards that cracked and flaked as he moved. The pant legs were damp from the knees down, dark with moisture where the ground hadn't let go. His socks had soaked through hours ago, stained by his boots—rust-colored rings biting into his ankles.

Sam followed him into the kitchen. Before he could say anything else, she reached for a towel from the back of a chair and knelt in front of him. She peeled one sock down gently, then the other, careful where the skin looked raw. She gathered his socks in the towel and folded them tight, setting the bundle aside.

CHAPTER 4

small kicks

The first snowflakes fell on a Saturday morning, drifting past the apartment window and dissolving against the blacktop below. They didn't stick. They left dark marks where they landed, then vanished.

Eric stood at the window with a cup of home-brewed coffee, watching the spots appear and fade on the roof of the FJ.

Sam came up behind him and slipped her arms around his waist. Her cheek rested between his shoulder blades.

"Wait," she said.

She moved around in front of him, took his hand, and guided it down, pressing his palm against her belly.

He felt nothing at first.

Then—there. A small, sudden thump.

He looked down at her.

It happened again.

He left his hand where it was and reached back blindly to set his coffee on the counter.

"I'm sorry," he said.

"For what?"

"For everything. For not being what you needed."

Her expression tightened. "Don't." She searched his face. "You're working hard for us. I love that."

"And I love you."

He took a breath.

"There's something else."

Sam pulled back enough to look at him.

"There's something I didn't tell you," he said, eyes drifting to the window behind her. "About the FAA. About what they found."

She stilled. "What didn't you tell me?"

Eric looked back at her.

"They asked to see my logbook."

She waited.

"They went through it. Compared it to the Hobbs meter readings. And Bruce's records."

"Okay," she said carefully. "What did they find?"

"They said I padded my flight times."

"They said?" Her voice remained even. "Or you did?"

He let out a slow breath.

"Did you?"

He held her eyes. "Yes."

The room seemed to narrow.

"It started small," he said. "Minutes here and there. Taxi time. Shutdown. Nothing that stood out. But it added up. Enough to change the totals."

Sam stepped back.

Just one step.

But it felt like a mile.

"So even if the crash hadn't happened," she said, "they still could have taken your license."

Outside, the wind shifted, sending the snow slanting against the glass.

"Why didn't you tell me?"

"I was ashamed."

"And now?"

He didn't answer right away. "Still am." He swallowed. "I'm grounded. And not just because of David Roseman."

She watched him steadily.

"You thought you could get there faster."

"I know how it sounds," he said. "I wanted to get there faster—for you."

"I never asked you to do that."

"I know."

"I would have waited."

"I know."

She nodded once.

She wrapped her arms around herself now, not him. Watching him. Measuring him.

The baby kicked again.

She looked down at her stomach.

Then back at him.

"Okay," she said.

He flinched at the word.

"Okay?"

"That doesn't mean it's fine." Her voice was calm. "It means I'm still here."

He stood very still.

"You could have kept this to yourself," she said. "You didn't."

She stepped closer, though she still didn't touch him.

"This time you told me."

He nodded.

"But hear me." Her face tightened. "No more lies. Not small ones. Not helpful ones. Not the kind you think don't count."

"I won't."

She searched his face.

"Ever," she said.

"Ever."

For a moment neither of them moved.

Then she stepped forward and rested her forehead against his chest.

He closed his arms around her, careful, as if the air between them were fragile.

After a few seconds she pulled away and crossed to the kitchen counter. She opened a drawer and took out a white envelope, already torn along the top.

Oklahoma City.

The FAA seal in the corner.

She returned and placed it in his hands.

"It came three days ago," she said. "I read it."

He looked from the envelope to her.

"I needed you to tell me."

She leaned into him again. This time he held her without hesitation.

Between them, the small life shifted once more.

Outside, the snow continued to fall.

Now it began to gather in the cracks of the parking lot, settling into the seams.

CHAPTER 5

This is Eric

Eric's palms were already raw under the second pair of work gloves when his phone buzzed in his back pocket.

Unknown number—New York City area code. Probably Bruce Payne's lawyer. Or worse—someone from the Roseman family. He slid the phone back in his pocket.

Rumor was the job site would shut down for winter in two weeks.

After that it was unemployment.

He looked up and saw a small airplane passing overhead. For the first time in a while, he let himself think about it. He'd grown up reading Richard Bach and Saint-Exupéry, imagining thunderstorms and night flying. He'd seen it for himself—storms building, fireworks below him on the Fourth of July. It had been a hell of a view.

As he lifted the next load, he felt no bitterness toward David Roseman, or the FAA. They hadn't forged his logbook. He had.

He watched the airplane disappear, sunlight flashing off its wings. Then he drove the shovel into the mud.

The phone buzzed in his back pocket again. He threw another shovelful of mud, wiped the sweat from his forehead, and pulled his phone out.

Unknown number—New York City area code.

Deal with it.

He put the phone to his ear.

"This is Eric."

"Good afternoon, Mr. Young. My name is Conrad Oldman." The voice—crisp, polished, edged with the formality of an older man. "I hope I'm not interrupting anything you can't step away from."

Eric wiped the back of his neck with his sleeve.

"I'm working."

"I'll be brief," Conrad Oldman replied. "I represent the estate of my late brother, Randall Oldman. Certain matters have come to my attention involving the final affairs of David Roseman—a name I understand you and your wife, Samantha, are familiar with."

"You're a lawyer?"

"Yes," Conrad Oldman said. "And I would consider it both a courtesy and a necessity, if you and Mrs. Young could meet with me tomorrow afternoon."

Eric pinched the bridge of his nose. "Where?"

"Mount Pocono Airport. Two o'clock sharp. We'll find somewhere private to talk."

He hesitated, staring across the job site, the wall rising block by block.

Two weeks.

Sensing it, Conrad Oldman added, "I would strongly recommend canceling any prior engagements, Mr. Young."

"Young!" the foreman shouted from across the yard. "Clocks runnin'."

Eric turned away from the noise.

"Alright," he said. "We'll be there."

"Excellent," Conrad Oldman said. "Until tomorrow."

The line went dead.

Eric slipped the phone back into his pocket and stared across the job site as smoke curled from the fire pit where they burned empty mortar bags and scrap lumber.

"Break's over!" The foreman yelled.

A cement truck began backing up, the high-pitched beep-beep-beep slicing through the air.

Eric picked up his shovel.

"Move, Young!" the foreman barked.

He moved.

CHAPTER 6

Gravy Pit

"I got a call today," Eric said. "A lawyer from New York."

Sam didn't look up.

At the small table in the corner of the kitchen, Samantha sat with her legs swinging off the chair, her plate pushed close, steam still rising from her dinner. She wasn't eating yet. She was sculpting. With the back of her spoon, she pressed careful indentations into her mashed potatoes, then caved in the center. She reached for the saucepan cooling on top of an oven mitt. Her mom guided her hand. Her dad made silly stories of potato hills. She tilted it and spooned in two heaping spoonfuls of the thick brown liquid, letting it pour into the gravy pit. It filled slowly, seeping into the edges, coating the walls of mashed potatoes. Across the table, her parents were smiling.

"Sam?"

"What did he want?" She pressed the spoon back into the crater of the gravy pit, deepening it. She poured the gravy in and watched it rise, stopping before it spilled. She dragged the spoon once more around the edge, tightening the border where the gravy had thinned the wall.

"He represents the estate of Randall Oldman. Somehow, he's tied up with David."

"Who's Randall Oldman?" she asked. "Wait, yeah, he's a lawyer for the Rosemans. I read about them. You think it's about . . .?" She let it trail off. Her spoon traced the rim of the gravy pit, but her mind traveled backward. When she was that little girl, her dad had sat across from her, much like this, and her mom had laughed at every odd shape she made with her food. Her spoon hovered, and she blinked. Their kitchen was still the same: bikes hanging in the corner, the hum of the light, the plate of mashed potatoes. But the little girl wasn't real.

"I don't know," Eric said. "But the lawyer wants to meet us tomorrow. At the airport."

She pressed her spoon deep into the potatoes. A slope caved in. She spooned more gravy in, letting it flood deeper. It broke the wall and spilled over.

Eric reached across the table and found her hand. "It's gonna be okay," he said.

"Yeah."

Later that night, steam fogged the bathroom mirror as they stood beneath the shower, hot water rinsing concrete dust from his skin. Sam stood with her forehead against his chest.

They didn't mention Randall Oldman again.

CHAPTER 7

Ming Vase

Wind whipped across the tarmac at Mount Pocono Airport, rattling a loose panel on the old hangar and carrying the sharp tang of jet fuel. It snapped the windsock straight over Runway 13, then let it fall limp, and sent a plastic coffee cup skittering past the self-serve pump toward the taxiway.

Eric looked around and checked his phone. 1:58 p.m. The lot stayed empty. Just a salt-stained F-150 and an airport maintenance van.

Sam followed his gaze toward the parking lot, half expecting to see an old Cadillac or maybe a polished town car glide up, the way you'd expect for a lawyer from New York.

Eric frowned, scanning the access road.

Then—

A low whine rose behind them, over the tree line.

They turned toward the runway.

A sleek silver Learjet descended onto the asphalt. It touched down so smoothly it barely seemed to land, then rolled toward the terminal, engines humming in a high, steady whine.

It came to rest on the apron. The whine tapered off. The cabin door hissed open.

An elderly Black man stepped down the stairs, sharply dressed in a dark velvet overcoat, polished shoes flashing in the afternoon sun. He carried a mahogany cane but didn't lean on it—the cane, a statement, not a necessity. He moved with the careful pride of a man who had walked into many rooms where he wasn't expected—and owned them anyway.

At his side walked a tall woman, silver hair tucked beneath a cream-colored scarf. In her gloved hands, she carried a white-and-blue Ming vase.

Sam's fingers gripped Eric's sleeve.

The elderly couple crossed the tarmac slowly, as if Mount Pocono airport had been built for their arrival.

"Mr. and Mrs. Young," the elderly gentleman lifted one hand in greeting.

"Thank you for meeting us," his voice rich and rolling like an old hymn.

He turned slightly and rested a hand at the woman's lower back — gentle, practiced.

"I'm Conrad Oldman. This is my wife, Madeline."

Madeline inclined her head with quiet majesty, the Ming vase still cradled in her arms like it held the heart of the afternoon inside it.

Eric stepped forward and clasped the offered hand.

Conrad Oldman's grip was firm but measured. Lawyer grip. The kind that didn't waste motion.

"My brother Randall was a founding partner of Oldman & Oldman," he continued. "Many years ago, he traded the noise of New York for the quieter echoes of the Poconos."

Eric turned to Sam. She was already looking at him.

"I presume this is not quite what you expected," Conrad Oldman said evenly. "My brother was particular about details, and we do so hate to arrive anywhere without making a bit of a scene."

Conrad Oldman adjusted a gold cufflink—on it, the glint of an old family crest.

He leaned closer to Eric.

"Besides, after a certain age, my boy, you either disappear, or you make damn sure they see you coming."

A gust snapped the windsock again behind them.

Sam surprised herself by smiling. She glanced at Eric.

Catching the flicker of their confusion the way a seasoned lawyer reads a jury, Conrad Oldman's mouth curved into a wide smile.

Beside him, Madeline Oldman chuckled softly—a sound like glass chimes stirred by the wind—then gave the Ming vase the slightest, most affectionate squeeze.

"My brother kept a private office in Stroudsburg, near the courthouse. It would ease my spirit if we could conclude our more delicate business there . . . among his papers." He paused—not from hesitation, but ceremony. "If it would not trouble you terribly, Mr. Young, I would consider it a courtesy if you would drive us there yourself."

Eric looked up. "You want me to . . . drive us?"

"Not *chauffeured* today," Conrad Oldman said precisely. "*Taken*."

Eric glanced at Sam. She lifted her shoulders in the faintest shrug.

"Sure," Eric said. "I'll take us."

Conrad Oldman clapped a hand on his shoulder. "Good man. We shall ride in your chariot, Mr. Young. Lead the way."

Behind them, the Learjet gleamed in the Pocono sunshine.

CHAPTER 8

Hand Signals

Eric's old FJ rattled down Route 611, the tires humming over snow dusted road. Conrad Oldman sat in the back seat with his knees nearly under his chin. Madeline Oldman perched snugly beside him—the Ming vase cradled in her lap. Eric gripped the wheel, aware that the interior smelled faintly of stale coffee, and whatever had fallen in the vents over the past decade.

"I'm, uh . . . sorry about the Toyota," Eric said, checking the mirror.

From the backseat Madeline Oldman said, "Oh, I do love these old safari vehicles."

Sam choked on a laugh, disguising it as a cough. Eric shot her a look.

He took a turn too quickly. The FJ leaned hard. Conrad Oldman tilted sideways, knees knocking against Eric's seat.

"Marvelous!" Conrad Oldman said, chuckling as he steadied himself with his cane.

"Mrs. Young," Conrad Oldman continued, his voice smooth, "do not tell anyone this, but when Mrs. Oldman and I were married, we left the synagogue in the plumber's pick-up truck."

"Full of pipe wrenches in the back seat." Madeline Oldman added.

"Oh, really," Eric said.

Sam looked at him and raised her eyebrows.

The FJ Cruiser fell into silence as the woods thinned and signs for Stroudsburg appeared.

Conrad Oldman broke the quiet. "I'm sure by now you've heard," he said, almost absently. "Mr. Payne's little lawsuit."

Eric glanced at Conrad Oldman through the rear-view mirror. "What happened with that?"

"Tried to sue the Rosemans. Filed some desperate little action—emotional distress, reputational harm, all that sort of thing. Thought he'd cash in, I suppose."

"What did they do?" Sam asked, glancing into the backseat.

"The case was thrown out in summary judgment. Judge didn't even take a recess."

Conrad Oldman paused, watching the trees pass. Then, like it barely mattered, he added, "Some time later, I'm told he was in a rather terrible accident in Newark."

Eric snapped his head around. "You're kidding."

"What?" Sam gasped.

Conrad Oldman's voice didn't waver. "Awful thing. Truly awful."

Sam studied him.

"I wasn't there myself," he added. "But those cargo ramps do get terribly loud I am told."

"Did he . . . die?" Sam asked.

"No, my dear," Conrad Oldman said. "He survived. Lost the hand. That's all I know."

Mrs. Oldman rested a hand on Conrad Oldman's arm and said softly, "Some men only learn the hard way."

Eric shook his head once, eyes back on the road. "Jesus. Bruce."

Sam looked straight ahead. "Oh, my goodness."

Eric wheeled into an open parking space on the courthouse square in Stroudsburg. In the back, Conrad Oldman unfolded himself with a grunt. "Splendid ride," he tapped the cane against the door frame. "I do love these old four by fours, as well."

Madeline Oldman adjusted the Ming vase in her lap and leaned forward. Sam opened the door for her, and the older woman stepped out like she was disembarking from a royal carriage.

The office in front of them was a low, stately brick building tucked between updated business suites. A plaque read:

Randall Oldman, Esq. — Private Counsel

Conrad Oldman drew a key from his coat, paused, then unlocked the door and pushed it open. Inside, the air smelled of leather and old books. A mahogany desk filled the room. A globe occupied one corner, a stack of heavy law tomes on a bookshelf on another.

Madeline Oldman stepped forward and placed the Ming vase at the center of the desk. The blue dragons curled around the porcelain surface seemed to shimmer under the gray light. Eric and Sam stood side by side, their hands clasped tightly together.

Conrad Oldman turned to them. "My brother Randall passed several months ago. Shortly after David." He paused, his gaze lingering on the Ming vase. "This was his sanctuary."

He reached into his satchel and withdrew a single envelope.

To Samantha.

"I've been instructed to deliver this to you. Personally."

She took it, the weight of it impossible to ignore.

"We'll give you privacy," Conrad Oldman added. He and Madeline Oldman stepped out, closing the door behind them.

Sam looked at the envelope, then handed it to Eric. They sat together on the leather sofa by the window. Bare branches tapped the glass outside. Eric broke the seal. The letter inside was written on the same thick, cream-colored paper as the envelope.

He unfolded it.

Cleared his throat.

CHAPTER 9

To Samantha

To Samantha,

If you are reading this, then I am gone, and my brother Conrad has honored my request.

My name is Randall Oldman.

In my lifetime I was many things—a lawyer, a brother, a son. The one title I never claimed publicly was David Roseman's partner.

When we met, I left New York and the firm and came to the Poconos. We built a life together.

He began flying lessons. He learned about Eric's freight routes. He worried about the cargo plane.

He told me he intended to fly it to the strip behind Honeymoon Hideaway. To hide it. Dismantle it, piece by piece.

But the storm caught him.

As for what remains:

David left his personal holdings to me.

I now leave everything I inherited from him to you, Samantha.

-Honeymoon Hideaway.

-And the condominium in Boca. (Funny, isn't it? He spent years lamenting about couples fleeing to Florida instead of driving to the Poconos.)

This is not a gift.

It is a legacy.

You see, David carried something long before he met me.

Years ago, he was responsible for a car accident. Two people died. A child survived.

A little girl.

When he took you to Honeymoon Hideaway, I believe he suspected who you might be.

Your article then confirmed it.

There is one condition, and it's mine.

The vase before you contain our ashes.

I ask that Eric take to the sky and scatter half over New York City. The other half over the Pocono Mountains.

Yours,

Randall Oldman

P.S. One thing always puzzled me. David knew the road to the Hideaway had washed out. I never understood how he thought he'd make it back.

CHAPTER 10

Necessitas non habet legem

Eric finished reading and looked at Sam. She wiped her cheeks with her sleeve and stared at the letter. Then at the vase. She reached for Eric's hand.

"I remember his eyes," she said. "From the backseat of our car. And after. On the road."

She swallowed.

"And the way he looked at me at Honeymoon Hideaway."

"Residue."

She looked at the vase.

Eric pulled her into him.

"I don't know how to hold all of this."

Footsteps approached along the hall—measured, unhurried—then paused outside the door.

Conrad and Madeline Oldman entered and closed it gently behind them. The latch settled with a soft click. The room returned to stillness.

Conrad Oldman removed his hat. He bowed his head for a moment, offering a silent benediction—for the broken and for the saved. Then he held the hat in both hands before placing it carefully on the corner of the desk, aligning it with the grain of the wood.

Across the room, Madeline Oldman adjusted the Ming vase. She turned it slightly so the painted face caught the light from the window. Satisfied, she stepped back and folded her gloved hands in front of her.

They did not speak.

They stood.

Waiting.

Eric felt their presence and looked up.

Conrad Oldman spoke at last.

"I imagine this is quite a lot to take in."

He allowed the words to settle before continuing.

"My brother believed this is what David would have wanted. Rightly or wrongly."

He paused.

"It was David Roseman's money that did most of the talking—even in death."

Sam's eyes flicked to him.

"When you've had time to process," Conrad Oldman continued, his voice returning to its steadier tone, "we can begin the planning. Scattering the ashes. Transferring the assets. All of it."

Sam's fingers tightened around Eric's.

Eric looked at her.

She held his gaze for a second.

He cleared his throat.

"Mr. Oldman," Eric said. "There's something you should know."

Conrad Oldman turned, one eyebrow lifting.

Eric shoved his hands into his pockets. "I don't have a pilot's license anymore. The FAA took it after . . ."

He glanced at Sam.

"After what happened."

"I don't have a plane; I can't even rent one.'

Conrad Oldman regarded him for a long moment with the kind of look that had talked hundreds of clients off a ledge. Then he stepped forward and rested a hand on Eric's shoulder.

"Well then," he said evenly, "I suppose you'll just have to steal one."

CHAPTER 11

The Broken Hearted

The door to Randall Oldman's law office closed behind them, the late afternoon sun turning the courthouse square into a wash of long shadows with gold edges. Sam cradled the Ming vase and shifted her grip carefully.

A breeze tugged at the hem of Madeline's scarf, and Conrad's coat flared as he buttoned it. He adjusted the cuffs of his overcoat, then turned to face them both.

"Well then. I've done what he asked of me."

He gave Eric a slight nod, the kind usually reserved for the closing of a courtroom deal.

"The terms of my brother's estate have now been delivered," he continued. "After your . . . airborne obligation is completed, I will, of course, execute the necessary contracts and see to the transfer the properties. Cleanly. Quietly. Legally."

He slipped on his leather gloves. "Assuming, of course, that you choose to proceed."

"It's a conditional bequest," Conrad Oldman said. "Odd, but enforceable." His gaze settled on Sam. "It is my understanding the old resort requires rather a great deal of attention." He rested his gloved hands atop the handle of his cane. "You are under no obligation to accept it, my dear."

"Honeymoon Hideaway—what remains of it—is something of an *aut Caesar aut nihil proposition.*" He lifted the cane a fraction.

"Rule it," he said quietly, "or let it rule you."

He paused. "But, of course, there is always Boca. Boca does not ask to be conquered. It does not demand resurrection. It does not require history to be repaired. Sometimes preservation is wiser than restoration. *Imperium* is not the only measure of a life well lived. The ocean is steady. Predictable. Warm. One may build something new there."

He tapped the cane once against the pavement.

"Just something to consider."

Conrad's gaze stayed on Sam. He drew off one glove, pressed his bare fingertips lightly to his chest, and gave her a small nod.

"In the meantime," he slid the glove back on, "Madeline and I will summon a car. An Uber, I believe they call it. We'll spend a few days here in the Poconos. I am told there's a heart-shaped hot tub involved. God help me."

Madeline linked her arm through his.

"We look forward to your return," Conrad Oldman said. "Don't keep us old folks waiting too long."

"We won't," Eric said.

They began to part ways, but just before Conrad Oldman reached the curb, Sam called out softly: "Mr. Oldman?"

He stopped and turned.

"Yes, my dear?"

She hesitated, then asked, "How did Randall die?"

Conrad Oldman held her gaze.

"My dear," he said gently, "I'm afraid I'm not at liberty to share those details."

He looked down, smoothed the cuff of his sleeve, then lifted his eyes again. "But let me just say this—"

"My brother died of a broken heart."

He gave Sam a small, gracious nod—holding her gaze just long enough for her to feel it.

Then he tipped his hat, turned, and took his wife's arm, and together, they crossed the courthouse square in Stroudsburg.

CHAPTER 12

Swan-Boat Dock

"He stole a plane and flew into a storm for me."

The apartment was quiet. A cup of coffee sat untouched on the milk crate beside them. The faded Uncle Sam top hat still leaned crooked on the TV. The Ming vase sat between them. Eric rested his hand over Sam's. She let it stay.

She stared at the vase.

"I was six. My mom was singing. My dad was driving. I pretended my hand was flying." She squeezed his fingers. "Then my whole body was flying. And that's it. That's all I remember."

Outside, smoke from a chiminea on the next balcony drifted through the window.

"He saved you," she said. "For me."

Her voice broke.

She drew a breath.

"Now he's sitting on our coffee table."

She looked at Eric. "I don't hate him. Is that crazy?"

"No," he said. "That's not crazy."

"One random night. One random road. Everything changed for me, you know . . ."

"And now we own two properties."

"Do we—"

"One of which," she continued, "has a swan-boat dock."

Eric stared at the vase, then back at her. "Jesus Christ."

"Right?"

"Of all the details in that story," he said, "it's the swan-boat dock that really gets me."

She elbowed him, then leaned in.

"Are you okay?"

"No," she said. "But I'm here."

She nudged him. "You know what we have to do now, right?"

He looked at her.

"Steal a plane?"

She nodded.

"Steal a plane."

CHAPTER 13

Mona Lisa

The Cessna 150 idled on the runway at Mount Pocono Airport, engine purring, propeller slicing the chilly morning air. The rising sun caught the windshield, flashing gold across the asphalt.

Inside the cockpit, Nasser sat in the left seat—back straight, brown bomber jacket zipped tight, white silk scarf tucked beneath his collar. He was ready to fly a mission he would never log.

His Ray-Bans reflected the pale sky like polished glass.

He keyed the mic. "Mount Pocono Traffic, Cessna One Niner Two Niner Six. Runway Two Three for departure. Solo student. VFR local."

He scanned the tree line to his left.

Nothing.

Then—

From the edge of the woods, Eric and Sam burst into view at a run. Sam crossed the grass in worn sneakers, both arms locked around the Ming vase against her stomach. She was breathing hard.

Eric ran beside her, boots thudding, jacket flapping open.

Nasser climbed out and met them at the door.

"Did you bring the extra headset for Sam?" Eric called over the engine.

"Yes—yes, Eric," Nasser said, already reaching back into the cockpit. "It is here."

"Good." Eric leaned in, gripping the doorframe. "First—thank you for renting it. We'll pay you back."

"Eric . . . I am sorry. The FAA asked if you knew about David. I told them what I saw. They twisted my words."

Eric shook his head once. "No. That's not on you." His voice stayed steady, but it carried weight. "You didn't do anything wrong. It's on me. I made some bad decisions."

Nasser's eyes held on him. "Eric—"

"I mean it," Eric said. "You did what was right."

He glanced down the runway, then back. "Second—logistics. You rented the airplane, so you'll have to return it to the flight school." He looked at his watch. "We'll be back in one hour and fifty-two minutes."

Nasser looked at his watch. "One hour and fifty-two?"

"Yeah. I'll land Runway Five," Eric said. "I'll roll to the end, turn off onto the taxiway, and shut down. We'll swap seats there. You taxi it in and turn it in to the flight school like normal."

Nasser nodded. "Okay, Eric. I'll be here."

"Thank you. Seriously." Eric released the doorframe and turned to Sam. "Headset on. Keep the vase steady. Let's go."

Nasser's eyes flicked to Sam—then dropped. He cleared his throat. "And, Mrs. Young . . . I am also very sorry."

Sam frowned. "Sorry for what?"

Nasser swallowed. "For . . . seeing something I should not have seen. By accident."

He didn't wait for an answer. He turned and jogged into the trees.

She climbed into the right seat, wedging the Ming vase carefully between her feet, then pulled the door shut.

The latch clicked.

"What's he talking about?"

"Nothing," Eric said, already reaching for the throttle.

"What did he see by accident?"

Eric scanned the panel—oil pressure, tach, suction.

"Eric."

"Tell me."

He exhaled through his nose. "I'm pretty sure Nasser saw . . . your tits."

"What?"

Eric kept his eyes forward. "That picture. The bathroom one. The day you—" He pretended to unbutton his top button. "He was sitting across from me at the picnic table. I looked down at my phone and—"

"Oh my God."

Eric winced and kept his eyes on the panel.

Sam shifted in her seat, the Ming vase clinking against the rudder pedals.

"Great," she muttered. "Nasser saw my tits."

He glanced over finally. "Come on. We really gotta go. Ready?"

Sam's eyes stayed on the windshield. "Go."

Eric shoved the throttle forward. The engine surged.

"Mount Pocono UNICOM, Cessna One Niner Two Niner Six departing Runway Two Three. VFR eastbound," he called.

The Cessna rolled—fast, eager—tires humming over the asphalt.

Sam didn't say another word as the nose lifted and the runway fell away beneath them.

They turned east toward New York. Eric knew the route and the air traffic control frequencies by heart.

Soon, Pennsylvania and New Jersey slid away beneath them. The skyline of Manhattan rose into view—jagged and majestic through the haze.

They leveled at 2,500 feet, skirting the edge of Class Bravo airspace. Eric called New York Approach and received clearance to cross Midtown Manhattan at 1,500 feet.

He banked gently, tracing the southern edge of the skyline.

"There," he said, pointing.

Sam lifted the lid of the Ming vase and looked down—at the rooftops, the narrow streets, the couples on benches in tiny parks, the place where memory folded in on itself.

Eric flew steady.

Sam reached into the vase. She hesitated. "Are we doing this?"

"Yeah."

She let go.

The wind caught the ashes as she released them over Greenwich Village—lifting them above sidewalks and fire escapes, across rusted tin roofs, drifting over Bleecker Street, where she'd met her boy from New York City, who was from Pittsburgh.

Another handful. Then another.

When it was done, she closed the vase.

Neither of them spoke.

The radio stayed uncommonly quiet.

Sam placed her hand on Eric's knee, and he covered it with his.

They were clear of the skyline when Eric spoke.

"Wait," he said.

Sam looked at him.

"Before we head back," Eric said, "you've got to see this."

He eased the nose down and brought them lower.

He keyed the mic. "New York Approach, Cessna One Niner Two Niner Six. Westbound at one thousand feet. Requesting the river to the Lady."

A pause. Then the controller came back.

"Roger, Cessna One Niner Two Niner Six. Stay to the right on the river. Contact Newark Tower one two seven point eight five."

"Right on the river. Over to Newark Tower, one two seven point eight five. Cessna One Niner Two Niner Six."

Eric switched frequencies.

"Newark Tower, Cessna One Niner Two Niner Six. One thousand feet, westbound, request the Lady."

"Cessna One Niner Two Niner Six, roger. Maintain one thousand. Stay to the right on the river."

"Maintain one thousand. Right side. Cessna One Niner Two Niner Six."

Ahead, the Statue of Liberty came into view—small from the air, torch lifted.

"That's incredible," Sam said.

Eric set a gentle bank and started the first turn. He kept the statue just off Sam's side, steady and centered in her window. The second turn was smoother. On the third, the water and the statue stayed steady in her window. Sam took out her phone and snapped some photos. After the third turn, Eric rolled wings level and brought the nose up a touch.

He looked over.

"I'll probably never get to do this again," he said. "Not like this."

Sam tightened her fingers around his and nodded once.

Then Eric banked west, and they turned toward the Poconos. Soon, they were back over Pennsylvania. The ridgeline unfolded beneath them, and then—Honeymoon Hideaway. He glanced at Sam.

She nodded.

He eased the throttle back. Ten degrees of flaps. Slow flight.

Sam cracked the window. Cold air rushed in. Before reaching for the vase, she slipped a hand into her jacket pocket and pulled out her phone. She tapped once. Then again. She looked at Eric and shook her head. "I don't know what the perfect song would be," she said. "Feels too heavy."

"If there was ever a time for *On the Wings of Love* . . ." Eric said.

She gave him a look. "That's a little too cheesy. Even for us."

"Fine." He nodded toward her feet. "Take your boots off. We'll pretend we're back in the Luscombe."

"Not like that—be serious." She frowned. "This is important. I don't think there is a song for this."

Eric took off his sunglasses and reached for her phone. "Let me try."

Sam didn't hand it over right away. Her mouth tightened into a small pout, like she'd been holding it in and couldn't anymore. "I can't believe Nasser saw that pic," she muttered. "You shouldn't have told me that."

Eric gave a short huff—almost a laugh, but not—and kept the airplane in its slow, keeping the airplane steady in a slow circle over Honeymoon Hideaway. "Yeah. I know." Then he took the phone, scrolled her playlist with one hand. He found the song and pressed play.

A soft piano melody filled their headsets.

Sam tilted her head, listening.

"Oh."

He'd chosen their wedding song—*Beautiful in My Eyes.*

Eric glanced over, locking eyes with his wife. Then, without breaking her gaze, he slid his Ray-Ban Aviators back on.

She smiled and held his gaze. "That was pretty cheesy." Then she reached into the Ming vase. The cool porcelain rested on her lap as she scattered the last of the ashes.

When the vase was empty, they climbed—

and turned gently on a wing toward Mount Pocono Airport—

and flew *home.*

Epilogue

The old Honeymoon Hideaway sign still creaked in the mountain breeze—but now it was freshly painted. Sam stood at the edge of the parking lot, watching workers patch potholes and plant maple trees along the road. In her arms, she cradled their son.

They named him David Randall Young.

Eric came up beside her, brushing dust from his work jacket. He smelled like sawdust and paint—still looked like the boy she met under the fireworks, only stronger.

He slipped his arms beneath the blanket and took the baby from her. "They're finishing the roof on the Swan Suite."

"Good. It deserves to shine again."

Sam had sold the Florida condo to begin the renovations. It was enough to get them started. The rest they would have to figure out.

Eric's phone buzzed. He glanced at the screen, then handed it to Sam.

A selfie: Nasser and Aaliyah beside a yellow Piper Cub—Nasser in his bomber jacket and white scarf, a *DeNunzio's* takeout bag in Aaliyah's hand.

Sam smiled and handed the phone back. "Looks like they made it."

Just inside the renovated lobby, a bronze plaque had been set into the cornerstone on the first day of construction.

It read:

In Honor of America's Older Generations

Rebuilt by America's Young

"Not many people will get it."

"That's okay," Eric said. "They don't have to."

They started with the road. Then the piano. They stripped it, re-lacquered it, re-stoned it—one glittering piece at a time. Eric glued each rhinestone in place with tweezers, methodical and unsmiling.

In silver ink across the fallboard, Sam stenciled: *Sinatra was here.* She leaned in and blew on it.

Eric shook his head and kept gluing.

Sam never went back to newspaper work. She wrote for *Seen in the Poconos* once a week—short pieces about real people, diners with neon signs, cozy coffee shops, hidden bike trails, candle shops, comic-book stores, chainsaw-carved grizzly bears, and Lukas's occasional UFO sightings near Lake Wallenpaupack.

He had turned his idea into a digital storytelling platform people actually followed—something like *Humans of New York*—only with heart-shaped tubs.

Constance—defying all logic—agreed to serve as managing editor. "It's not editing," she told people. "So much as it's curating Lukas's rural delusions."

Seen in the Poconos didn't have an office. Every Thursday at nine, they met by the windows at Small Mountain Coffee, laptops open.

"I still think we should change it to *Scene in the Poconos*," Lukas said one morning. "*Seen* is just past tense. Flat. Sad. *Scene* is edgy."

"It's branding," Constance said. "We already have the logo. The mugs. The *Seen in the Poconos* safety vests you made us wear—for that highway cleanup you forgot to mention."

"What if it had a semicolon?" Lukas said. "Like *Seen;* —"

"Lukas," Constance said calmly, "you are one misplaced semicolon away from being strangled with my charging cable."

That evening, they left the work at Honeymoon Hideaway behind and followed the winding road north, their baby asleep in the backseat. Big Pocono Ski Area rose ahead—2,131 feet up. Sam tilted her face into the summer air, breathing it in deeply as the wind tumbled through her hair. She flew her hand on the current, riding the air in slow, weightless arcs. They spread out a blanket beneath the chairlift to watch the fireworks.

"You can see forever from here," she whispered to the baby.

The fireworks rose and fell above the ridge, the finale lifting and twirling, colors flaring before breaking apart and falling away. Red and blue flashes lit the hills and reflected in their baby's eyes.

Above the fading sparks, a jet etched a contrail through the sky.

Eric watched it.

Sam watched him watching it.

The line stretched clean and white against the dark.

He looked down at her then, and at the baby in her arms.

The wind lifted around them, carrying a trace of campfire smoke. Sam shifted the baby against her shoulder. One bootie had come off. She slipped the other one off too.

The FAA review was still pending.

It didn't matter.

They were still taking *flying lessons.*

Author's Note

I started writing *Pocono Flying Lessons* in 2003, when the airline industry was still reeling from the September 11th attacks. That year my airline offered voluntary leaves of absence. I asked Melissa if she'd be okay with me taking guitar lessons in New York City and trying to write a novel.

She said yes. I took a year off, went to the city to learn some chords, and started writing.

Over the years, life kept moving. I changed airlines, we raised four kids, and I carried this story in my flight bag for twenty-two years.

It isn't our story. Not exactly. But it carries pieces of our life.

This year, on July Fourth—her fiftieth birthday—I gave it to her. That's what this book is: a love note to her, and evidence of her patience.

—C.A.

Acknowledgments

This book exists because of a few people who believed in it.

Sarah Lyn Rogers provided sharp editorial guidance and made the manuscript stronger. Connie Olszewski supported this story from the beginning and helped it find its shape. And to Melissa and our kids—who lived with this book for a long time—thank you for your love, humor, and patience. To everyone who offered time, attention, encouragement, or belief along the way: thank you.

Playlist

"BOY FROM NEW YORK CITY"—The Manhattan Transfer
"1812 OVERTURE"— Tchaikovsky
"YOU TAKE MY BREATH AWAY"—Rex Smith
"TENDER LOVE"—Force MDs
"LET'S GET IT ON"—Marvin Gaye
"DO YA THINK I'M SEXY?"—Rod Stewart
"JUST THE WAY YOU ARE"—Billy Joel
"LOVE BOAT THEME"—Jack Jones
"AS TIME GOES BY"—Dooley Wilson
"STRANGERS IN THE NIGHT"—Frank Sinatra
"TOO MUCH HEAVEN"—The Bee Gees
"JUST THE TWO OF US"—Grover Washington Jr., Bill Withers
"HAVE I TOLD YOU LATELY"—Van Morrison
"SEASONS OF LOVE"—Original Broadway Cast of Rent
"I'LL COVER YOU"— Jesse L. Martin, Wilson Jermaine Heredia
"MOST OF THE TIME"—Bob Dylan
"COME FLY WITH ME"—Frank Sinatra

"ENDLESS LOVE"—Lionel Richie, Diana Ross
"LANDSLIDE"—Fleetwood Mac
"EVERY ROSE HAS ITS THORN"—Poison
"WE CAN WORK IT OUT"—The Beatles
"WONDERWALL"—Oasis
"YES"—Merry Clayton
"HUNGRY EYES"—Eric Carmen
"ON THE WINGS OF LOVE"—Jeffrey Osborne
"BEAUTIFUL IN MY EYES"—Joshua Kadison
"NEVER KNEW LOVE LIKE THIS"—Stephanie Mills

About the Author

C.A. Pensiero is a Boeing 747 captain living in western Pennsylvania. He lives on a small farm with his wife and four kids, twelve Highlander cows, two German Shepherds, and about a hundred chickens.

www.ingramcontent.com/pod-product-compliance
Lightning Source LLC
LaVergne TN
LVHW100502110826
845146LV00002B/488

* 9 7 9 8 9 9 3 8 6 4 7 0 9 *